Ten Thousand Heavens

Also by Chuck Rosenthal

Loop's Progress

Experiments with Life and Deaf

Loop's End

Elena of the Stars

Jack Kerouac's Avatar Angel: His Last Novel

My Mistress, Humanity

Never Let Me Go, a memoir

The Heart of Mars

Are We Not There Yet? Travels in Nepal, North India, and Bhutan
(Magic Journalism)

Coyote O'Donohughe's History of Texas

West of Eden: A Life in 21st Century Los Angeles
(Magic Journalism)

Ten Thousand Heavens

Chuck Rosenthal

Whitepoint Press
San Pedro, California

A Whitepoint Press First Edition 2013

Cover design by Monique Carbajal
Cover photograph © Michael Eastman. Used by permission.
Author photo by Gary Goldstein

ISBN-13: 9780615744995
ISBN-10: 0615744990

Library of Congress Control Number: 2012955943

Published by Whitepoint Press
www.whitepointpress.com

For my mare, Jackie O, my first horse

In the afterlife there are eighteen hells,
but on earth there are ten thousand heavens.

- - Anonymous Tibetan Buddhist saying

Not a Pasture

If horses had gods, their gods would be horses.

- - Heraclitus

The hills were green now. The rain had stopped and it was spring. Along the riding paths grass sprouted, and wildflowers: yellow daisies and Arizona blue eyes, wild sunflowers, orange monkey flowers, white Estevez's pincushion, red bottle rockets, blue and yellow lupine, pale lavender ceanothus. Anastasia stopped to smell them when Bird took her out of the pasture for a ride, though Bird didn't call her Anastasia, he called her Annie.

And she called him Bird. Because he wore bird feathers in his straw hat, all stained with sweat and dirt. That was his smell. Sometimes, when he smelled like something else, when he smelled sweet, or he had the smell of another person on him, particularly his Other, she didn't like it, and she pinned her ears at him. Well, in the old days she did. Now it mattered less. He was her Hum, her very own Hum, and many horses had bad Hums, as she once did, or infrequent Hums, or no Hums at all.

Most of the time was pasture time anyway, and she liked to stand in the sun or lie in the sun, if only everyone else left her alone. It was hard to be left alone, because the other pastured horses had no Hums of their very own and had to rely on each other for attention and that often meant any kind of attention. When that started, things usually spilled over, and she was forced to get involved.

Some times somebody just needed her, especially little white Rumi who was young, 100% Arabian and 100% ditzy. Like the others, Dummie, Tasha, and Precious, Rumi was a drop-off. In general, the pastures were

9

for drop-offs. Their own Hums stopped coming, and the ranchums, helper ranch Hums, took them from their stalls and brought them out here where no one came to clean up their hot plop or care for their feet, but twice a day ranchums came on a rumble and threw dry alfalfa bales over the fence and into the dry, dirt corral. It wasn't really a pasture. There was no grass. It had a water faucet where you could release water with your nose into a bowl, and there were two big metal tubs that Bird filled up when he came.

Bird just liked keeping Annie outside. It was better than standing around in a stall with nothing to do. Stall horses who didn't get out every day got crazy or dull or both. They didn't know anything about anything, only what they'd been trained to do.

Annie nibbled some alfalfa hay and watched the road outside the corral where rumbles rolled by. Rumi walked up beside her.

"Do you think Bird will come?" Rumi said.

"Bird always comes," said Annie.

"And why do you watch the rumbles?"

"Bird comes in a rumble. I've told you and told you and you always forget."

"I don't forget," said Rumi. "I just don't bother to remember. Bird just appears. Hums are here or not here."

"Hums come from rumbles," Annie said.

"Hums and rumbles are very different," said Rumi. "Different things don't come from one another or stay with one another. Remember the brah-brah, Harley?" He meant a donkey that once stayed in the pasture. "He was different. We didn't like him."

Annie didn't care about Harley any more or less than she now cared about Dummie or Precious or Tasha. Or even Rumi, for that matter. Some horses always felt the need to be next to other horses and grew anxious when they were not. They were herd bound. Annie wasn't. She only cared about Bird. Though it wasn't always that way.

"What about the ranchum rumble?" said Annie.

"They're one thing," Rumi said.

"Why do they come?"

10

"Because someone cares," said Rumi. "Because even when your Hum stops appearing, someone cares. That's why everything works. There's not much to think about it."

It was true enough that most horses didn't like to think about much or even move much. Tasha said that if the water weren't far away from the food, she wouldn't move at all. And they didn't like change. Some didn't even believe in change, no matter how often things changed around them. That was another thing Tasha said. Change was illusion. But Annie had seen five ranches and watched the cycle of seasons change fourteen times.

That's one thing about horses. They can count. Some higher than others. Though a horse wouldn't think fourteen. They counted in fours like people count in tens. Animals had four feet. There were four basic directions, four different seasons. All movement, walking, trotting, running, came in fours: one, two, three, four. Annie counted four complete cycles of the seasons three times, then two more times. Four fours, sixteen years, was one life. Four more, two lives. That was a lot. Few horses reached a third life. Two was another useful number, one and three not as good.

When Annie first met Bird he tried to teach her to change her lead running legs on his command. Of course, any horse can change leads while running. Any horse can already do anything people think they train them to do. When they lope or gallop, horses throw one foreleg out and push off harder with the opposite leg behind. When they tire or change directions, they change their lead. It's easier to take a left turn while leaning left, with your weight on the left leg. Hums called changing leads at a gallop a flying lead change, as if they'd invented something. Hums liked to make a lot of sounds and often, when they matched a sound to something, they thought they invented the thing they matched the sound to.

Back in the early days, Bird tried to get Annie, his sweet little Annie, though she wasn't little, she was well over fifteen hands and 1,100 pounds, he tried to get her to change leads on the fly whenever he asked. But she understood the game immediately and automatically changed leads between barrels or between poles or before she had to turn. Or if he wanted her to change on every fourth beat, or every other, she just counted and after the second request she'd change her lead before he asked. This kind of thing drove Hums crazy, and there was a person who often came and watched Bird ride Annie, and then yelled at him; that person yelled a lot when Annie changed leads before Bird asked. When the yeller, she was called a trainer, came around, Bird tried lots of tricks to fool Annie into not knowing what he was going to ask next, but Annie always figured out the pattern. This made the trainer yell a lot more, but it made Bird laugh and Annie came to like it when Bird laughed. She knew he was proud of her for being smart and tricky, and, over time, Annie herself even became a little proud of the things they did together, though she had to be in the mood.

Anyway, horses can count. All of their movement comes in beats and rhythms and rhythm is everything, rhythm is unchanging change, the sun, the moon, the stars, the rain, the grass, the warm, the cold, the seasons, the day, the night, deep rhythms that horses understood and Hums only made sounds about.

Annie was a dark bay with black feet, black mane and tail, a white star on her forehead. Her father had been a thoroughbred, a stallion, of course, her mother Arabian, like Rumi. Horses, ranch horses anyway, had three sexes, stallions, mares, and geldings. Rumi and Dummie were cut, or gelded. The stallions were kept by themselves, up in the barns. She could smell them when Bird rode her by, or took her up for a bath. Then she called to them sometimes and they screamed back. They didn't have it good. They couldn't even meet with mares but had their life drained from them by Hums who put it in the mares, called broodmares. Precious was once a broodmare. At least Rumi and Dummie got to run around in the pasture. Sometimes they pretended to be stallions and that was tiresome, particularly from Dummie who was very big.

He came over now, leaving Precious and Tasha who grazed in the corner of the corral. Dummie was light brown-red with a white nose and white hooves; he was over sixteen hands, a thoroughbred, and very broad. He had some other name. When his Hum dropped him off, she called him something. "Good-bye. Good-bye. I love you," she said, standing near her rumble. And then she never came back. Dummie liked to lope right up to you to make you move. Rumi jumped and stepped aside. Annie didn't budge.

"Come over here with me," Dummie said to Rumi.

"I was just talking," said Rumi.

Of course, horses don't talk like people, like Hums; they murmur and whinny, nicker and scream, they emit smells, they touch, they position themselves in significant attitudes, they urinate and poop, kick, bite, nibble, nip, swish their tails; everything has its place and everything says something. Much of how horses communicate is tactile, and horses can even communicate tactilely from a distance.

Rumi lowered his head and turned slightly away, submitting to Dummie. Annie faced him with her ears perked. "Go away," she said.

"I need him to brush away flies," said Dummie.

"You have two mares over there," said Annie.

"He's the best at it," said Dummie. "Unless you'd like to."

He stepped toward her. She turned, feigned a kick. He stepped back. And then she walked away. Rumi followed Dummie to the bottom of the pasture. Annie walked to the gate. A rumble came by. A red one. Not Bird.

Inside Each Other

Look at the birds of the air; your heavenly father
feeds them. Are you not much more valuable than they?

- - Jesus, Gospel of Matthew

Before Dummie, Precious ruled the pasture. She was a big, red saddlebred, almost as big as Dummie. There was no Rumi or Tasha then, just Precious and her two broodmare daughters when Annie moved in. Annie wouldn't submit. She and Precious fought every day, biting and kicking. Bird showed up. Put salve on her wounds. She didn't know it then, but he thought of moving her, he just didn't know where. But eventually, Precious just gave up. The others left Annie alone, too. Then the Hums took the daughters away to breed. There were some others, new geldings then, for a while; one, Bernard, who was soon taken away, and another, Howard, a gentle gray roan, who died. Those were the days of what Bird called The Great Alliance.

Hums generally saw things in very simple ways: this causes that and then that causes something else. Hums had simple, linear ideas of time and place and behaved as if they were somehow separate things. Tactilely they were almost deaf, and though they had eyes they could only see a few, select things that were directly in front of them. They thought one horse must be in charge, then came the next horse in line, and then the next. They must have lived that way themselves and assumed that all the other animals did, too. Most Hums must have very boring lives.

But one lead mare doesn't necessarily submit to another lead mare, and geldings don't generally behave like stallions, who just fight, fuck, and follow the herd. Herds, no matter how small or how large, consisted of

14

shifting political alliances based on circumstance and issues, strength, brains, persistence. All horses know these things, because they're born with the knowledge. Somehow Hums are born without knowledge and have to figure everything out with the sounds they make. They could surprise you sometimes with how creative and wrong they could be.

Precious picked on those two geldings, Bernard and Howard, constantly. She kicked them and bit them, chased them away from the food. Finally, one day, Howard walked away from Precious. He approached Annie, who stood alone in the far corner of the pasture, waiting for Bird as far away from Precious as she could be.

"May I stand with you?" Howard said.

Annie just twitched her ears. When Bird came, he shared some carrots with Howard. In a few days, Bernard came over, too.

"Would you stand up for me?" he said to Annie.

"I'll let you stand with me," she said.

Furious, Precious pranced up in a rage. And though she could take any of them individually, she couldn't take on all three. Domineering Precious was suddenly alone.

Bird showed up that day and teased Annie. "I see you've got your own little herd," he said. "Must be my carrots."

Annie didn't understand much English, but she knew carrots and she knew from his tone he was teasing her. She was a lead mare, too. If she did it with her brains, her diplomacy, her stubbornness, instead of her muscle, all the better. She gave Bird a hard time that day. Bird thought it was because bossing two geldings around had gone to her head, but she didn't care that much about Howard and less about Bernard. They could stand with her if they wanted. Or share her alfalfa. But she didn't like it when Bird used that tone, and she wanted to make sure that if Bird was going to spread carrots around, then it wasn't coming out of her share.

"The Great Alliance," Bird said.

Howard died of colic in the night. It was a miserable death. Soon after, the Hums took Bernard away. Now there was Tasha and Rumi, and Dummie who took over immediately. Precious submitted to him the first day, letting him nibble her neck, take the best food; she folded like a foal. That's the kind of horse Precious was. Annie had no respect for her.

Later that day, when Dummie was preoccupied with Precious and Tasha, Rumi came by again.

"What do I do?" said Rumi. "I want to stand with you."

Well, she really didn't want to stand around with Rumi. If he was bright, he talked too much and much of it was nonsense. If there were anyone, she preferred Tasha who at least had seen a few things; in fact, according to Tasha herself, she'd seen and done everything, race tracks, moo ranches, even worked where Hums lived together in great bunches of barns. With Rumi here, eventually Annie'd have to deal with Dummie who'd come over to dominate him.

"Fight back," said Annie.

"He'll hurt me."

"Hurt him back."

"He'll hurt me worse," said Rumi. "He'll win every time."

"Hurt him some," said Annie. "Make it hurt for him to win. Make him get tired of winning every time."

Rumi let out something between a moan and a squeal. Rumi was a gelding, and geldings were seldom stubborn and if they were, not for long. That's how she'd beaten off Dummie, as she had Precious. If they want to fight, fight them. Never be dominated because they'll just pick on you again and again whenever they want. It'll go on forever.

"They don't pick on you because they like fighting," Annie told Rumi. "They pick on you because they enjoy picking on you. Make it unenjoyable."

In the sky, a jet left a white tail. Annie watched it.

"Why do you watch those things?" Rumi said.

"Sky rumbles," Annie said.

"That doesn't rumble," said Rumi.

"It's like the ones that do." She meant the helicopters that buzzed around the mountains like giant dragonflies. "There are Hums in them."

"There are no Hums in those things," said Rumi.

"How did you get here?" said Annie.

"I was put in a can. Then I came out of the can."

"A rumble dragged the can," said Annie. "It's a trailer. Watch when a big one goes by. The polo ponies will be inside."

"Why drag the polo ponies in a big can?" said Rumi.

"Before Bird," said Annie, "my female Hum wanted me to jump things."

"With her," said Rumi, "you were a jumper?"

"Yes," said Annie. "She put me in a trailer, and the rumble took us someplace else where we jumped."

"Why go someplace else to do the same thing?"

"We went to a place where there were lots of us, and lots of Hums, jumping, and more Hums watching and making noise like the Hums always do."

"That's ridiculous," Rumi said.

"The rumbles go on big paths, like our paths, only there are many, many rumbles on them."

"Rumble herds!" Rumi jumped and ran around a little bit. The story was getting him all worked up.

Across the way, Dummie lifted his head and Rumi, seeing it, stopped. That's all it took. Dummie could control him from a pasture-length away.

"The Hums take the polo ponies to another place where they play a ball chasing game. Hums watch and make noise. Then they bring the ponies back." She'd done it once or twice herself, but she preferred jumping even then, though not without ambivalence because she didn't like that Hum, and sometimes jumping made Annie crazed and high, then the little female Hum got scared and upset and hit her and spurred her, then Annie bucked her off or dumped her. Then the Hums panicked and ran around and pulled on her and sometimes hit her. Anyway, that's how that went, but she didn't need to tell Rumi.

"The rumble paths lead to other rumble paths. They go all over. The Hums ride inside the rumbles like they ride on top of us. They get inside and agitate them to make them rumble. If you see a rumble, even a sky rumble, then there's a Hum inside keeping it agitated."

"The rumbles should fight back," said Rumi.

"You're funny," said Annie. "That's refreshing. The rumbles need the Hums more than we do. They can't do anything without a Hum."

"Maybe there's somebody inside running us," said Rumi.

"You can see Hums getting inside rumbles," said Annie. "You just have to watch. You don't see anyone getting inside us."

"Maybe what's inside running me is very tiny or invisible," said Rumi.

"I think you're right," said Annie. "What's running you is very tiny."

Often Annie was saying more than one thing at once, Rumi could tell by the way her ears tilted, one back, the other sideways. At least she wasn't hurting him.

"Or invisible," insisted Rumi.

That made Annie's ears go all goofy for a moment. If only he could just translate some of that into standing up for himself once in a while. But he'd thought something, she had to give him that.

"Anyone can go inside a rumble if they're small enough. Hums even take the woofers inside," Annie said.

"Woofers don't do anything," said Rumi. Dogs. Horses knew that Hum sound. A horse could learn any Hum sound that mattered. "They just follow Hums around. Hums need lots of attention."

"Maybe there are tiny woofers inside running the Hums," said Annie.

"Who's inside the woofers?"

"Everything is inside each other running each other," said Annie.

"This is what you do when you stand around," said Rumi. "You make up all this silly stuff."

"Do you only believe in what's in front of your face?" said Annie. "No. Don't you picture?"

"Why?" said Rumi.

"To think about better times," she said. "Or to get ready."

"To get ready for what? Like Tasha says, everything is always the same," Rumi said.

"Some things are always the same and some things aren't. Which ones?"

"Some things are and some things aren't," muttered Rumi.

"Which ones?" said Annie.

"What's to get ready for?" said Rumi.

"For Dummie coming over here and biting you," Annie said.

"That's always the same!" said Rumi.

18

"If you get ready, you can make it one of the things that aren't always the same," said Annie.

Horses, like most animals, though for the most part not like people, think in pictures that mean things to them. Some of those pictures are smells or tastes, touches or sounds, some are feelings and some are visual pictures. A smart horse, like Annie, when inclined, could place one picture next to another, learn to associate one picture with another, and so have expectations, make predictions, even figure out how to do things, like remove a halter from the fence to ask a person to take her out or, if need be, to unlatch the corral latch. You watch the Hums, connect the pictures, then do what they did. It's a little harder without hands, but you use your mouth and be patient. When a dog brings you his leash, there are dozens of pictures, smells and feelings going on, and expectations. Those pictures are signs, just like the little woman on the door of the women's room.

People once thought like that, long ago, before language, but now the words have got in the way of everything and most people don't even notice the pictures that they're thinking, unless they daydream or, even more true, sleep dream or have nightmares, but now people are so far removed from their picture life that they don't even understand it. Some people are so busy listening to the words (that they think are in their heads, though really they don't have any idea where they are) that they don't even see or hear or smell or touch what is right in front of them. In fact, they might not even notice the words themselves spinning by. They barely notice anything at all. That's why a person will speed around a blind curve and a horse would never do that unless a Hum made her. People, Hums, lived their lives running around blind curves.

"So when you stand by yourself, you think like that?" said Rumi.

"What do you think about?" she said.

"As little as possible," said Rumi.

On the hill above them, the new mothers had been released with their foals. Five this year. Sometimes Bird rode Annie past them. Some of the mothers pinned their ears and kept their babies from the fence, others let them come forward and Annie smelled them, though if they were male she screamed at them because you had to let the males know from a very young age, while they were small and impressionable, that you might not

19

be worth the trouble. Later, if she wanted to have union, the decision would be hers.

Once, a long time ago, she gave birth. She was very young, not even three cycles old, still untrained. She did not like the stallion, a white Andalusian, and refused him, so a Hum came, a vet – she learned that word because they came pretty often – and soon she was carrying. Carrying was painful. She wasn't built wide like many of these mothers. She was slender. Then the birth was troublesome. The foal turned around the wrong way and came out rear first. It almost killed them both and at that point she no longer cared. But she came to love the foal, a colt, a dark bay like her, and guarded him ferociously. She didn't get along well with other horses, even then, and so they separated her and her baby in a small corral where he lay in the sun as she nuzzled him. Sometimes he ran about her, playfully. Sometimes he suckled. And then one day the Hums came and took him.

They took all the foals from their mothers that day. The mothers cried; they screamed day after day, and then the screaming stopped but for Annie, back then called Anastasia, who continued to scream. Now, sometimes, cycles later, she still screamed for her child. She began not to trust Hums then. And she didn't want to have another foal.

"See the mothers and babies on the hill?" Annie said to Rumi.

"One thing takes care of another," said Rumi.

"And when the Hums take them away?"

"For some good," said Rumi.

"Whose good?" said Annie. "Where is your mother?"

"I believe in the Great Caregiver," said Rumi.

"I believe in Bird," said Annie.

"There is a great caring. It cares for everything," Rumi said. "Without it, even Bird wouldn't come."

"Bird comes in a rumble," said Annie.

Though later, Annie saw Rumi standing by himself, near the corral fence, watching the road. A rumble came up the road. It was the color of a rain cloud. It slowed as it approached the pasture and Annie looked across the field. It was Bird.

Before Bird

Parvati loved it when she didn't understand. What attracted her most was obscurity. Otherwise the world that surrounded her would have been too transparent.

- - Rig Veda

After her colt was taken, a small female Hum, Mitzi, took Anastasia in a trailer to a new place where she was kept in a long barn of horses in stalls, in her barn only mares. She couldn't touch the mares next to her, even if they both stretched their necks around the wall. Across the way she could see the other mares. She was fed at dawn and at dusk and once a day a man came who placed a chain over her nose and hit her on the chest with a whip, this to make her behave, to control her, because she was young and full of fire and banged with madness in her stall and when she got out she wanted to fly. The man took her into a big fenced area and let her go. She ran and bucked and ran and bucked until she was covered with white foam and grew so tired she could barely stand. She wouldn't let them catch her until then, until she could barely move, and then it took three of them, two who roped her neck while the man put the chain over her nose again. Then he took her to an area where he chained her head immobile between two poles and rinsed her with water. She liked that, the bath, but then he left her there for hours and this she did not like. Learning to stand still for hours. It was something she was supposed to learn. She learned that she hated to be chained up.

Then, sometimes, Mitzi came. The man saddled Anastasia and tacked her, took her to the ring where Mitzi hopped on her from a platform. Anastasia ran. Mitzi tugged and pulled the bit against Annie's teeth.

Annie ran. And jumped. There were lots of things to jump inside the ring and when Annie came to one she jumped it. But jumping made her even more excited and she snorted and sweated and Mitzi tugged and Annie bucked her off. The man caught Annie, whipped her chest, Annie reared, the man hit her more. None of this was any fun, but it beat standing in the stall. Well, running was fun, and jumping was fun, and bucking Mitzi off was fun, but there was too much pain in between.

Anastasia didn't mind Mitzi. What was there to mind? She showed up, jumped on, you ran, you jumped, you bucked her off. Want to try again? But after that happened a few times she started hearing the Hums use the sound bad a lot. It was an ugly sound like a goat made, only when goats made it, it kind of trembled in their throats in a soft, natural way and when Hums made it they kind of spat it out at you. Also, a goat was willing to spend time just hanging around near you, nibble some grass, just spend time with you doing nothing, and every time a Hum showed up they wanted you to do something for them. Hums never relaxed.

A new man came. Even among the horses it became apparent that things were changing a little bit, and though some of the Hums still tried to break horses by jumping on and riding them into submission, some others were talking about watching horses and trying to communicate with them. "Horses are horses," this new man said. "They aren't people. They aren't dogs. They're horses." It was another good example of how the sounds Hums made took a long time to catch up with what was in front of their faces. Then the Hums would stand around and say the sounds over and over. "Horses are horses. Just remember, horses are horses." That's when you knew that the Hums were stuck on those sounds and some new stupid thing to do was going to replace the old stupid thing to do.

"First, you have to get her attention," the new man said to Mitzi. "She's a herd animal. You're a herd of two. You going to be the lead mare, or her?" He took Anastasia to a small ring with high walls to do something called soft breaking.

He stood in the center and chased her with a long whip, first one direction and then the other. This went on for a very long time because Annie could run and run for a very long time, partly because she was young and bred for it, and partly because the last guy who chased her around in the big ring, in order to tire her out, just got her in better and better shape.

The new guy chased her with the whip – he didn't hit her, he just cracked it behind her – and when he put it down she stopped. Then he tried to walk toward her, but when he did, she took off. Then he went back to the center and picked up the whip. It only took her twice to realize that "getting her attention" meant she'd have to notice when he put the whip down. By the third time, she noticed that he put the whip down when she tilted her ear toward him or lowered her head. So then it was whip in hand, run, whip down, stop. Then he'd try to walk up to her.

She could refuse to run at all, but then she'd have to let him walk up to her, and after being whipped and struck on the chest by the last guy she wasn't ever going to let anybody touch her there again, so the next time he put the whip down she just kept running. Trotting could be as much work as galloping, but she could slow down to a steady lope and go forever. He figured that out, though, and started whipping behind her when she loped. She was foaming and a little tired, but after a couple hours of that he put the whip down and walked out. Some other guys came in with the chain. She didn't like the chain on her nose, but it meant the session was over.

The new guy came back the next day and they did it again. Same results.

"How long can she go like that?" he said to Mitzi.

"Forever," said Mitzi.

"She's hard and smart. And somebody hurt her. She's in a deep hole. It could take a long time."

"I'm paying you by the hour," Mitzi said. "What about your clinic?"

"I don't want her in my clinic," said the new man. "Horses are horses. Herd animals. Her behavior could be contagious."

"Why can't you get her attention?"

"Well, that's just it," said the man. He put his hand on the brim of his hat. "I think I did."

That was the way it was supposed to go. Once he got your attention, then he'd get you to pay attention to something else, then something else, and the next thing you know, you're getting trained. Well, fine, but let's make a game of it. Hums took it all so seriously.

23

And horses might be horses, but that was just something the Hums thought meant something and it didn't mean anything. Horses weren't all the same. And if a lot of Hums were mean and dumb, the smart ones could be just as bad because once they thought they'd figured something out, then they expected the same thing to happen all the time. As soon as you didn't do what everybody else always did when the Hum did the thing he'd figured out, he was stumped, and maybe irritable.

"But you can ride her?" said the man.

"It depends what you mean by that," said Mitzi.

So then this guy did what the last guy did. He took her in the big ring and turned her loose and let her run, though if she stopped he came toward her with the long whip and she took off again, though this guy wasn't mean like the last one, he didn't yell and he never hit her, he just kind of pushed her around with his body movement. She liked running around, and she didn't even dislike him. But here in this big ring, if he didn't give up eventually, she'd tire out. The sun moved, and he was still out there with her. She'd have to change the game.

If he put the whip down she let him come up to her, but not touch her. If he tried to touch her, she took off again; she didn't care how tired she was. But after doing that a few times, he figured it out and just connected her lead line to her halter and led her out of the big ring. She was foaming and tired. He put her in the cross ties, those chains that immobilized her head, then he saddled her, tacked her, and got on. She stood. So he took her to the big ring and sat on her there. They ran around a little bit.

He rode her over to Mitzi. "Well, maybe this'll do it," he said.

"I can get on her," said Mitzi. "It's staying on her."

"Well, she seems all right now," he said. "Herd of two."

This guy wasn't like Mitzi who sat on her back like a bee, nervous and buzzing. He relaxed and put his weight into her. He was the first person to do that. He took her out on the trail. She walked nice and slow, almost as if she didn't want to even bother.

"Why, you're a good girl," the guy said and petted her neck.

When they got out good and far, she bucked him off and ran home. Herd of one.

It took a little longer than Mitzi, but she got him. Any horse can buck anybody off. Some horses just got tired and gave up. Hums called that a "broke" horse. To Annie's mind a broke horse was a dead horse, at least mentally, if not physically. A horse that wouldn't try to buck you off once in a while was no companion at all. And Annie never gave up. If she failed the first time, and she seldom did, she just tried again later. They never expected it the second time. And she could always use a tree or just roll over.

She should have run somewhere else instead of back to the barns, but she didn't know anywhere else. When the new man came back in a rumble with some other men, Mitzi said to him, "What should I do?"

"Sell her," he said.

"Who's going to buy her?"

"Ship her to France for dog food," said one of the grooms.

How about a carrot? thought Anastasia. Everything should begin and end with a carrot.

But it had gone way beyond carrots. The new guy had been better. She didn't hate him, she just bucked him off. Had some fun. He gave up really easily. Next day, Mitzi showed up with another new guy. He was big and wore a hat that made him look like a duck.

"That soft stuff is baloney," he said to Mitzi. "You have to break her."

"I paid a fortune for her. Break her," Mitzi said.

That break word sounded really bad. First, he put something over her nose, a hackamore that forced her mouth closed and really, really hurt. He pulled her head down. He picked up a big spur and poked her side. He poked her again and again until she bled. "You'll move away from me when I tell you to, damn it!" said the man. She began to bleed. He jabbed her hard and she jumped. He pulled her nose down and went to the other side. "When I say jump you say, 'How high?'" the man said.

She was bleeding on both flanks now, and the man pulled her to the side of the barn and put a heavy Western saddle on her back. He took her to a small corral. "You can buck forever," he said. "Try." And he got on. But Annie just stood.

"What's her problem?" the man said to Mitzi.

25

"She'll just do the opposite of what you want," said Mitzi. "She's a bitch."

With that the man dug his spurs deep into Anastasia's wounded flanks. She jumped forward into a trot. He brought her back around to the gate. "This was nothin'," he said. "This horse is already broke."

Annie waited. Had anyone bothered to notice, they'd have seen her nostrils flaring with rage, though her body waited calmly. Then Mitzi opened the gate. Anastasia broke into a gallop, almost pulling the man off. She headed straight for the barn roof that sloped down low over the sides of the barn. The man pulled her head to his knee and she almost tumbled over, but she recovered and, neck bent, ran right through it. She ran him into the overhanging roof and he came off with a loud thump. He hit the ground already unconscious.

Then everything exploded. Grooms screamed and ran at her. She reared. Mitzi was there. "Oh my God, I'm going to get fucking sued!" she screamed. She whipped Annie's chest. Annie struck out at her with her fore hoof and knocked her down. A groom struck Annie on the head with the butt of a whip. The hackamore had loosened, and she grabbed him by the shoulder and threw him twenty feet. Then there were ropes all around her. Mitzi screamed and screamed. The grooms held Annie down with the ropes. After a while, two big rumbles came, put the man and Mitzi on beds and took them away.

Annie spent a lot of time in the stall after that, but everyone left her alone and by now she felt that being left alone was better than running around and being beaten. But by this point the only thing keeping Mitzi from selling Anastasia for dog food or glue was the loss of the investment.

Then a rumble showed up with big can on the back and they put her in and took her someplace else. It was a very nice place on top of a mountain. The horses were kept in stalls in a square around a courtyard. There was a big woman there named Paddy with yellow hair who told the other Hums what to do.

"What do you want me to do with her?" said Paddy.

"Sell her," said Mitzi.

"She's gorgeous," said Paddy. "Look how her eyes are bright and always moving. See those deep furrows above her eyes. The white star on her forehead. She's a thinker."

"But she thinks about killing me," said Mitzi.

"She hasn't killed anybody," Paddy said.

"She's tried," Mitzi said.

Mitzi's plan was location, location, location. If she kept Anastasia in a beautiful stable like this, on a mountaintop overlooking the Pacific Ocean, a first rate facility, then people would think that Anastasia was a first rate horse and not only buy her, but pay a lot of money for her. For Anastasia, it seemed like a good plan but for the selling part.

Every day Paddy turned her loose in a corral for an hour or so. Out there, when she wasn't running around, she liked to stop and look out at a pond across the way where tall birds, some white and some blue, swooped in, then stood in the shallows, moving very slowly and smoothly, their heads turning slightly. They were nice to watch. More things should move like that, Hums in particular.

After the corral, a groom came and rinsed her with a hose and put her away and fed her. It was all right.

Sometimes a prospective buyer came by and got on her and Annie got rid of them, sometimes by just going wild in the ring – she could gallop off sideways as fast as a lightning bolt – sometimes by stopping quickly in front of a jump; sometimes she waited till she got them out on the trail. They'd leave and it was back to the routine: corral, bath, dinner. Things were working out great!

Paddy dropped by the stall and brought her a carrot and said, "You're really talented. You'd be one hell of a horse for somebody if you don't end up dead first."

And unbeknownst to Anastasia that's exactly where things were headed. Mitzi came by and gave Paddy one more month.

"Why don't we try working with her?" said Paddy.

"She's bad," said Mitzi.

Bad. Annie pinned her ears and bared her teeth at Mitzi.

"See. Bad. A dangerous horse," Mitzi said.

Paddy knew horses. And though there were certainly ways in which Anastasia was dangerous, she wasn't mean. She'd been hurt. For one, you couldn't touch her chest.

"And she doesn't like me," Mitzi said.

Well, what was there to like? But it was out of Paddy's hands. Horses came and went. Some, like the thoroughbreds, only got a year or two; they died on the track or failed on the track, were bred for hell and running and nothing else; it took years to work that out of them and it might be worth the effort and it might not. Who had the money and time? Animal shelters were full of abandoned dogs and cats, thousands of them put away every day. But horses had it the worst. Most of them bred, trained, and used for one thing and if they didn't do it well, didn't do it better than almost all the others, then they were history, dog food. Even here, their owners came by once a week at best. They were moved around and isolated, despite being social animals who lived in herds. Forgotten hobbies of the wealthy. Or, like Anastasia, not what was expected. Just a half-ton of too much trouble. So in a month it would be off to auction and at the auction the highest bidder was usually a Japanese meat merchant. A horse's meat was worth more than his mind and heart.

Three weeks went by. Then another five days. Mitzi came by and informed Paddy that she'd have the trailer show up on Saturday for the auction. And then Paddy got a phone call. Some guy was looking for a horse.

Bird, Bow, Ride, Think

Bird

Whoever's calm and sensible is insane!

- - Rumi, "Where Are We?"

Friday morning, the day before the trailer arrived to take Anastasia to auction, Paddy looked Anastasia in the eyes. "Do you know what's at stake here?" Paddy said.

The answer was no. It had been a while, but usually that tone meant somebody was coming and somebody was going to get bucked off.

And this time Paddy figured there wasn't a chance in hell. Her old friend Bob had called on Thursday. Bob was a lawyer who had a little ranch in another canyon, four stalls and a couple turnouts, a riding ring. Paddy went there every week and helped him train his reining quarter horse; reining was a kind of rodeo dressage where the horse is taught to stop and slide at a dead run, then reverse direction and do it again, change leads on the fly in the middle of the ring, spin around on its hind legs.

Bob was temperamental, too temperamental to ever be a good horseman; moody and jerky, too fast moving; horses liked things slow and steady. Besides that, Bob got pissed off all the time and getting mad at your horse never accomplished anything. Eventually he'd get fed up, sell his horse and buy a more expensive horse, destroy that relationship, get fed up and buy an even more expensive horse, though eventually he was going to run out of money or the world was going to run out of horses. Anyway, he always boarded two or three horses besides his own – that paid for his horse – but his boarders, a husband and wife, had twins and that ended their horseback riding, and now Bob had an empty barn. Lucky for Bob, his telephone repairman, Telephone Bill, knew everybody's business in the canyon and found out that one of Bob's neighbors was looking for a horse.

"Has he ever owned a horse?" asked Paddy.

"No."

"What's his experience?"

"Trail rides," said Bob.

"Glorified pony rides? He's never even leased a horse?"

"He's had some lessons."

"I really don't think I have anything for him," said Paddy.

"What about that mare?"

"Anastasia?"

"I need a boarder," said Bob. "Or I can't afford my reining lessons."

Well, she knew that was baloney. Bob owned a million dollar ranch. He was just cheap. But what was another rider bucked off? Saturday Anastasia would be auctioned for horse meat.

"You better come out tomorrow morning because she's going to auction on Saturday."

It was a cold April morning when Bob showed up with Bird who had a straw hat with lots of feathers in it. He smelled like a bird. He even moved a little like a bird; like one of those tall water birds in the pond; he kind of stopped cold, then moved a little, stretching out, then stopped again. Steam poured off Anastasia's back and out her nose as Bird leaned on her paddock door.

"What are you looking for?" said Paddy.

"I don't want a bay or a mare or a thoroughbred or an Arabian," said Bird.

"Well there she is," said Paddy. "All of the above."

Well there she was.

"She's pretty," said Bird.

Paddy said, "Let's get her out," and they saddled her up Western. Bird led Anastasia into the training ring where there was a little bridge to walk over, a water trough to walk through, a big, blue plastic tarp to walk on (things horses were supposed to be afraid to do), barrels to run around, lots of small fences to jump.

"What should I do?" said Bird.

"Let's try getting on," Paddy said.

Bird got on and Anastasia took off. She never had anybody this ignorant on her back before. It was impossible to outguess him, he was too stupid to trick; she couldn't anticipate what he wanted because he didn't want anything. She ran over the bridge, around the barrels, over the tarp, jumped the fences. Bird hung on. Anastasia got bored and just ran up to Paddy and stopped.

"What do you think?" Bird said to Bob.

"I think I made a big mistake," said Bob.

"She can sure run around," said Bird.

"That horse is a maniac," Bob said.

"High strung," said Paddy. "I've never seen her go over the bridge or the tarp for anybody before. How did you ask her?"

"I didn't," said Bird. "She just did it."

"Let's try the trail," Paddy said.

Anastasia and Bird followed Paddy and Bob out to the trailhead.

"Do you think this is wise?" said Bob.

"What do I do?" Bird said.

"If you come back together that will be a new thing," said Paddy.

And out they went. Anastasia walked and trotted, she bounced Bird around with her highest trot. Bird hung on. When she got to the top of a hill Anastasia spun and crow hopped a few times (that's a small buck). Bird didn't even say whoa. She stood. Bird kissed for a lope. She flew. She ripped. Everything became a blur. When Bird pulled back slightly on the reins, she slid with her head down but he didn't go over the top, so she broke back into her vertical lope, a lot of up and down, it pulled even good riders off the saddle and knocked their crotch into the horn. Up top, Bird was laughing. "This is scary!" screamed Bird. So she stopped. She stood. The wind whistled around them. She could smell sweat on him, but she didn't smell fear. She smelled something else. It was a Hum smell, but she couldn't place it.

"What do you think, Annie?" Bird said.

31

She gave him a hard buck and ran for the barn.

Bird yelled, "Whoa!" and pulled back; she stopped only because he surprised her. Then she began to trot back.

"I guess I'll let you trot, seeing as you're not running," said Bird.

And that's how they got back. Anastasia stopped in front of Paddy and Bob. She didn't quite stop completely, she sweated and danced. She hadn't gotten rid of Bird, but Bird never asked her to calm down, so there was never really a moment when she could trick him. Once again, he'd been too clueless to surprise.

"Well holy shit," said Paddy.

"She likes me," said Bird.

"Did she try to get rid of you?" said Paddy.

"Maybe a little," Bird said.

"That horse will kill you," said Bob.

"She was your idea," Bird said.

"That horse wasn't my idea," Bob said. "I think that's too much horse for you."

"When I bought my first motorcycle, it was too small. I outgrew it in a few months," Bird said.

"That horse will keep you interested till the day she dies," said Paddy.

"The day he dies," said Bob.

Anastasia spun and looked at Bob. Bob was making sounds she didn't like.

"I love her," said Bird.

"You don't love her," said Bob. "You don't know anything about her."

Bird got down and gave Anastasia a carrot. "Carrot," said Bird. Carrots were a good thing and carrot a good word. She twitched her ears.

"You shouldn't do that with the bit in," Bob said.

"She likes me," said Bird. "She won't hurt me."

"She doesn't like you and she doesn't care if she hurts you," said Bob.

"I think she does like him," said Paddy. "At least more than she's liked anybody else."

That kind of summed it up. Anastasia didn't like Bird or dislike Bird, though at that moment she just disliked him less than she disliked Bob. In

32

general, she had a really low opinion of Hums, who were idiots, though it seemed you'd never live a day without them. She saw Paddy making other horses do ridiculous things all the time, and she figured if she stayed here much longer that's how it would end up. She pinned her ears at Bob.

"I don't want her on my ranch," said Bob.

"Then I'll keep her somewhere else," said Bird.

Yeah, we'll keep her somewhere else, felt Anastasia.

"If he doesn't take her, tomorrow she's glue," said Paddy.

That glue word was getting thrown around far too much to mean anything good.

"If it doesn't work out, he can bring her back," said Paddy.

"Minus his money," Bob said.

"And then? said Bird.

"Glue," said Bob.

See? Bob said glue. Bird didn't.

"I'll take her," Bird said.

The next morning, before dawn, she got in a trailer and when she got out, there was Bird. He led her up a road and into the woods. She hated the woods. She couldn't see what was around her or what was up ahead. Smells and sounds came from everywhere and nowhere. She jumped, she pranced, she sweated, she pooped. The road narrowed to a path. She pulled up.

"Easy, Annie," said Bird. "Easy now."

They stood there a long time, but after a while it was scarier to stand in the woods than to walk in the woods so she took off, but Bird pulled her back to him and then trotted along beside her at her head until they broke into a clearing where there was a sandy track that ran along two big corrals, above that a place to hitch up horses. Near the tie-ups lay a hose – she liked hoses, it meant baths – then a line of stalls, four of them, like four hooves. Bird slid her into the first stall. Half of it was enclosed and in the other half she could walk outside, though behind the outside part there were a lot of trees and she didn't trust them. Bird took off her halter and left her in there. He stood at the stall door and watched her. She watched him. Then Bob came out of nowhere and she pinned her ears and lunged at him.

"Jesus Christ!" said Bob.

But she didn't like Bob, so to hell with the formalities.

"Did she try to bite you?" said Bob.

"Not yet," said Bird. "She didn't like the woods."

"What does she like?" said Bob. "Anything?"

Carrots. She liked carrots.

Bird pulled out a round thing that smelled sweet. He bit it and took the piece out of his mouth and put his hand over the stall door. She smelled it. Ate it. It was sweeter than a carrot.

"Apple," said Bird.

She liked apples. She knew the word before she finished the apple.

"She likes apples, too" said Bird.

"I give this a week," said Bob.

"If I could ride her, I could ride anything," Bird said.

"If you live," Bob said.

As Bob walked away, Anastasia snorted into the cold air. She arched her neck and stared at Bird. Steam poured from the sweat on her back and she pranced sideways in her stall.

"Annie," Bird said. "Holy Mackerel. Annie."

That was his word around her. Not Anastasia. Annie. She guessed he'd want to do some things. But no matter how much his stupidity could keep her guessing, if his plans had anything to do with the woods, Bird was in trouble. Hell, Bob was right, he was in trouble anyways.

Bow

All things are full of Gods.

- - Thales

In the pasture that wasn't a pasture, years later, Bird stopped his rumble and looked out the window. "Annie," he said. "Sweet Annie." He was by himself. It meant a ride. Maybe a bath.

"Do you see him?" she said to Rumi.

"I see a rumble," said Rumi.

"Bird is inside," Annie said.

"Is he in all the rumbles?"

"Just some. If this one comes, Bird is in it."

"Why doesn't a rumble come with my Hum?" said Rumi.

Yes, why not? Though it was sometimes hard to know whether the rumble brought the Hum or the Hum the rumble.

"Maybe your Hum's rumble ran away," Annie said, though she doubted it. She didn't see rumbles without Hums, it's why she assumed the sky rumbles had Hums inside. Yet it was a mystery to her why the others, like Rumi, didn't see the Hums at all. Maybe blindness was better than hope. She wouldn't say it to Rumi, because she found the price of her sentience worth it, but emotions and thoughts were often painful and it was difficult to know whether or not Rumi would be better off with them or without them.

Certainly he had some thoughts and feelings. He waited expectantly for food. He was afraid of Dummie. When Bird showed up and Rumi was reminded of his Hum, or his lack of one, she sensed his melancholy. Dummie, on the other hand, often went into a rage. As Bird drove off to return without the rumble, Dummie pushed Tasha and Precious aside and pranced forward, scattering Rumi. He circled Annie, as if this time, if he just made a big enough show of his giant self, Bird would choose him. It was as if he had no memory at all, though surely even Dummie had to know that Bird was hers; it had to be what prompted his rage in the first place. But Dummie couldn't hold two things in his head at once, and as Bird approached he was bouncing at the top of the corral fence, nudging his old halter and feeling, Choose me! Choose me!

Annie calmly turned, spread her legs, and urinated, taunting Dummie with her sex, though she always urinated when Bird came for a ride; she didn't like to do it while being cleaned and tacked, and it was easier to do it now, without Bird on her back, though if she needed to, she stopped and spread her legs and Bird stood in the stirrups, taking his weight from her kidneys and petting her neck as she peed. Bird, like most Hums, thought it meant something, that it was some kind of good sign if the horse beneath him was relaxed enough to stop and pee, but it wasn't necessarily; sometimes she just had to pee, especially if she was in season, and sometimes, in the early days, just to fool him, she'd blow sky high after taking a long, relaxed pee, not that it changed anybody's opinion, not even Bird's. When Hums got something in their heads, forget changing it.

Annie could tilt herself forward and urinate between her legs, like a stallion. Stallions and geldings urinated forward because they were built that way and most mares, whose organs tilted the other direction, peed behind themselves. Annie could do that too, if she wanted to put it in someone's face. Sometimes a Hum who was afraid, for some reason, to get close enough to see a horse's sex, just looked at the front of her back hooves to see if there were pee stains on them; if they saw urine there they thought the animal was a gelding. Just another thing the Hums thought they'd figured out.

Annie could bend her neck in an arch, pitch her ears forward, snort out her nostrils and make that deep, throaty sound that stallions made. Because of all that, lots of Hums, looking straight at her, if they didn't look closely, assumed she was proud gelded, that is a stallion cut in his maturity.

Right now she walked behind Dummie and went to the gate. She rumbled at Bird, grprrurrturrurrtr, purgurgurtrpurrtr. Some Hums called

36

it a nicker, but she didn't know any horses who ever said nicker-nicker. Bird came to the gate with a carrot and she raised her nose and touched his lips with hers. He liked that. "Kiss," he said. That was his word for it, though sometimes, when the ranchums were there, he said, "Beso." He opened the gate and put his hands together and lowered his head to her and then she put out one leg and put her head down between her forelegs. That was a bow. He bowed to her and she bowed to him. Then he offered her another carrot and put his arms around her neck, something she used to hate but came, lately, to accept.

"I love you, Annie," Bird said.

Ride

There is a way between voice and presence
where information flows

- - Rumi, "Only Breath"

Then he opened the gate. If it had been a wet spring, then fresh grass was everywhere and Bird let her graze. He didn't even put the halter on her anymore, let alone the lead line. This drove the other horses crazy with jealousy. Sometimes other Hums came and yelled at Bird. "Your horse is running loose!"

"She's not running," said Bird.

"But she could run away."

"Where?" said Bird. "The carrots are here. The grass is here." And Bird was there.

In her younger days she did run away. At another ranch, the one after Bob's, she'd run to the stallion pens and throw her tail in their faces. She'd pick fights with the mares, arching her neck and striking out with her fore hoof. She could still pick a fight. She would not share Bird.

This spring it was dry and there was little grass, so Bird broke carrots up and put them in a round, black rubber dish. Bird brushed her coat and cleaned her hooves, saddled her as she grazed. This was the compromise. Though she loved a bath, she hated brushing and cleaning. There were too many spots on her body that remembered pain and when they were touched, that's where she went, back to the pain, it didn't matter, and she'd have to kick or bite or strike. And in time, Bird learned it, slowly, over time, Bird learned to accept her and adapt.

The Hums had somehow forgotten that they were animals, too; they thought that thinking was somewhere in those sounds they made, that everything was occurring somewhere behind their eyes. They forgot that their hands had thoughts, their feet, their legs, their bodies, their hearts; that every cell strived with intention. And that everything around them was thinking too. Hums forgot that you think with your body, your whole body. And because a horse's body was not like their own, they couldn't understand it. They looked at the eyes of a horse, trying to see what was behind them, trying to see if there was something behind an animal's eyes that was like a Hum, but Annie was not behind her eyes, she was everywhere she was, 1,100 pounds of thought and feeling right in front of your face, huge, agile, tactile, capable of feeling another body through space the way you see and hear and smell and, yes, even taste at a distance. Hums had forgotten how to do that, how to feel at a distance.

At the very last minute, Bird showed Annie the headstall and she lowered her head into it. Bird still used a bit, a soft snaffle, but she could barely remember the last time he pulled on the reins; he just shifted and she knew what to do. He wore spurs, too, out of respect. If he didn't wear them, then she'd kick his ass until he put them on. Once they were on, he didn't need them.

The other horses, but for Precious who sulked at the other end of the pasture, stood at the corral fence, their heads stretching forward, watching Annie and Bird. Tasha eventually hung her head and walked away. Rumi followed. Dummie began to scream, "Take me! Take me!" He just didn't get it. There was even a time when Bird felt sorry for him and spread carrots for Dummie and Precious, Tasha and Rumi, but Dummie and Precious thought it meant that they were moving up on Annie and picked a big fight with her. Dummie really hurt her that night. He took a bite out of her neck and put a hoof into her ribs that caused a huge welt.

The next day when Bird showed up and saw the wounds, he dressed them, made sure her feet were sound, then saddled her up and went into the corral on her back with a lasso. They chased Dummie all over the place. Boy, that was fun! Dummie didn't remember much, but he remembered that. Now, Dummie was so desperate for attention that he wanted Bird to chase him, but Bird had figured that out; chasing Dummie every day would make him feel good about himself and cause more trouble for Annie, and lucky for Annie, though Dummie knew that Bird would scare him if he hurt her, he wasn't capable of manipulating that to get Bird's attention.

"Where do you want to go today, Annie?" said Bird.

Nowhere. She just wanted to eat carrots and have a bath. But Bird had this riding thing. They never ended up anywhere but back at the pasture, so why leave at all? But they didn't fight about it much anymore. If Bird wanted to go somewhere for a while, then let's go. Besides, once she got him out there she'd try to get him to cross through the ranch to Mick and Adele's. They were a retired Australian couple who rescued horses and dogs. They kept lots of carrots in a garbage can, and Annie liked to drop by and take the lid off the can.

"Smart, but a bit of a snob, that one," Mick always said. Because when he passed her pasture on the way out of the ranch, he always made sure the water tub was full and left carrots for everybody, though Annie wouldn't stand with the others; he had to take her carrots down the fence aways. Annie liked Mick and Adele and their carrots.

In the old days she drove Bird crazy. Back then, they often went to the ring and trained. She hated the ring, but not as much as she hated the trail and the woods. Now, as they sauntered along, if she caught him with his mind wandering she just stopped until he noticed. Some Hums called it horse telepathy, but it was just feeling. When they were riding in tune, she could feel Bird's eyes move inside his head. And when a horse is concentrating that much, you needed to be in complete control of every part of your body, because you could send a dozen different signals at once and drive a good horse mad.

Wherever they were, she knew the shortest way home. Bird liked to play as much as Annie did, and sometimes he took her to a crossroads where one road circled the long way back and the other the short way, but she knew that yet another road went off the short way home, a trail that led up a mountain, though it also could lead to Mick and Adele's. If they went up the mountain, Bird would ask her to lope up to the top, so she had to remember how long they'd been out on the trail. If it was early in the ride, then the short way would lead to a mountain run. She stood, calculating. Bird laughed and laughed.

When they got back, Bird loosened the cinch and took off the headstall, gave her a carrot, then dropped more carrots in her dish while he undressed her, combed her mane and tail, brushed her sweat, cleaned her eyes. If she had any nicks or cuts, he put lotion on them. If there were flies, he sprayed her with fly spray and sponged her down. He gave her pieces of apple, opened the gate and she walked back into the pasture.

Bird circled back to the fence and gave her a good-bye carrot. "Good-bye, Annie. I love you. I'll see you tomorrow," said Bird. And almost always, he did. If there was one thing she'd learned about Bird, it was that he always returned.

Think

*It's getting hard to find anyone who realizes that when
you think, you risk losing your head.*

- - Varuna, Rig Veda

"Where do you go?" said Rumi. "Do you go see the wild horses?"

"I am the wild horse," Annie said.

"No, you're not."

"You're the wild horse," said Annie.

"I'm not a wild horse," said Rumi.

"What is a wild horse?"

Tasha had wandered over and Dummie stared across the pasture at the three of them. How had it happened that he ended up alone with Precious?

"Here you are, back," said Tasha. "Nothing has changed."

"Wild horses have wings," said Rumi.

"That's better," Annie said.

"You'll make him crazy," said Tasha.

"I'm already crazy!" said Rumi and he began to jump around and buck and run. "I want to go out!"

"You just end up back here," said Tasha.

"Every time I see Bird it's different," Annie said to Tasha.

"Nothing is ever different," Tasha said.

"Annie and I are going to sprout wings!" said Rumi. "We're going to leave!"

"Are you going to take him when you leave?" Tasha said to Annie.
"No."

42

"She won't want to, but she'll have to," said Rumi.

"He's excitable," Annie said to Tasha.

"You're no good for him," Tasha said. "You end up where you end up," she said to Rumi.

"Rumi is waiting," Annie said to Tasha. "Like I wait for Bird. When you wait you see what's going to happen."

"Then you make it happen!" said Rumi. He jumped some more.

"You just made Dummie come over here with all that jumping around," Tasha said. "That's what you made happen."

"Something happened," said Annie.

"The same thing happened," said Tasha. "The same thing always happens."

"I need some flies swiped from my face," said Dummie.

"Now watch," Annie said to Rumi. She walked between Tasha and Dummie and stopped with her face at their rear ends. She swished her tail. They swished theirs.

Rumi ran around and faced Annie. "Submission?" he said.

"They think I'm servicing the both of them, but in fact the two of them are servicing me." While she had neither flank exposed and their two tails brushing flies from her face, they had her one tail brushing their two faces and each had a flank exposed. Off on the far end, Precious stood alone.

"Who cares what they think about it?" said Annie.

"You care what I think," said Rumi.

"I care a little that you think," said Annie. "I don't care much what you think."

"Does Dummie think?" said Rumi.

"Don't call me Dummie," said Dummie.

"Was that a thought?" Rumi said. "Do you think, Tasha?"

"Only when I have to."

"I think you should come over here and brush some flies off me," said Dummie.

"Most Hums don't know that we can think," said Annie. "The few that do know, don't know how we think. The ones who think they know, don't know. You can use it to your advantage."

"He doesn't have a Hum. He doesn't have an advantage," said Tasha.

"He has a tail he's not using," said Dummie.

"He has a mind he's not using," said Annie.

"He doesn't need it," said Tasha. "Anyway, what makes you think that the Hums can think?"

That was a good question. Tasha had been around the Hums a long time.

"She's thinking," Rumi whispered to Annie.

"Damn it," said Tasha and walked off. "Now leave me alone." But Precious, seeing the opening, rushed up to her and chased her from the alfalfa bin.

"There's what all your prancing around did," said Dummie. He trotted at Tasha and Precious, pushing them with his chest.

"It got rid of you," whispered Annie.

Rumi came forward and stood head to tail with Annie. "Did I get rid of him?"

"Yes," Annie said.

"You just used me."

"Yes," Annie said.

"So you got rid of him."

"Maybe," said Annie.

"Maybe?" said Rumi.

There was a tiny difference between intelligence and stupidity. The difference was this: Unintelligence just moved from one thing to the next as it came to it. Intelligence chose the next thing to come. It didn't matter what you were, a horse or a Hum. It made all the difference.

"Does Bird think?" said Rumi

"He tries," said Annie.

"Do rumbles?"

That was a good question. "I don't know," Annie said.

"Ha!" said Rumi. He jumped once, twice. "I have to run around!"

"You need a Hum," said Annie.

"News!" screamed Rumi.

Dummie, Precious, and Tasha raised their heads.

Rumi ran and kicked and jumped.

"You're making him crazy," yelled Dummie.

"Dangerous to himself," said Tasha.

Rumi ran around and around and finally stopped in front of Annie's face. "What do we do?" panted Rumi.

"We'll need Bird," Annie said.

The First Days

In every important relationship, generation is reciprocal.

- - Satapatha Brahmana

*I lift up my eyes toward the mountains;
when will help come to me?*

- - Psalm 121

The very first morning at Bob's ranch, when Bird took Annie out of her stall, she tried to bite him. She backed up. She pranced in place. Bird stood. Annie pranced. Bird stood. She pranced to the back of the stall where it opened up, but there were woods behind the opening and she didn't like the woods, so she trotted at Bird and knocked him down. She could have run over him and run out of the stall then, but she didn't. She didn't know where to go. Bird hadn't hurt her, why hurt him? And the same thought hit Bird then. She didn't run over him and she didn't run out. Bird got on his feet. "You like me," Bird said, though maybe this was a big mistake. Maybe Bob was right and this was too much horse.

With great suspicion she let him put the halter on her, pinning her ears, baring her teeth. He led her to the tie-ups and tried to brush her, but she nipped at him again, so he attached one chain to her halter and gave up on the brushing. She let him clean her hooves, it was the only part of her that didn't remember pain. Then he unhooked her chain and took her up a little slope to a small riding ring beyond the barn. Inside, he unhooked the lead line from her halter and tried to send her forward. She knew this routine, a lot of running around in a circle, one way, then the

46

other. But Bird didn't have a whip, so she turned and looked at him. Bird clucked. Bird made a kissing sound with his lips that meant lope. He twirled the end of his lead line. Nope, that wasn't going to do it. She could stand there all day.

Then Bird began walking toward her. She'd have to let him touch her or run. She ran. "Ha!" laughed Bird. She stopped. She ran as far away as she could get, the far end of the ring, and turned her butt to Bird. She lifted her tail and pooped.

Bird walked toward her. "How much poop do you have in you?" said Bird.

Well, you'd be surprised. She turned and looked at Bird and they stood looking at each other. After a while, Bird stepped toward her and she took off for the other end of the ring. After an hour or so of that, Bird opened the gate and she came forward and let him put the lead line on the halter.

"So that's how it is," said Bird. He took her down to one of the big corrals, called turnouts, and turned her loose. He threw a big square of alfalfa in there.

She stared at Bird. How about a carrot?

"You have to do something for me to get a carrot from me," Bird said.

She pinned her ears at Bird. Carrots first.

Bird pulled out a carrot and stepped back. Annie stared at him. Bird folded his arms. Okay, the heck with it. She lifted her ears and began to turn away, but then Bird offered the carrot. She lunged at it. He stepped away. She tried lifting one ear. "Okay," said Bird and put the carrot down in front of her and walked out.

Later in the day Bob came down and rode his little gray reiner, Gray Dog, up and down the path next to the turnouts. He ran him to one end of the path, pulled him to a halt, turned him hard and ran him down to the other end, then he'd curse and do it again. Each time he did it, things got worse. Gray Dog ran slower, stopped slower, turned slower. Bob spurred him and hit him on the neck and butt with the long reins. Gray Dog started bucking. Bob cursed. After all that, he put Gray Dog in the other turnout and left.

47

Before dark a little Hum named Manny showed up and put food in the stalls. He tried to catch Annie, but she wouldn't let him so he just opened the stall door; then he opened the corral gate and she ran to the stall. That's how things went for weeks, the difference from all the other situations being that unlike the other Hums she'd had to deal with, Bird showed up every day. Every day the same thing, standing around in the little ring looking at Bird. She wondered how long Bird would do it before he got rid of her. Then one morning Bob showed up with him.

"What the hell?" said Bob.

"She's smart," said Bird.

"She's a horse," said Bob. "They don't think."

"She thinks," said Bird.

"Get a whip," Bob said. He went in the tack room next to the tie-ups and came out with a long whip. He came into the ring and cracked the whip at Annie. She reared up and ran at him and Bob ran out of the ring.

"That went well," said Bird.

"Sell her," said Bob.

"To who?"

"Anybody."

"I just got her. Give her some time," Bird said.

"A lifetime?" said Bob.

The next day was Manny's day off, so Bird showed up with him the night before and watched him put Annie away, so to speak.

"I'll be damned," said Bird.

"Do not tell Bob," said Manny.

Bird walked up to Annie's stall where she was eating and shut the door. She lifted her head and pinned her ears at him.

"You don't want to run away," said Bird.

No, she just wanted to be left alone.

"Who hurt you?" said Bird.

Everybody. Hums hit her and chased her and took her baby and moved her around.

Bird brought out a carrot.

She kept her ears pinned at him. But she was eating alfalfa now. Get lost.

Bird bit the carrot and it snapped. Her ears went up. He gave her the carrot. When she finished it, she pinned her ears and bared her teeth at him. He stepped back. Waited. When she put her ears up he gave her another carrot. Well, if that's all it took to get a carrot, fine.

Bird hadn't been around horses or horse people much, but from what he could see, horses had it about as bad as any animal who had to deal with human beings. People bought them like they bought bikes and ski equipment. Buy the skis, buy the clothes, now you're a skier. Buy the bicycle, buy the colorful spandex suit, helmet and spiky shoes, now you're a bicyclist. Buy the Jeep and you're an off-roader. Buy the horse, the hat, the boots. But the skis, the bike, the Jeep, even the hat, the boots could all rot in the garage. Not the horse. The horse had a belly and more, a mind and a heart. In this case, more mind and heart than he knew what to do with.

The next day he tried something different. He saddled her up in the ring and hopped on. Annie took off. She ran and ran and ran and then she ran some more. When she got a little tired and slowed down, Bird yelled, "Whoa!" but she took off instead and Bird yelled, "Run!" After a long while she got tired again and slowed to a fast trot and Bird said, "Trot. Trot, Annie." Then she broke into a gallop and he said, "Lope. Excellent." Bird didn't know how to ride and he was bouncing all over her back, but whenever she did something he made a sound, "Run, lope, trot, whoa."

Whatever she did, he had one sound for it and he could make that sound as fast as she could change what she did. She wondered if he had a sound for getting bucked off, but she was too tired, so she just stopped. "Okay," said Bird, "whoa, excellent." And he got off and offered her a carrot. He took her out of the ring, undressed her, rinsed her off with the hose and let her graze till she dried off. Then he put her in the corral and walked out. He didn't even look at her until he was pretty far away, and then he turned. Sometimes when he did that she remembered the ride, but more often she remembered every Hum who ever hurt her. Then the next day Bird came again.

Bird came every day. Every day he got on and she took off and he said his words, though sometimes he just showed up at the door of her stall and looked in. She never went up to him unless he held an apple or a carrot, and when he did he always said, "Annie," then "apple" or "carrot" and that was it. She tried being more trouble in the ring, but the ring was pretty small; there weren't a lot of options. She ran sideways or backed up really fast (Bird said, "Back up" when she did that), and she did buck him, but she wasn't a bronco and it was hard to catch him by surprise. Once she did. Bob came down the road behind the ring. He was inside a rumble. Suddenly the rumble stopped and Bob jumped out. Bird turned in the saddle. She bucked hard and threw Bird over the fence.

It was only an accident in that she hadn't thought of it ahead of time. She'd never seen a Hum jump out of a rumble before and it really did startle her. Bob ran around like a chicken, yelling, "That horse is going to kill you!" and "You're going to die!" The same old noises. She looked at Bird lying on the ground and didn't even hate him. Not with Bob there. She even took a step toward him. Then Bird stood and crawled through the fence. He walked up to Annie and got back on her. And without even thinking about it, Annie was standing there under Bird. "Stand," said Bird.

Bob made a lot of noises and eventually got back in the rumble and went away. Annie took off. Bird said, "Run."

That went on for a long, long time. For months. Every day. Every day Bird came. And in the ring it got to the point where it was hard to tell what came first, the doing or the sound. Until one day after running and loping and trotting for an hour or so, she just plain walked. "Walk," said Bird. And when she stood and he said, "Okay, whoa, excellent," and he didn't get off. He urged her forward. She walked a few steps. "Okay," said Bird and he dismounted.

Sometimes, when she was deep into grazing, so deep that she forgot he was there, he touched her side. And sometimes, instead of turning and baring her teeth at him, she let him.

Then some things happened. One day Paddy came. Annie looked to see if there was a rumble with a trailer, but there wasn't. She was relieved. That was an odd feeling. It was one of the things that happened. She wanted to stay here. Some people question whether animals have emotions, whether they can feel anything at all when, in fact, many animals, particularly horses, can feel several things at once, sometimes opposite things. Horses, by nature, are profoundly ambivalent. That's how Annie felt when she looked at Bird that morning with Paddy standing there, and Bob, too, and no trailer. Ambivalent, relieved, trapped, uncertain, both wanting Bird to go away and never take her into the ring again and wanting to stay here with Bird and eat carrots, have a bath, and graze. Bird came to her stall.

"Annie," said Bird. "Sweet Annie. Want a carrot?"

Yes.

Then they did what they always did, only this time Paddy and Bob watched; well, Bob watched, Paddy made a lot of noises and Bird laughed and made his sounds. Annie didn't behave so badly. She didn't buck. When she ran sideways Bird said, "I need a word for that."

"It's called a side pass," said Paddy, "but most horses do it at a walk."

"In time," said Bird.

"A lifetime?" said Bob.

"A decade?" said Bird.

"In a year," Paddy said, "that horse could lope backwards."

"She already does," Bird said.

"I can show you how to ask for it," said Paddy. "She can do anything."

"Except obey," said Bob.

Bird laughed. "I'll have to learn how to ride," he said.

And in that moment, Annie felt something new again. In those moments when Bird wasn't splattering his feet and legs and butt all over her back, when he was there moving as she moved, as if they were both doing the same thing, in that moment when they were one she held a feeling of accomplishment, almost pride, in herself, in herself and Bird, and Bird felt it too, a moment of perfection, of absolute joy, a bit of heaven; and then it was quickly replaced by humiliation and Annie's desire to dominate him, to disobey him, to disobey all Hums, all horses, to disobey.

Later, while Annie grazed, Bird said to Paddy, "Watch." Gently, he placed his hand on her side. She turned her head toward him, then went back to grazing.

"This mare will hold your interest till the day she dies," said Paddy.

"Till the day he dies," said Bob.

"You just going to run around in that little ring all your life?" Paddy said.

"It's just a thrill to be on her," Bird said.

"Bring her down to the big ring," said Bob.

"You'd like to get my death over with," said Bird.

"I'll go with you," Bob said.

Annie'd heard of the big ring from Gray Dog, though it was hard to communicate with him. For one, he was taciturn and moody, too much like Bob himself. Bob needed to keep Gray Dog pristine for shows, so he always kept him in one corral while any other horses, however many, were turned out in the other. Gray Dog had to wear jackets so his coat wouldn't grow, fly masks over his face, had to get shaved for his shows, then because he had so little fur he had to wear heavier jackets when it got cold. Bob was so afraid of Annie hurting Gray Dog that he kept him at the opposite end of the four stalls, with two empty stalls in between. Outside, the space between the two big corrals was about ten feet, too far away to touch noses. What little Gray Dog intimated to her, he did to feel superior.

Sometimes instead of running up and down the reining track, Bob and Gray Dog headed into the woods. Gray Dog didn't like the woods either, no horse does because you can't see ahead of you or around you; but though Gray Dog spooked on Bob occasionally, earning him a whipping over the neck and a quick back up, he'd grown resigned to the trek, at the end of which was the big ring. There were noises down there from a road where rumbles constantly swept by on one end, on one side a stream, and then a place where Hums made a lot of noise, on the other two sides, woods. The good thing was that it was huge and you could run like crazy, though Bob never let Gray Dog run like crazy, Gray Dog was a special kind of horse and what he did required a lot of control and discipline.

"Well, okay," said Bird. "We'll try that."

But before that big day yet another thing happened. Bird showed up with a female Hum. But she wasn't like Paddy and she wasn't like Mitzy. She smelled soft. When Bird showed up he usually smelled Hum-sweaty, sometimes a little soapy, more often than not his clothes smelled a little like Annie herself, and then there was that feather smell on his hat. Then there was another smell that Annie could never quite figure out till now, just mildly sweet like a mare with a foal and a little bit edgy like sex. It was this female Hum's smell. The female Hum stood really close to Bird. She even touched him

Annie pinned her ears and showed her teeth.

"She doesn't like me," said the female Hum. Bird called her Gail.

"She doesn't really like anybody," Bird said.

Annie turned and pooped at Gail.

"She hates me," said Gail.

Annie raised her tail again and popped her vulva at Gail.

"Wow, I can't do that," Gail said.

Annie turned around and glared at Gail again.

"You can have him here. In my barn, he's mine," Gail said to Annie, which didn't make any sense to her, but it sounded vaguely domineering.

Annie spit at Gail.

"That's a new one," said Bird. "You're pretty special."

But it was, without anybody noticing, another turning point. Toward Gail, Annie felt something she'd never felt before. She didn't dislike her because of anything she was. She disliked her because Bird liked her. Without even knowing just yet what she felt about Bird, she'd taken possession of him.

"That horse loves you," Gail said.

"I don't know if that's the word just yet," Bird said.

"If I were you, I wouldn't leave with me," said Gail. "She's jealous."

After that, as bad as Annie could be at any given time, if Bird showed up with that Gail smell on him, he was in for a long bad day. Even Bird figured that out.

And then came the first trip to the big ring.

Woods, Ring, Woods

Action is a mysterious and terrible word.

- - Satapatha Brahmana

Bird didn't smell like Gail so Annie let him saddle her. Across the way, Bob saddled Gray Dog. Some new thing.

"Maybe I should lead her down there," said Bird.

"That'll take forever," said Bob. "You're going to want to ride her down there eventually, you may as well start now."

Bird didn't try to groom Annie before tacking up anymore. He cleaned her feet, inspected her back, then threw the saddle on, bathed her after the ride. Now, before putting her headstall on, he offered her a carrot.

"What are you doing?" said Bob. "You'll never get a decent ride if you give her a carrot before you start. Herd of two."

Annie hated that "herd of two" phrase. It always meant the Hum was going to ask you to do something you didn't want to do. And it was the wrong tone of voice to have around you while you were eating a carrot.

Bird jumped on Annie.

"I'll lead," said Bob. And he headed for the trail into the forest.

Not the woods, Bird.

Bird touched Annie's neck. "Don't worry," said Bird.

Not the woods, she felt to Gray Dog. But by now Gray Dog was feeling pretty superior and plodded off toward the dark opening in the trees.

Not the woods, Bird.

But woods it was. Annie ran up behind Gray Dog, bumping him. Gray Dog kicked at her. She dodged it. Bit his butt. Gray Dog bucked. "What the hell?" said Bob. Gray Dog bucked again and Bob bounced left, almost off. Bird clucked Annie forward and caught Bob, pushing him back onto his saddle. Annie nipped Gray Dog's neck. Gray Dog bit back. Bob backed him up hard. Everybody stopped. But now, in the chaos, she'd entered the woods without noticing with Gray Dog behind her.

"Control your damn horse!" Bob said to Bird.

"Can we go back now?" said Bird.

"That would be the worst thing you could possibly do," said Bob. "Go ahead, you lead."

Bird pushed Annie forward. She took one step, stopped. Wind shook the oak leaves. The whole place smelled of predation and she couldn't see more than twenty feet ahead. Bird pushed again. She took another step.

"What's the matter?" said Bob.

"She's walking very, very slowly," said Bird.

"We haven't got a decade to get there," Bob said.

"Maybe we can do this later by ourselves," said Bird.

"Not on my property," said Bob. "I'm a lawyer."

"You think I'd sue you if I got hurt?"

"Everybody sues everybody," said Bob. "Okay, we'll ride next to each other."

And so they did, kind of, all the while Annie trying to bite Gray Dog and Gray Dog biting back.

"Goddamnit," said Bob. So she took a nip at him, but Bird caught her in the nick of time. Bob swatted at her with his hat. She caught it in her teeth. "Goddammit!" said Bob. They rode along like that for a while with Bob pulling Annie along by his hat.

"This is working," said Bird.

"This is not working," said Bob.

Gray Dog stopped paying attention to her, so she bit him. Bob pulled his hat away. Gray Dog jumped. Bob screamed. She could feel the nervous electricity in Bird's legs. She broke into a sweat and lay down a wet poop.

"She's scared," said Bird.

"She's not scared, she's a bitch," Bob said.

In fact, she was a little scared.

Anyway, that's how they got to the ring, the four of them sweating and exhausted.

Let's go back, felt Annie.

"Let's go back now," said Bird.

"What's the point in that?" said Bob. "We should at least walk around in here a little."

The big ring was pretty much what Gray Dog had led Annie to expect, woods all around, rumble noise, but at least inside it, she could see everything. She could feel that Gray Dog didn't like it down here, because it meant a lot of work, but he wasn't afraid and this comforted her. They walked around the huge ring together. Bird kept her on the inside, so Gray Dog was between them and the edge of the woods. There was some cooperation here, a herd of four, cooperating.

"She's walking," said Bird.

"This is more like it," Bob said.

They turned and walked around the other way.

"Okay, we're heading back," Bird told Bob.

"I'm going to stay and work a little," said Bob.

Gray Dog moaned.

Bird got down and led Annie out of the ring, then remounted. She sent her excitement and fear into his thighs. There had to be some other way to get back to the barns. Even a rumble and trailer.

"Easy, Annie," said Bird.

And she tried. She really tried. She jogged up the hill above the big ring. Bird asked her to walk again and again, but she couldn't do it. A strange smell came in the wind. The leaves rattled. She couldn't see! She leapt. Bird turned her. She crow hopped. She spun. She blew up.

An hour later Bob and Gray Dog came up the hill and found Bird and Annie standing in front of each other, the both of them pouring in sweat, Annie still snorting and covered with white foam.

"What happened?" said Bob.

"Everything," said Bird. "I'm going to walk her back."

"That's a big mistake," said Bob. "A capitulation. It'll only set you back. Get back on."

So Bird did. Annie went for the moon. She was crazy now with fear. She spun and bucked and screamed. Bird slid off.

"Sell her," Bob said. "Before she kills you."

Bird stood in front of Annie. She felt a little calmer now with Bird on the ground in front of her. "Are you going to kill me, Annie?" said Bird. But she couldn't even hear Bird. In fact, she could barely see him. The woods collapsed around her in a rush of wind, threatening voices of a thousand things, the smell of blood; she just wanted to run, run away, if only there were somewhere to go.

The Meaning of Rain

Parvati said: Then I hear the sound that dwells in the space within the heart: like a river, like a bell, like a chariot wheel, like the croak of a frog, like the rain . . .

- - Brihad Aranyaka Upanishad

One night it began to rain. A horse can stand in the rain. It's just rain. Though the pasture had an awning in the corner nearest the road, at the opposite end from the gate, and if you wanted to get out of the rain for a while you could stand under the awning and turn your tail to the wind. If it got cold, the horses stood together and warmed each other. Stay still. Moving wastes energy. Even Annie did this if she had to. She stood between Tasha and Rumi as the dawn came and turned the air from blue to gray. The rain pounded on the metal roof.

"What does the rain mean?" said Rumi.

"Butt to the wind, wait it out," Tasha said.

"Mud," said Precious.

"Grass will come," said Annie.

"Outside the fence," grumbled Dummie. "Outside the fence!"

"But Annie gets to eat it because Bird comes," said Rumi.

"Don't get me mad," said Dummie. "You'll be standing in the rain."

Annie shook herself and walked into the pasture, letting the rain fall on her back. In the rain, the ranchums did much less rumbling; fewer Hums, none riding, fewer rumbles on the road or in the sky, the dust settled and the dirt filled with a prescient, fecund smell. The brown hills turned purple, hinting at dark green. After a while Rumi followed her.

"You see," Annie said to Rumi. "It's not that hard."

"But now I'm standing in the rain," said Rumi.

"It doesn't rain forever."

"I'm wetter."

"It's quieter," said Annie.

"Colder," said Rumi.

"And getting noisier," Annie said.

When the rain let up a little, the ranchums came and threw bundles of alfalfa under the awning. When it was dry, the ranchums threw five bundles around the pasture so each horse could eat separately, though often Dummie went from pile to pile pushing the others away, Precious first, then Precious chased Tasha away from her pile, then Tasha pushed Rumi from his, then Rumi came to Annie who let him eat with her. Then Dummie came over and chased Rumi out. Of course, he couldn't chase Annie and they fought. And fought. Annie didn't like to talk to Dummie, but finally she said to him, "You know, while we're fighting, everybody else is eating." Then she walked over to the last unoccupied pile.

Dummie followed, but he didn't do anything, he just ate. After a while he said, "Ha! I'm eating with you."

Neither Tasha nor Precious liked that. All their submission and then Dummie went off and ate with Annie who couldn't care less. In the beginning they even tried to pick on her, but she fought back. They got tired of fighting and now they just came over and tried to share with Dummie and Annie. Annie walked away to a free pile. Dummie followed. Rumi watched. Something was happening that wasn't supposed to happen. Dummie was following Annie around. Wasn't he in charge? Then why was he following Annie? This was ear twitching stuff.

Now, in the rain, they all had to eat together under the metal awning or not at all.

"Hungrier," Rumi said.

"And noisier," said Annie, looking Rumi right in the eyes.

The rain let up to a drizzle. Small birds sped out from the trees like black dots crossing the sky. Annie sniffed the air. Something else. Leapers. Deer. Six doe emerged from the brush across the way. Annie knew them. They were smaller than Rumi, about the size of an early yearling, with big, floppy ears. In some ways they moved like the birds she

59

used to watch when she lived at Paddy's ranch on the mountaintop; one step, then quickly raising their heads to the air, ears and noses twitching. Like horses, they could feel each other through space. They were quick and could jump their own height. They could change directions even faster than a horse, but they were not as powerful or fast.

Sometimes, out riding with Bird, they saw these female leapers on the side of a hill where they often fed. Annie always stopped and watched them. In fact, now Annie always stopped there whether the leapers were there feeding or not. Bird petted her neck and said, "Looking for your friends?" He always said that. That was a good thing about Bird. A lot of Hums just made noise, but Bird always made the same noises in the same places. "Apple" when there was an apple. "Looking for your friends?" meant that they stopped and looked at the spot where the leapers fed.

If they were there, the leapers followed Annie and Bird down the trail, then, when Annie and Bird headed up the mountain, into open air, the leapers cut through the brush and met them at the top. There they stood together. Leapers were afraid of Hums, but when Bird was on Annie, the leapers didn't see him or smell him or feel him, they just felt Annie and stood quietly in a kinship of hooved sentience. That's one thing they shared, the ability to stand absolutely still, listening, smelling, feeling the same things around them.

And in that way they shared other things as well. Annie learned what was edible in the woods and where to look for it, what the wind was carrying on its back, whether or not the leapers would have babies in the spring. For the leapers, whether or not the wild woofs were moving in packs or if the death hiss was about. They told each other if the rattlers had started to sun themselves on the trails, and now, in what had been a dry year when food was scarce in the woods, Annie pointed to the safest place to find alfalfa droppings that fell from the ranchum rumbles.

It began to rain again and the leapers raised their heads, ears twitching. They crossed the riding path. Only in the rain would they venture this far from the woods, because the Hums were in their own barns and the eaters like the wild woof and the death hiss and rattlers didn't like the rain and though the rain sat on smell and might have made it easier to sneak up on prey, eaters didn't like to be inconvenienced. They'd rather

move behind the wind or, like the death hiss, just wait; Annie had se..
death hiss squat and wait, unmoving, for a day. Even the hawks and eagles
and owls stayed put in the rain, and the small furs that they ate, ground
squirrels, mice, rabbits, emerged to scour the wet ground because the rain
sat on sound, too, and the eaters that used sound as well as smell, like the
rattlers, were now at a disadvantage. In this way, prey and predator
danced inside the world's beating heart.

The leapers stepped cautiously toward the corral, in unison, one step,
then raised their heads, each nose pointing in a different direction. Out in
the open now, they were as if one body with a dozen eyes and a dozen ears,
six noses, two dozen sharp hooves. Many animals can do this, share their
bodies and senses, move as one: fish, migrating birds, herds, team predators
like wolves and lions and orcas; it's only people who think that we are
trapped inside our bodies, beneath our skins, living alone in the world; not
knowing that we live inside each other, that the natural world lives inside
us and we can share everything in every moment.

Annie took one small step toward the leapers. They stopped.
Watching. Finding her shape and her motion in their memory. This could
take a long time, though there was no time now, there was just this motion,
this ever-constant reading of air and light and the odor of wind-rain.

"Do you feel it?" Annie whispered to Rumi with her body.

"I couldn't live like that," Rumi said.

"Then you don't want to be wild."

"I want to be wild and safe," Rumi said.

"Then you don't want to be wild," said Annie.

In fact, they said this back and forth to each other many, many times.
When animals communicate there's often a lot of repetition; it keeps things
unambiguous and certain. Hums moved forward inside their too many
sounds, inside both ambiguity and uncertainty, and this made them
unpredictable and impossible to understand. When riding you, they
wanted you to move inside their uncertainty, unless they wanted to do
something in which the outcome was uncertain, like racing blindly to the
top of a hill. They were almost always certain about that kind of thing, and
that's why sometimes you just had to get rid of them or buckle under the
way Precious did with Dummie.

Slowly the leapers came forward, cautious of Rumi, though he was hooved like them, and stood with Annie whom they knew to be safe and reliable. Now they stood on the other side of the fence on the far end away from the awning. Annie had moved with them, matching their steps. They stood in front of her, Rumi at her hindquarters, the eight ungulates standing motionless in the rain.

"Are the wild woof in packs yet?" the leapers asked. "Wild packs? Wild packs? Wild packs?"

Till now, it had been a very dry year. The leapers didn't have babies and so neither had the wild woof, but now the rain, if it kept up, would bring pups in the winter, sooner than the leapers would have their fawns. Singly, the wild woof hunted the small furs, rabbits, ground squirrels, and mice, but with mouths to feed they began moving in groups for larger prey and the fawns in particular would be vulnerable. Annie had the advantage of being too big for the wild woof.

"No," said Annie. "No. No. No. No."

"Death hiss? Death hiss? Death hiss?" Over and over.

"No. No. No."

Everyone grew silent.

Annie had seen their male when she was last out with Bird. They didn't call him a stallion. It was a feeling that was deeper, a sign horses remembered as when they escape and join wild herds and then remember all the things that were in them but that they'd never before done, the deep memories, the before life memories, the memories that you were born into. That was what she felt from these does about their male, only something different because these leapers didn't have herds, in fact sometimes they were completely solitary, especially the sexual males.

Unlike the female leapers, the male, the buck, had a rack of horns on his head. The day he spotted Annie he leapt the stone barrier between the ranch and the rumble path, a tremendous leap, twice his height; it startled her. "Holy shit!" said Bird, his surprise sound.

"I've seen him," Annie said.

"We've smelled him," the leapers said.

Everyone stood silently now in the downpour, feeling the rain and all that was coming; if you were a Hum you might call it prayer. A rumble growled from the road below, and the leapers exploded up the hill beyond the pasture. Annie listened for the gate that opened to the ranch rumble path, though she knew it wouldn't be Bird. Bird never came on the first day of heavy rain. He did once, when she first came to this place. Then, she'd pastured on the hilltop where the foals and mothers stayed now. It was windswept and cold up there, worse than here. Now, with the rain, they'd separate the foals and move them to the pasture under the hill, away from the wind, but away from their mothers, too. There'd be screaming. It made her remember her colt with a pain that ran from her heart to her womb. Maybe now, with Bird, she could have a foal and keep it.

At first, when she stopped hating Bird, she thought Bird could give her a foal. She smelled male on him and she displayed for him, popping her vulva and urinating at him. She didn't think he was a gelding because she smelled female sex on him, too; in fact she smelled Gail, the Other. She hated Bird's Other and if he showed up with her sex smell on him he was in for a really bad time. Jealous, Gail said.

Annie didn't quite understand that word, but she felt the same thing Gail felt.

"You have to shower before you come here," Gail said.

Anyway, Bird wasn't going to make a foal with her. It wasn't that kind of relationship. But maybe she could still have one. Maybe Bird could find her foal, the one the Hums took away.

That first cold rain when Bird showed up, she left the other mares and came to him. It was a strange moment because even then, after years and years, though she'd come to tolerate Bird, she wasn't happy to see him when he showed up and when he left she only wanted to forget about him. That she might have wanted his foal, too, well that was just something else. However much or how long you might want a stallion, it didn't mean you wanted to spend time with him. Annie was both jealous of Gail and not that crazy about Bird.

So when Bird showed up in the middle of that storm, Annie looked up. It was miserable out there and maybe, just maybe, he'd do something about it. That's what Hums were good for, doing things about stuff. She walked up to him. The cold wind and rain beat on them both, beat much harder than now. The heat left her back and she shivered. She didn't mean to say that to him, but suddenly Bird shivered, too. Sometimes Bird showed up not even knowing why he was there. "Oh, Annie," said Bird. He saw that her moving took her away from the others where she could share heat, and now here she was standing in front of him shivering and, well, vulnerable, and Bird never thought of Annie as anything but trouble and fire, never vulnerable. After that, Bird always waited for the rain to stop, then he came, and she knew that.

Now Rumi had wandered back under the awning. The rain pounded on the metal roof like thunder. She walked over, wedged herself in. It was warmer. A little drier. Rain made partners.

"What did the leapers want?" said Precious, who seldom spoke to Annie anymore.

"Nothing," said Annie.

"They wanted something," Precious said. "Nobody communicates unless they want something."

"So what do you want to know now?" said Rumi.

Precious bit him.

"They wanted to know about the yippers," said Tasha. When Tasha rode the range as a cow horse, they called the wild woofs yippers because of the sounds they made at night. "Leapers always want to know about the yippers. It never changes."

"They want to have babies," said Annie.

"Leapers always want to have babies," said Tasha.

"Is that what the rain means?" said Rumi. "Having babies?"

"The rain doesn't mean anything, you idiot," said Dummie.

"I'm not an idiot," said Rumi. But when Dummie snarled at him he turned to Annie. "Am I?"

"There's nothing wrong with being an idiot," Annie said.

Even Tasha and Precious had to nicker a little over that.

Of course you must remember that horses don't converse like this anymore than leapers or small furs or anybody else; there's a kind of pushing of bodies and murmuring, farts and nips, so this is only a vague translation and synopsis of a tactile dialogue far too complex for human language, too patient and repetitive for human minds.

"The rain means everything," said Rumi.

"It means all that happens when it rains," said Tasha, "and what happens every time it rains."

"And what about before and after?" said Annie.

"Ha!" whinnied Rumi. "That's change!"

"Everything is the same before and after every time," said Tasha. "Just watch."

"I hate standing in here with all of you," said Dummie.

"That's what the rain means for you!" said Rumi.

"Horses have meaning, rain is just rain," Precious said.

"Will you all just shut up," said Dummie.

"Speaking of mean horses!" said Rumi.

"Get out of here!" screamed Dummie and bit Rumi hard on the butt, driving him from the covering.

Rumi stood in the rain, staring in at the four others. He stared at Annie, wanting her to come out. She moved through the slop to Rumi.

"You fought with Dummie," she said to him.

"I did?" said Rumi.

She said nothing.

"I did," Rumi said. "I wonder if he knows."

"He might figure it out eventually," she said.

"Ha! And then it will be too late!" He jumped around, the mud flying. The others stared from underneath the awning. He was making fun of all of them, even himself. He was thinking now, if ever it did anyone any good. Rumi quivered with comfort; Annie felt his pleasure up and down. He murmured something as he panted in the rain. "Change, change. Everything is one big changing thing," whispered Rumi. It was almost a prayer.

"Be still," she said, moving beside him. "You'll waste energy." And she stood with him in the rain, in the rain that meant that today Bird wouldn't come.

If You Go Into the Woods

*Prajapati said: "That whoever goes in search of you
in the form of a horse shall find you." From that day on
horses have red mouths, as if seared, and delicate eyes.
They are the marks left by that wound we call knowledge.*

- - Baudhayana Srauta Sutra

This whole woods thing was a real impasse. Every day Bird showed up, saddled Annie, and rode her into the woods. Every day she blew up, sometime, somewhere, even if she made an effort, and occasionally she did. But it was no good. The woods surrounded her with blindness and sounds, predator smell, cold, dangerous invisible air, butterflies! And Bird somehow just figured that if he took her in there often enough she'd get used to it, because being a Hum he thought the woods were something you got used to instead of a world both inside you and outside you, a world that changed and threatened every second and was always different and always everywhere and always frightening, and so things didn't get better and better, they got worse and worse.

Back then, Bird stopped giving her carrots at the beginning of the ride because Bob told him that if you gave carrots to your horse before the ride you were spoiling her, then the horse wouldn't give you a good workout. Annie hated being groomed before a ride because every touch remembered pain, though she could tolerate it after the ride if there were carrots and apples involved. She was still waiting for Bird to figure that out before the ride. As it was, Bird simply didn't clean her until after.

Tire her out, that's what Paddy said. So Bird found a little clearing in the woods and every time Annie blew up, which was every day, he got off and walked her there, then tried to chase her around him in a circle until she got too tired to go crazy. But the reins were too short, so he had to put her headstall on over her halter and wrap a long lead line around her neck so that when he took her to the clearing he could twirl the end of the line at her butt. He had to learn to do it right and left handed, first one direction, then the other. Every day, round and around out in the woods until Annie frothed and sweated and got so tired she'd compromise and walk home, really fast; if she broke into a trot Bird took her back to the clearing. She thought he'd give up, but he never did. Every day he showed up and they did it again.

Who knows how many months it would take for Bird to figure out that what he was doing wasn't working? Bird met an Indian who told him to tie Annie to a tree in the woods and leave her there for a few hours. When he got back, Annie would be so glad to see him that she'd behave. That's what Indians did and it always worked. So Bird tied Annie up in the woods and went and hid. He didn't have the heart to leave her there without watching her, she felt that, so even when he hid she could feel him and smell him and when he came back she was madder than ever. Back to the clearing where it took longer and longer to tire her out.

"You have to distract her," said Paddy. "Make her so busy she forgets about being scared." So Bird had Annie walk sideways, first one way, then the other. He backed her around rocks and trees. No good. Then Bird tried to make her walk backwards all the way home, a mile walking backwards in the woods, uphill, downhill, around bends. It was dangerous! Boy, did she get good at that. She learned how to run backwards and when she almost backed off a cliff, that put an end to walking backwards in the woods.

They'd get back from the woods, the two of them dripping in sweat, Bird cursing and muttering. He'd dismount, walk her until she cooled down, then give her a bath, some carrots, but by then she was so pissed off at Bird that when he put her away she'd try to bite him. He had to hightail it out of the corral and stay away from the fence because by that point, if he got close, she tried to bite him again.

But the next day, there he was. He always came back. He never hurt her. By the next morning, when he showed up, she didn't hate him so much until he put her away again. Why didn't he give up?

"You're nuts," said Bob. "That horse is going to kill you."

"She doesn't hate me," Bird said.

"You can't even ride her through the woods to the ring. What good is she?"

"I just have to convince her that I'm always going to be here."

"Maybe that's exactly what's pissing her off. You won't be here after she kills you," said Bob. "Sell her."

"All that passion," said Bird.

"How many horses have you owned before this?" Bob said. "I've owned twenty. Sell her and get something you can ride."

Well, somebody had to change something and it looked like Bird wasn't going to change anything, so it was up to Annie. The next day when Bird took her into the woods, she tried not to be scared. Bird petted her neck. He started to make some strange sounds. "Annie, Annie, my sweet Annie, Annie my sweet little horse," Bird sang. Maybe singing was the answer. Annie tried to listen to Bird. She heard her name inside his sounds. Her ears went back. They went forward. They went back. Bird rode her up a steep hill. But the ground was too loose and she couldn't walk on it, she had to lope. Up the hill she went, the woods all around. She tried. She tried. Then just at the top of the hill, a big dog! Annie spun downhill. Bird flew off.

She looked back at Bird. She hadn't meant to dump him, but now that he was on the ground she felt relieved, though when he didn't move she felt sorry, then scared. Then he sat up. She ran home.

It took awhile, but Bird found her waiting for a bath. Let's have a bath and forget about the whole thing, felt Annie. Instead, Bird got back on her. "We have to go back in, Annie," Bird said gently. "I can't let you dump me and get away with it." Why not? felt Annie. Why don't we just stand around and eat? But it was back to the dark gaping maw of the forest. Annie shivered. She sent lightning into Bird's butt. How could this end? What good could come of any of it? The wind turned the trees into a blur. The ground rose up and sucked her feet. The air screamed like a mad mare. She tried to spin and run. Bird spun her all the way around. She bucked. Bird pulled back on the reins. But she wouldn't back up. She lowered her head. Bird pulled more. She jerked her head forward and broke the reins off where they met the bit.

Bird fell backward but he didn't come off. Annie spun and headed back for the barn. Bird reached forward and grabbed the headstall. He pulled Annie's head around until it touched his knee, but that stopped nothing. She could run like that. And run she did. Bird let go of the headstall just in time for her to spot the cliff ahead and she swung back onto the path, thundering now through the woods, blur and thunder, the outside inside, the dark green everywhere threat, uphill, downhill, past the lumbering trees, and then, suddenly, the opening to the ranch. She plunged for it. She felt Bird kicking her on the right and she swung left onto Bob's reining run and then, at the end of the run, clueless, she skidded to a halt. It was over. That fast. "Whoa," Bird said, if a little after the fact. That was Bird. And that was it for the woods, wasn't it? The woods thing was settled.

Bird got off, shaking. He'd never been more scared. Annie, too. She was white with foam; the air shivered around her as her heat rose. Bird's shoulders sagged. He put his hands over his eyes, then lowered them enough to look into hers. He took her by the headstall and led her up the path to the tie-ups. Let's take the saddle off now. Let's have a bath. But he walked into the tack room, emerged with a new headstall, removed the old one and put the new one between her teeth, over her nose. He led her out, got back on and pointed her to the dark opening that led into the woods.

When she didn't budge he moved his spurs into her belly. She stepped forward slowly, slowly, then, at the woods' edge, she stopped. She spun. Bird kept her spinning until she faced the woods again. When he tried to spur her again, she bucked him. She wasn't going in. She didn't want to kill Bird, but he might die. She felt his fear and something else, not determination, something breaking. Something breaking. And then it stopped and she felt him firmly again.

Bird got off her back. He took the reins and walked forward in front of her. That wasn't so bad, having him in front of her. She felt a little safer being able to see Bird. In a little while he turned and they walked back. Then he led her back in again, stopped, jumped on her back. They stood there in the woods. Not too far in. She could see the entrance behind her.

"What am I going to do with you, Annie?" said Bird. "What am I going to do?"

Horse for Sale

I don't want to be useful to anyone.
I just want to burn.

- - *Agni (God of Fire),* Rig Veda

One had to wonder what Bird got out of all this. Bird, for his part, couldn't quite figure it out either.

"Let's look at some other horses," said Bob. So one Sunday morning Bird and Bob drove out to horse country, north of town, to look at some quarter horses. They all seemed very nice, but Bird didn't like the way a quarter horse spread under his legs; they were too wide, and their lope, like their bulky workhorse bodies, was short and choppy. Bird liked how lean Annie felt underneath him. And when she ran she had a long, smooth gallop; it almost felt as if she were stretching out, into space, and he was stretching with her, though she had a vertical gallop, too, almost straight up and down; he could hardly stay in the saddle when she did it, but as he learned to hold his seat -- it only took him five years -- it enabled her to dance underneath him, forward, sideways, backwards. Every time Bird hopped on a horse, it reminded him of something he liked better about Annie.

Back at the barn he met a young trainer, Suzy, who used to work with Paddy. "Hey," said the girl, "you're the guy who bought that crazy horse. Who'd you sell her to?"

"I didn't," said Bird.

"But he's going to," said Bob.

"I got tired of getting bucked off," Suzy said. "You'd fix one thing and she'd break someplace else."

"You didn't like her?" said Bird.

"I hated her," said Suzy. "She's crazy."

The stable owner, a woman in her forties wearing English riding boots, dark auburn hair pulled back, walked up and shook Bob's and Bird's hands. Her name was Lynette. Bob wanted to ride a reining stallion she had there, so Lynette had the horse saddled up and Bob hopped on and rode him into the ring. Bob looked like a midget on top of that big stallion.

"It doesn't matter how big you are or how big they are," said Lynette. "If it's a contest, they win."

She was right enough about that. If it was a contest, Bird figured he had no wins, a few hundred defeats and a dozen draws.

Lynette was one of those types that liked to stare straight ahead, looking at something, in this case Bob, and talk to you like that without looking at you.

"What are you riding now?" Lynette said.

"An Anglo-Arab mare," said Bird.

"Dark bay? That one from up at Paddy's?"

"Yes," Bird said.

Lynette stared straight ahead. "Thought that horse would be glue by now," she said. "You have much experience?"

"First horse," said Bird.

Lynette was quiet for a while. Bob skidded the stallion, rolled back, came to the center and spun the animal right, then left. "Whoopee!" said Bob. He spurred the horse and rode toward the other end of the big ring.

"She shouldn't have sold you that horse," Lynette said to the air. She turned to Bird and looked him in the eye. "That's too much horse for you." Then she turned and walked away.

Pretty dramatic, that's what Bird thought. Bob jumped off the stallion and Bird met him outside the ring.

"You should get a horse like that!" said Bob.

"I don't have forty thousand dollars," Bird said.

"I have forty thousand dollars," said Bob. "Maybe I should get him."

"Lynette says Annie's too much horse for me," said Bird.

"She knows Annie?"

"Seems everybody does," said Bird. "She says Paddy shouldn't have sold her to me."

"Mistakes get made," said Bob. "You just have to correct them."

Down the road they looked at some Arabians. Bird liked their quirky personalities, but they were a little short, and even they seemed round and choppy compared to Annie. At a third stable Bird rode a Morgan mare and a big palomino gelding. Bob liked the palomino. "A nice big horse for a big guy," said Bob, but Bird thought the animal was a blockhead and sensed a mean streak in him. (And it turned out he was right; Bob arranged for some wealthy friends of his to buy the palomino and the horse bit the husband and kicked the wife.) Bird liked the mare, a tall bay like Annie, with a relaxed gait, but she came up lame during his ride. Still, it was his first inkling that there might be another horse out there, somebody easier, more accommodating, and less dangerous than Annie.

He rode a thoroughbred gelding at a fourth ranch. Bob rode him first, English. "Ah, he's an old slug," Bob said. But isn't that what Bird wanted, something safe? The ranch owner, who was selling the horse for one of his boarders, didn't have a saddle big enough for Bird, so Bird had to ride bareback. He'd never ridden bareback before, but the ring sand looked thick and soft enough to break a fall. The gelding was fifteen years old and very forgiving, coming back to Bird anytime there was a danger of him losing control, and unlike when he was under Bob, for Bird the animal moved out, gliding along; he backed up and side passed, stopped on a dime.

"He likes you," said Bob.

But he was fifteen years old and they were asking $10,000. "That's too much money for an older horse," Bird said.

"How much is your life worth?" said Bob. "He could live to be thirty. Offer them five."

"Four would be too much," said Bird.

"Offer them four," Bob said.

But one thing Bird was learning was that he somehow knew more about horses than Bob. Sure there were thousands of people out there more experienced than Bird, Bob included, and some of them, Bird knew, were great with horses. But others didn't really even listen to them, feel them, or watch them; in some ways they didn't even see them. You couldn't get into an animal's head unless you could get outside your own.

That late afternoon Bird wandered over to Bob's ranch. Of course, Annie was already out in her pasture. He'd missed a day, and she stared at him, both mad and relieved. He'd never catch her now. He guessed there probably were other horses out there. He walked home and placed an ad in The Horse Trader.

Anglo-Arab Mare, dark bay

7 yrs. old, 15.2 hands

flying leads

$4,000

Immediately he got a lot of calls. They went like this:

"Can she jump?"

"Yes."

"What about the lead changes?"

"On a one beat."

"Every time?"

"Nothing happens every time," said Bird.

"Broke?"

"Kind of."

"Kind of?"

"She's a lot of horse."

"What about the trail?"

"She hates the trail."

"Bucks?"

"Runs home," Bird said.

"Do you like her?"

"I love her, but she's going to kill me."

That's how that went.

After a few phone calls like that, Gail pulled Bird aside. "Are you trying to sell that horse?" she said.

"Yes," said Bird.

"No," said Gail. "You try to talk everybody out of buying her."

"I'm ambivalent," Bird said.

"Lie," said Gail.

"But they'll have to meet her," said Bird.

"Maybe, just once, she won't act up," said Gail.

So Bird lied the next time. Said Annie was sweet, smart, great in the ring and on the trail. A woman named Robin agreed to come by and take a look.

Meanwhile, back at the ranch, Bird had been acting suspiciously. He took Annie out and grazed her or walked her, sometimes took her into the small ring and rode her around. He'd grown quiet around her, and undemanding. She liked it, maybe even preferred it, but she was getting bored. And it was a change. When one thing changed, then other things changed. In the past, when somebody stopped trying it meant a move was coming. Leaving this place. Dealing with somebody else instead of Bird.

Then Bird showed up with Robin, a big woman in a billed cap and high boots. Bird and the woman made their sounds. Robin made short, curt sounds. Women like that rode English; small, light saddle, a softer bit but a lot of contact, constant pressure from both the bit and legs, extra reins and a lot of pulling on your face to make you run with your head bent down. She came in a big rumble, the kind that you could put a can on the back to put a horse inside.

Bird and Robin walked down from the stables and onto the reining track, staring at Annie who stared back from the middle of her pasture.

"She's pretty," said Robin.

"And smart," said Bird.

Bird opened the pasture gate and went inside. Annie let him walk up to her because she was afraid of Robin. Bird put the halter on Annie and led her out. Annie, behaving, maybe this was his lucky day. Bird took Annie to the tie-ups, cleaned her feet, saddled her.

"You're not going to groom her?" said Robin.

"I groom her after," said Bird.

"That's odd," said Robin.

Then Bird led Annie to the little ring and hopped up. She sprang into a lope. "Lope," said Bird. She trotted. Bird said, "Trot." Annie backed up. "Back up," Bird said. Stopped. "Whoa," Bird said. "Excellent." He hopped off.

"It's almost as if she anticipates your commands," said Robin.

"Well, she's smart," said Bird.

"Does she go English?"

"Broke English," said Bird. He didn't know that, but he knew Annie'd been a jumper so must have been ridden English.

"I'll bring my gear tomorrow," said Robin.

"I'll meet you down at the big ring on the other side of the hill," Bird said. He figured he'd walk Annie through the woods and Robin could saddle her down there.

"I'll bring the trailer and my vet," said Robin. "If she gives me the leads we can knock it all down right there."

Bird led Annie out of the ring, brushed her off. "I'll probably ride her later, then I'll clean her good," he said to Robin. He just didn't want to give Annie a chance to act up.

"$4,000 isn't much," said Robin.

"I just want her to have a good home," Bird said, but by now he was feeling pretty lousy. Still, it was the right thing. Annie could kill him. Bob said it everyday. Everybody told him that Annie was too much horse for him. Maybe it could work out for her with somebody who knew what they were doing.

Bird led Annie back down to her pasture and Robin followed. He opened the gate and turned Annie loose. He never spent any time in there because even if he had carrots she got pissed off when he stopped feeding her and might try to bite him. When he came back out, Robin went to the fence.

"I've got some carrots here," said Robin.

"I don't usually feed her over the fence," said Bird.

Robin pulled a few carrots from her vest. "It's carrots," Robin said.

Annie took a look at Bird. She took a look at Robin holding those carrots. Wrong person with the carrots. Can rumble, new person watching and now holding the carrots. She took a long look at Bird again. Bird was beginning to recognize different looks on Annie's face; sometimes she was afraid, sometimes screaming mad, wild scared, calm, apologetic, even soft, but this look was alert and quizzical, her waiting-for-something-to-happen look, ears a little perked, eyes shifting ever-so-slightly.

"Look at her watching you," Robin said.

"Well," said Bird. Well. Well what? What could he say?

Annie stepped toward Bird and Robin. Robin held out a carrot. Annie bit her hard on the wrist.

"Ow! Jesus!" yelled Robin. "She bit me!"

"She was just trying to get the carrot," said Bird.

"She bit me hard!" said Robin.

Then Annie bit Bird on the bicep. Bird screamed. Robin took a swing at Annie with her fist but Annie dodged it and backed away.

"That horse is crazy. Look at your arm," said Robin.

Blood was oozing through Bird's shirt.

"You should kill her for that," said Robin.

"She didn't mean it," Bird said. He half believed that.

Robin's wrist was already getting black and blue. "Didn't mean it? $4,000. Right." She spun and headed for her truck. "You're lucky I don't sue you," she said.

Bird watched Robin blitz from the barns and head down the driveway. He rolled up his shirt and looked at the teeth marks on his arm, turning blue now, the blood still seeping out. Annie stood back from him, calmer now, if not, well, feeling a whole lot better about the situation. Bird looked at her. He didn't think she meant to hurt him. She wasn't mean or bad, well, okay, she was bad, but not in a mean way. Was she untrainable? Unreachable? But now it seemed he couldn't ride her and he couldn't sell her. What was he going to do?

Starting from Scratch

*. . . a falcon dives into the forest
and doesn't come back up. Every moment,
the sunlight is totally empty and totally full.*

- - Rumi, "Omar and the Old Poet"

Bird called Paddy.

"Heard she bit that Robin chick," said Paddy. "I'd bite her, too."

"That doesn't help," said Bird.

"She's a smart horse," said Paddy. "You're not going to ride that horse without thinking about what you're doing every second. She'll keep you interested till the day she dies."

"Or I die," said Bird.

"That horse won't kill you."

"Bob says she will."

"Only if you do something stupid," said Paddy.

"I am stupid," said Bird.

"Ignorant, not stupid. You love that horse, she knows that. Nobody has ever loved her before. She doesn't know anything about being loved; she doesn't know what to do."

"Me either," said Bird.

"Get some books."

"I've read dozens of books. Watched dozens of videos," said Bird. "What about the horse whisperer guy?"

"Nobody whispers to horses," Paddy said.

"Could you fix her?" said Bird.

"You couldn't afford it. Besides, even if I did, I'd have to give her back to you."

"Ignorant me," said Bird.

"Look at Bob," said Paddy. "He buys a million dollar horse, I train it, I give it back to him, in a few months they're both train wrecks. Bob's not me. Training can be trainer specific, not necessarily, but possibly. So even if I fine tune the animal, when Bob gets him he reinforces all the wrong stuff. The rider is as important as the animal."

"But you train Bob," said Bird.

"It doesn't stick. People are harder to train than horses," said Paddy.

"But you keep doing it," said Bird.

"Bob can afford it," said Paddy.

"And I can't."

"Can you?"

"No," said Bird. Bob was a millionaire lawyer. Bird was a teacher. A teacher with a horse dream he couldn't afford.

"Treat her like an unbroken horse," said Paddy. "Start from scratch."

Years ago, when Bird was a young hard head, he didn't believe that animals had thoughts or feelings or, more to the point, he didn't care. Hell, he didn't care if people had thoughts or feelings. What mattered was how they behaved. People had a thousand reasons for what they did after they did it. He didn't care why his girlfriend was leaving him or why his roommate stole his change. If somebody did something once, they'd do it again; if they lied to you once they'd likely lie the next time and after that if you didn't figure they were lying to you, you were a fool.

Back then Bird thought that language was thinking. People thought in language and animals didn't, so animals didn't think. But regardless, thinking was irrelevant. People did what satisfied them or gratified them or avoided what scared them and the rest was baloney. Highfalutin emotions like motherly love were biological; mothers protected their babies, even alligators did it.

Back then Bird had cats. Well, he still did. He didn't like dogs because dogs were needy and never left you alone. He liked the way cats quietly filled a house. Bird lived in an old farmhouse up north near a dark Great Lake and he used to keep a basement window open for his cats, but the cats started bringing in rats and rabbits, then possums and raccoons started following the cats into the basement to eat their food. So Bird had to shut the window. But he still had to let the cats get in and out.

Being a behaviorist, Bird hung a string of bells on his back door. He figured when the cats came to the door, screaming and yelling and hopping around to get in, they'd eventually knock into those bells and when they did he'd open the door. Sure enough, within a week, all seven of his damn cats were ringing those bells to get in the house. His friends marveled. "Simple behavioral modification. Positive reinforcement," said Bird. "I could teach a guinea pig to do it." You rewarded somebody for doing something and after that they did it again to get the reward.

Then one snowy day while Bird was working in his living room, happily reading someone who agreed with everything he thought, a cat rang the bells. But Bird was busy so he didn't get up to answer the door. So the cat rang the bells again. "I'm busy," yelled Bird to no one in particular, certainly not the cat. Then the cat rang the bells again really hard. Bird jumped up and went to the door and let the cat in. The cat, whose name was Egg Martin, said, "Rrr." Bird shut the door and turned and then it hit him. Why did Egg Martin ring the bells harder? Even if he was just pissed off at the bells, then, well, he was pissed off. That was a feeling. And he wanted the door to open. That was an expectation. Not only that, he might have even expected that Bird come and do it. That was a thought!

Thank God Bird was stubborn. He found Egg Martin and threw him out. Sure enough Egg Martin did it again. Bird found another cat named Mr. Puff and threw him out. Mr. Puff wasn't as irascible as Egg Martin and it took him four or five rings before he got pissed off and rang the bells harder.

Then Bird wanted to know if the cats rang the bells when he wasn't home. He got in his old Chevy Vega and drove away, parked it down the road and sneaked back to his house. He spied Mr. Puff and a few others sitting outside the back door, but none of them rang the bells. So if Bird wasn't home, the cats didn't ring the bells. They not only knew he opened the door, they knew he couldn't do it if he wasn't home. They had to watch him leave, know that meant he wasn't home, and remember it.

Then they had to come to some kind of... what? A decision?... not to bother to ring the bells because nobody was home to open the door.

Maybe it was the car. Bird tried leaving the car, walking away and then sneaking back, but it was the same. And those cats must have been keeping an eye on him all the time, because even though he didn't see all the cats when he left, they obviously saw him leave, either that or they were passing the information to each other, and he was a long way from believing that.

The next thing Bird did was go out and get a new kitten because he wanted to see how the cats learned how to ring the bells the first time. Bird put the kitten outside and watched out his back window. Before too long, Egg Martin showed up and hit the bells. Bird let Egg Martin in. Then, not too long later, the kitten walked up and hit the bells. Holy Mackerel! He didn't want to jump to any conclusions and he wasn't going to go out and get more kittens to see if it happened again, but it sure looked like the kitten hit the bells after Egg Martin hit the bells.

Back then Bird was studying to be a philosopher. His first instinct was to try and find out if anybody'd written anything about animals thinking, but there wasn't much, just some stuff in psychology that rigged a lot of confined experiments that concluded the stuff that Bird used to believe, that animals were like living robots. He read Jane Goodall's book about chimps and found some stuff about people trying to teach chimps and gorillas sign language. But did they start thinking only when they learned to sign? Or were they thinking some things, somehow, before? And how were they thinking before somebody plopped a few signs on them?

There's nothing like a young man with a new idea, even if it was only new to him, and especially if it was the opposite of his old idea. Bird was ready to run out and try to buy a chimpanzee and start talking to him. He jumped in his Chevy Vega and hightailed it to his university where he was studying to be a philosopher, ran down the hallway and into the office of his dissertation director, P. J. Rabbit, a famous William James scholar.

"Animal consciousness," panted Bird.

Rabbit looked up from his desk and smiled gently at Bird.

"I want to do my dissertation on how animals think," Bird said.

"Bird brains?" said Dr. Rabbit.

"Maybe," said Bird.

"That's not philosophy," said P. J. Rabbit.

"What is it?"

"I don't know. You've read a lot of Spinoza. Why not write about some aspect of Spinoza?"

"I don't want to do that anymore," said young Bird. "I don't want to write about what I think about what somebody else thought."

"Why don't you choose another career?" P.J. Rabbit said.

And so ended Bird's career as a philosopher. He thought about other fields, but psychologists, zoologists, ethologists, nobody wanted to talk about the thoughts and feelings of animals. Bird couldn't even get a job at the local zoo. "We don't need anybody around here thinking like that," the zoo director told him. "Who wants to imagine that these caged animals are in there thinking? It would be the end of zoos." That was refreshing honesty, if a bit depressing.

For a little while Bird tried to write about his observations of animals. He got a dog, a rat, watched birds and squirrels, pondered migration, hunting strategies, food storage. He speculated about how animals held images in their brains: smells, tastes, pictures, sounds, how things felt to the touch, even maps of how to get places they wanted to go, and their own feelings, and thus memories of all these things, too, and how one connected to another and became a kind of thinking. When his dog was excited to see him when he came home, he concluded the obvious, that his dog was happy, and that his dog had been waiting for him; that one could not wait for someone without anticipation, could not anticipate without picturing, could not picture without thinking.

Bird figured those images were signs, not like words because they weren't a language, but nonetheless ideas that stood for things; the image of a bone, its picture, smell, texture, stood to the dog for some actual bone; it might be followed by the memory of where the dog last left it, and then the dog could go get it. When a cat laid a mouse at your feet, it was a triangle. Cat, mouse, you. A sign. That's how animals could hold thoughts for longer than a split second, how a cat could watch the path of a squirrel along an electric line and soon be waiting on the other end. How a cat or dog or a horse could be jealous or hold a grudge. The memory, a sign, recalled the emotion. And it's how an animal could actually make decisions between doing one thing or another.

Oh, there was more, much, much more. Bird wrote down his ideas and sent his articles off to magazines and journals who responded, if they responded at all, by saying his ideas were very interesting, but what experiments were they based on and what were his credentials? Bird learned that when people said your ideas were very interesting it meant they weren't interested in them. And to get credentials he'd have to get a degree in a field that didn't believe the stuff he was saying. He'd have to study and do experiments about the opposite of what he believed and then write papers about them saying those things, not the things he wanted to say. Maybe it was what he should have done and then, after a decade of that, if there was anything still left inside him, he could start trying to slip a few of his ideas into the field. Maybe.

But he needed a job. Soon. So he went into the world and held his jobs and married his wives (and divorced his wives) and caught and released wild children into life; he lived with his cats and dogs and whatever else happened to come his way, frogs and rats and newts and snakes and birds and turtles, chickens and butterflies, and he kept them till their deaths or released them back into the world, watching and believing in their minds but keeping it to himself -- you don't have to be an astronaut or an astronomer just because you love the stars, in fact, Bird concluded, if you were an astronaut or an astronomer it was probably harder to love the stars -- and eventually he went back to school (because a very smart girlfriend who was moving back to France told him, "You know, a poor, nutty young guy can be interesting for a while, but a poor, nutty old man is pathetic," those French); so he became a teacher, working with the minds of young people and treating them as if they were as smart as animals, knowing it was much easier to learn than to unlearn and that neither was ever accomplished without encouragement, so soon he became very successful at it, in fact so successful that several of his superiors suggested he write a book about his teaching methods.

Bird tried, but Bird being Bird he couldn't write a book about teaching so instead he told a story about a teacher reaching out again and again to some unreachable kid, coming close to turning his life around, but then circumstances turn for the worse. In the end he fails to help him. Well, that wasn't the book he was supposed to write and, of course, the textbook publishers couldn't do anything with it, but it happened that, like any teacher, sometimes Bird read to his students and one student, in this case an adult, had a wife who worked for a book agent and he gave Bird's story to her. She gave it to her boss and her boss gave it to a friend who was an editor and one day Bird had his little book published.

It wasn't a children's book, though many people thought it was a book for kids or juveniles because it was written simply; like Bird, the complexities were underneath if you wanted to find them and most people did not try. For a very short while Bird had a book agent and a movie agent, but the book disappeared with little notice in a matter of months. It convinced Bird once again that the whole business of trying to get your ideas into the world was a waste of time. That was it for Bird and books.

And then he met Gail and fell in love, maybe for the first time. Isn't that how you always feel, that this time it's real? But this time it seemed to be. They bought a little house in the hills where they kept stray dogs and cats and rescued anything else that came their way and seemed to need them. They made love passionately every day and then Gail, who was a surrealist and a poet, went her way into some other worlds where her words fell like rain, and jungles and gardens and deserts and forests blossomed from them. She had so many separate worlds that even when they sat together touching, even when they stared at each other over coffee, wine, or dinner, even as they reached the ecstasies of passion, even as she spoke to him, he could see that she was dreaming her worlds, her separate lives, and even as they had their baby, Marlena, yet another world, who grew into a young girl who liked to carry snakes and wear wigs -- what else could have happened? -- their passion grew and grew, from their inwardness not their togetherness.

However much Gail traveled in and in, she had one thing besides Bird and Marlena that brought her emotions to the outer world, a ring, originally a brooch, that she inherited from a distant great aunt. It arrived by special mail one day after the woman died, with a note that she'd been saving it for Gail from the time Gail had admired the piece as a child. It

84

came, said the note, from another distant relative who was once a lady in waiting for the Queen of Romania, a woman named, well, Anastasia.

Bird didn't know if Romania ever had a queen, but he took the brooch to a jeweler who said it contained some of the finest diamonds he'd ever seen; you could buy a car with those jewels. He had the jeweler set the three finest diamonds in a platinum ring. Now, Gail wore it everywhere and seldom took it off. It was a material metaphor of distant gifts and mysterious intentions that transcended time, and it was one of the reasons that when she heard about Annie, then named Anastasia, she told Bird, sight unseen, "You have to get that horse." And why Bird changed Anastasia's name to Annie.

Now he had that horse, staring at him, the welt from her bite swirling on his arm like that big storm on Jupiter. And here was the thing: back home, where the cats and dogs and sometimes the birds roved among each other, and the possums and raccoons and squirrels dropped in, and even at times the coyotes and bobcats and pumas surrounded them, and the owls and hawks dropped out of the sky and wreaked their havoc, back there, Gail was an anarchist and there were no rules for anyone, just boundaries, food bowl boundaries, defecation boundaries, but the doors and windows were always open and everyone, everything, passed in and out, no one was ever scolded for their infractions on the social order, only rewarded for their cooperation. And it all worked.

Of course, amphibians and reptiles had cages, as did small birds and rodents, not that they didn't at times leave them, knowing when to leave, and not that they didn't, at times, kill each other. Outside the house, wild animals, coyotes and pumas, killed chickens and cats; domestic cats killed wild rodents and birds; but inside the house-- well, inside the house everybody minded their own business. At first Bird was convinced that this could never be and what they needed around there were rules, rules, rules, but, in fact, rules were irrelevant, even for their daughter, and Gail was right, you just gave them affection and rewards and let them find out on their own what was best for them, what behavior was best for everyone and, in time, it became what they almost always did.

Bird had a lot of animals around him then, but any time you love a lot of anything and have a lot of things you love, you always have a favorite, and Bird's favorite home animal was a silver Maine Coon cat that Gail gave to him for his birthday. He named her Mucha Plata and every night when he sat down to read she danced into the room and flirted with him for an hour, burgling and murpling and tossing her long thick tail before settling down next to his thigh. Before Annie, Mucha Plata was Bird's diamond ring. If this were another kind of tale there would be hundreds of stories of Bird and Mucha Plata inside it, how she taught her kittens to hunt by placing live mice in their food bowl, how she raised her paws to Gail and Marlena when they did each other's nails, asking for hers to be done, too, her politics and alliances with the dogs, but this is not Mucha Plata's story; suffice it to say that Bird had many animals he dearly loved, maybe too many.

So Bird lived along and lived along with his love and his child and Mucha Plata and all the animals and somehow, amid them, as part of them, he forgot all about his theories of animal consciousness without ever really forgetting; he didn't forget that the animals around him thought things nor treat them as if they didn't, he just forgot about the theory part.

But now, this horse. Who outweighed him by a thousand pounds and who was twice as fast, ten times as strong, twice as stubborn and twice as quick. Did he love her? Did she know it? And suddenly he knew why Annie bit Robin. She refused to be sold. And why she bit him. She was mad at him for trying to sell her. Even if she didn't know it. Even if the whole world thought that was absurd.

"Okay," Bird said to Annie. "No more chasing you." He brought an apple and some carrots into the pasture without the halter. Annie watched him suspiciously. He approached with the apple. "I've made a lot of mistakes," he said to Annie. He bit pieces of apple and offered them to her. She took them. "Apple," said Bird. He took out a long carrot. "Carrot," said Bird, and put it in his mouth. She took the end of the carrot from him, her lips touching his, and ate it. "Kiss," said Bird. He took out another carrot. "Kiss," said Bird, and Annie put her mouth on his. He gave her the carrot.

She was smart. It took her once to learn anything, if she wanted to learn it. The same horse who bit him could kiss him gently on the lips. So okay, they'd do it together; they'd start from scratch, slowly, with love, however long it took. Did that solve everything? Not on your life.

Some New Thing

Don't think all ecstasies are the same!

- - Rumi, "The Many Wines"

Rumi stood in the center of the pasture, eyes closed, nose in the air. Annie'd never seen him by himself before, not by choice. The rains had left and been replaced by a cold, dry north wind. Horses hate the wind because it makes things fly around; it made the trees roar and dance and swoop. The wind was an omniscient predator, an airy fist that opened and closed around you, surprised you, brought fright to your nostrils in one direction and hid all the rest of the threatening world on its invisible face, making all the other directions indiscernible, and so to turn your back to it made you blind and to face it brought fright with every breath. Worse, this cold, dry northern wind that followed every rain stung your eyes. Mucus poured down the horses' faces and dried on their cheeks or built up in the corners of their eyes, cementing them closed.

Of course, Bird came and cleaned Annie's eyes, not something she enjoyed; it was annoying and horses hated to be annoyed. It often hurt, so it required a lot of trust. In general, as prey animals, horses are not big on trust. But like everything else, Bird wore her down and she came to prefer her eyes clean instead of matted in dry mucus. But for all these reasons the other horses didn't have anyone to clean their eyes and they wouldn't let Bird do it either. Just as well, it would have made Annie really jealous.

Between gusts the sun was warm. Another good thing about the day, too windy for flies. But if it stayed like this for very long, the mud that had accumulated on their hooves and ankles would encrust and make their feet sore at the spot where their legs met their hooves. Annie had Bird to take care of that, too, and if he didn't do a good enough job, when he took her out for a ride she'd walk him right over to a hose and then Bird laughed and laughed. Sometimes Bird rubbed Annie's feet with cream and massaged it into that spot between her ankle and her hoof. This she loved and she'd raise her foot and place it in his hand when he approached it. Annie had fine, black feet that never cracked and she liked them taken care of. It made her feel light and fast. She'd never been lame, never lost a single day to bad feet.

Rumi stood head up, facing the wind.

"What's he doing?" said Dummie.

"Do you want me to find out?" said Annie.

"No," said Tasha.

"Maybe he's thinking," said Annie.

"I'm going to go kick him out of it," said Precious.

"I'm going to kick him out of it," said Dummie.

Annie walked over to Rumi and stood by him.

He let out a nicker, an odd thing to do while standing alone in the middle of a windy corral. "See how easy it is to make trouble?" he whispered to the air.

"Are you watching the sky?" said Annie.

"I'm letting the world feel me," Rumi said.

Whatever that meant, Annie said nothing.

"Bird lives in a barn," said Rumi.

"I suppose all Hums do," said Annie. "Like the stallions and the trotters."

There were several kinds of horses on the big ranch, most importantly the owner's polo ponies who often were taken from the ranch all together in two long trailers behind rumbles. Based on what happened to her when she was a jumper, Annie assumed that they were taken away to do the same things they did here, ride around chasing a ball. Bird taught her to kick the ball when the polo players left it in the big outdoor ring. She could kick it forward, in front of her, or backward behind her. He taught her to step on them, too, and how to step on dollar bills and shiny coins. Once, after the shiny medallion fell off her breast collar, she found it for Bird the next day by spotting the shine and digging it up out of the sand with her hoof. But the polo ponies couldn't do any of that, they just chased the ball and the Hums on their backs hit it with long sticks. Anyway, most of them stayed in the long barns with the horses that were trained to pull little two wheel carriages. Then there were the stallions. There was another barn where the mothers stayed with their babies for a little while just after they gave birth. It hurt Annie to go there.

There were other little buildings that the Hums went in and out of. Annie figured they were Hum barns. However dry and safe it might be in a barn, it was also confining and isolating. Whenever any of the barn horses got out, their eyes were wild and their bodies crazy to run, their Hums always angry at them for being that way. There were special ranchums, helper-Hums -- Annie remembered back when she had to deal with helpers -- they didn't belong to the horses nor the horses to them, but they came and turned the barn horses loose in a ring by themselves and chased them around so they wouldn't be so wild when their own Hums showed up. Some helper-Hums were kind, but most were unpredictable. They didn't care about you. You didn't mean anything to them.

"Bird isn't alone in his barn," said Rumi.

"The Other," said Annie. "And the Little Other." Annie wasn't fond of Gail, Bird's Other, but she'd come to accept her. She never hurt Annie. She even brought carrots sometimes, though it was years before Annie accepted them. The Little Other, Marlena, well, Annie was even a bit fond of her. When she first met Marlena she was very young; she still smelled like a baby, and all babies, it didn't matter, had to be protected.

There was a time, back at Bob's ranch, when the Other tried to be with a horse, a little mare, a stepper, one of those horses that never ran but glided along very quickly with high, kicking steps, a Paso Fino. Her name was Obleena and Bob kept her over in Gray Dog's pasture so Gray Dog could have company that wasn't dangerous like Annie. Annie remembered the Other taking care of Obleena who'd been overtrained and had come up lame. She became a broodmare and when her owner gave up on that, too, she showed up at Bob's having just been separated from her foal. When Marlena came to the ranch with Gail, Obleena pushed the child to her hind quarters with her head and let down her milk. Gail wept. And Annie ached. And she saw then, felt then, Gail's body move around

90

Marlena the way a mother moved, and at that moment, feeling the same things, they were the same, mothers, not so different, less Other, and Annie's jealousy for Gail, for a moment, fell away.

But Obleena was too lame and had to be taken away. Remembering that made Annie think about Gail for Rumi.

"About the Others. How did you know?" Annie said.

"I felt it," said Rumi. "When I let the world feel me, then I get feelings too." He sniffed the air. "I don't like this wind," he said.

"No one does," said Annie.

"This wind has fire on its back," muttered Rumi.

"It just rained," said Annie.

"It's somewhere in the world. A hot wind waiting, carrying fire," Rumi said.

"There's nothing to be done about it," said Annie.

"Don't sound like Tasha," said Rumi.

"There's more Tasha in all of us than you'd think," said Annie.

"She doesn't like anything."

"She doesn't have anyone."

Rumi brought his head down and stared at Annie.

"Come to the fence today when Bird shows up," Annie said.

Bird usually didn't like it when the other horses came to the fence when he was tacking Annie because Annie worried that he might give them carrots, so she became jumpy and annoyed and pinned her ears and kept moving around to keep her eyes on them. But today, after she and Bird bowed to each other and then Bird gave her his inevitable hug around her neck -- her eyes went screwy and her ears twitched and Bird laughed because he knew she was just putting up with him -- then Bird opened the gate and Annie walked out, sniffing the air for grass. She knew what spots outside the corral that grass would first sprout and once it did she never hesitated to head right for them, Bird following along muttering, knowing she'd had all day to plan just where she was going to go.

But it was too early in the year and there'd been too little rain and it was still too dry, so she sniffed for grass somewhere beyond sight, but no, that fresh smell was still not in the air. Sometimes, when that happened, she liked to take off and run around the outside of the pasture and the adjoining pasture where six polo ponies stayed, and even down the road a bit to the pregnant broodmares. Annie ran around them with her head and tail raised, snorting her freedom at them, snorting that she had Bird and they didn't, advertising that when the grass came, she'd be the one out there eating it. Sometimes she even called them to the fence and arched her neck, snorting hard, then screaming, bucking, striking out with her front legs. It drove them mad. Dummie, in particular, ran up and down the length of the pasture, screaming, bucking; sometimes he went into such a frenzy that he fell down, then jumped back up, furious. And sometimes Hums came and yelled at Bird for letting her loose.

Bird half expected it today. He'd brought the lead line which, like his spurs or the little crop he sometimes brought from the shed (he couldn't hurt her with that little crop), meant he was ready for shenanigans. But Annie put her head down and walked over to the carrot dish. Rumi came to the fence. Annie didn't even look up. Bird looked at Rumi who made a soft face like a doe. He walked around Annie's head, then touched her on her sensitive spot, the center of her chest. Nothing.

Annie gave Bird a good ride. They ran up the mountain. They ran in the ring and threw flying leads straight down the center. They walked home. As he cleaned Annie up, she raised her head and put her lips on his. "Aren't you nice today," said Bird, because even though she loved him, it was her nature to give him a hard time one way or another. After, he put her back in the pasture; it wasn't hard, he just opened the gate and she followed him in. He gave her an apple. Hugged her. "Good-bye, Annie," Bird said. "I love you. I'll see you tomorrow." He always said that. It meant he was leaving in his rumble and he'd be back the next day. If he didn't say that, she knew he'd be gone longer. Bird walked out of the pasture and closed the gate. He got a few more carrots and came to the fence. Annie approached and brought Rumi with her. Bird gave her a carrot. She placed her lips on his nose. She nickered. Rumi nickered. Bird put out a carrot and Annie let Rumi take it.

Bird gave Annie another carrot. "So," Bird said, "some new thing."

And Annie was right. It wasn't long before Bird figured it out and showed up with Gail, his Other. Rumi went to her immediately. They nuzzled each other.

"See," Bird said.

"It's interesting," said Gail.

"It's not my idea, it's Annie's idea," said Bird.

Gail studied Annie whose ears twitched ever-so-slightly and whose eyes did not look unkind. "There's a lot more going on in there than it might look," she said.

"There's a lot going on in there," said Bird. A horse's face didn't express like the face of a person, or even a chimp or a dog; like a cat, a horse spoke with her body, but with her face, too, as you learned to read it, with the texture of her eyes, the loosening and tightening of her lips, whether or not she showed her teeth, and a thousand subtle cues from her ears, as well as the position of her head, up, down and sideways, and then the movement between her neck and shoulders, all that for starters.

For all Bird knew, this was as much a plot to get rid of both Gail and Rumi as much as it was one to bring them together and, as a matter of fact, he was right. But as smart as Annie might be, there were a lot of complications she didn't understand. Hum complications. Rumi belonged to somebody, however much they ignored him, and you just couldn't jump on somebody else's horse; there were property issues and insurance issues for the ranch.

Then there was Gail herself. Horses weren't like cats and dogs and birds who came to you when they wanted you, you had to go to them; you had to get out of the house, leave your inwardness and your art and drive to them, and you had to do it often, and you had to clean their feet and brush their coats and tails and clean their eyes and worm them and exercise them, too. It took time. It was one thing to show up every few weeks to share some carrots and nuzzle, another to take care of a horse.

What else? Bird didn't know if anarchists could ride horses. You couldn't let a horse just do what he wanted. Horses were really stubborn and flighty and really big and strong. However nice and little Rumi looked now, he was a spunky Arabian and he still weighed a thousand pounds. What did Gail know about riding? Not much. Would Rumi listen to her? Maybe not. Would she listen to Bird? No. It wasn't that kind of relationship.

Then there were equipment issues, lease or purchase negotiations, then boarding, all of which took money that Bird and Gail might or might not have. And if they had to find out if Rumi was rideable or, if he wasn't, make him rideable, who was going to do that? Bird. How would that go over with Annie? It wouldn't. He bet Annie hadn't thought about that!

"Can I take him out?" said Gail.

Bird already had Annie at her bowl eating carrots. He found a halter and gave it to Gail who went into the pasture.

"You should take off your ring," Bird said to her.

"I'm only going to take him out," said Gail.

"Rings don't mix with ropes and horses."

Gail held her ring up to Rumi who sniffed it. "He likes it," she said.

She could damage it or hurt herself, but she knew he was saying that. She put the halter on Rumi.

When Rumi got out of that pasture his eyes got as big as polo balls; his ears went up, his neck stiffened, he began to dance. Annie lifted her head to look at him. What a knucklehead. But Rumi hadn't been out of that pasture in recent memory. Suddenly the whole world was all around him! If the world was feeling him earlier in the day, he was feeling the world now.

"He's trying," said Gail.

"It's pretty windy," Bird said. "Maybe on a calmer, warmer day."

Gail tried to pet his nose a little. He was almost too nervous to notice her carrot, but finally he did, gulped it, farted.

"Look at Annie," said Gail.

Annie's eyes were mischievous. Her lips soft, but tight.

Gail led Rumi in a tight circle and then led him back into the corral. He practically jumped out of the halter, then he galloped down the pasture bucking and squealing with excitement. He ran back up to Gail, jumped and ran back down. At the end of the pasture Dummie, Precious, and Tasha watched and swished their tails, heads up and forward.

Rumi stopped in the center of the corral, nostrils pumping like a diaphragm. Annie nickered and nuzzled Bird's ear. The carrot bowl was empty. He replaced the carrots. Rumi stood mid-pasture, hopping in place, back and forth from his front to his back legs. Rumi yes! Rumi yes! Rumi yes! felt Rumi. Gail put her elbows on the fence and watched him.

"He's cute," she said.

But if he could get that worked up over that little attention, out on the trail he could kill her.

"So let's saddle him up and you and me head into the sunset," Gail said.

"Rrrrgbrrr, brrrgrrrgbrr," said Annie.

Doing Nothing

Moment after moment, everyone comes out from nothingness.

- - Shunryu Suzuki, Zen Mind, Beginner's Mind

The first week after the biting incident, all Bird did was get Annie out of her paddock, take her into the small arena, and stand in the middle. Bird stood at her left shoulder. They stood for a week. It felt like they stood there for a week without moving, but maybe he put her away in between, or maybe they just stood there. If Annie could be stubborn for a week, or pissed off for a week, well, Bird could be patient for a week. What was a week? What was a month or a year for that matter?

Bob drove down the driveway behind the ring and stopped his truck. He stuck his head out the window.

"You've been standing around for a week," said Bob.

"Yes," said Bird. "Did you notice she didn't spook at your truck?"

"Great," said Bob. "You have a horse that you can stand around with."

"She bit that Robin woman."

"I heard," said Bob. "Everybody within a hundred miles knows."

"So we're standing now," Bird said.

"Are you having fun?" said Bob.

"I don't mind standing around with a horse," said Bird. And in fact, he didn't. And she didn't mind standing around with him. Horses like to stand around. You have to do something. Why not just stand around?

After Bob left, Bird reached up and touched Annie on the withers. He put his hand on her withers, then he took it off. That went on for days and days until one day she realized he was scratching her there. Bird dug his

96

fingernails deep into Annie's fur. He scratched hard up and down her neck and back. Annie pushed her head forward. Her lips puttered. She half closed her eyes.

Sometimes Bird gave her a carrot and sometimes he scratched her withers and sometimes they just stood. After weeks and weeks of that, one day while Bird was scratching her withers she noticed that he'd put his other hand on her shoulder. After a while, who knew? Maybe it was months, his hand was on her neck, under her mane, and then on the front of her neck. Then they shared some carrots. And one day, while Bird scratched her hard and she remembered how her mother bit her gently on the withers as she nursed, his hand appeared on her chest, right on the place that hurt so much, only just then it didn't hurt so very much. It only took months.

Then one day Bird scratched Annie's withers with his left hand and put his right hand on her left haunch. Annie felt his hand and moved into it, but Bird pressed a little harder. She moved away just a little and he took it off. They did that little dance for a long time, till one day when she moved away just a little Bird kept his hand there and she moved a little more. Annie didn't care. It wasn't much different than standing around. It didn't hurt. But soon enough she'd spin around in a complete circle with her hind legs and with her front legs stationary, and soon she'd do it for him in either direction. Then the front, circling sideways around her stationary back legs. And then, when Bird touched her side, she walked sideways, one way, then the other.

That was months and months. Winter passed to spring. But standing in the ring was easy and safe. And learning things was kind of fun. Bird never hurt her. And now she learned things almost immediately; she knew right away. Bird placed a rope under her front knee and tugged it slightly. She moved her foot just a little and he released. Immediately she knew he was asking her to walk. Now, in a blink, he could lead her with the rope by either front foot, or either back one, or wrap the rope around both legs and lead her like that, forward or backward. He could lead her by her ear or by her tail or by her nose. And if he touched her behind her front leg, she kicked out hard and walked beside him dancing. It was easy, like doing nothing at all.

Soon he could direct her without touching her. She watched him and moved as he moved. Backward, forward, sideways, at a walk or a run; he could take her outside the arena and she'd run around a tree or back around a post, follow at his shoulder or, if he asked her, run to him or back up. It only took a few months more.

For a carrot she'd touch her haunch with her nose, either side. And that's when she learned how to bow, too. Bird wanted her to go down on both knees, but she refused to do it. She put out a foreleg and bent her head beneath her chest, but she would not fall to her knees. She could tuck her head so far back that she touched her stomach or her hind feet, but she wouldn't go all the way down. Not going down on my knees, Bird.

Bird wondered whether this was the woods all over again, whether this was the point where one of them had to break. And then he stopped wondering. It was not about breaking her. Or her breaking him. And he understood that these other things meant nothing to her, but somehow, somehow she felt, she knew, that going all the way down on both knees was subservient, a circus act, and Annie was proud, if cooperative; cooperative, fine, but never obsequious, in fact, maybe not even obedient at all.

Paddy saw it when she showed up to work with Bob one day. Annie and Bird showed them all their stuff. Bird tugged Annie by the tail and she walked backwards in a figure eight.

"How come you don't teach me to do that?" said Bob.

"You don't have a tail," said Paddy.

Annie liked it when Bob made shrill noises. She liked upsetting Bob and she felt pleasure in the fact that doing these things so well with Bird got Bob upset.

Bird bowed to Annie. Annie bowed to Bird.

"She doesn't go all the way down?" said Paddy.

"She won't," said Bird. He held a carrot below Annie chest and she stretched to it without going down.

"I didn't think a horse could do that," Paddy said.

"She's athletic," said Bird.

"She's a counterfeit," said Paddy. "There are some horses that are so talented that they can do anything, but they aren't sincere. They always hold a piece of themselves back. That's Annie. There's a piece of herself she won't give up."

"She's a bitch," said Bob.

It didn't matter what you called it. What was the difference between a horse that did everything obediently, sincerely, and one who just did everything? Paddy answered that. She said it could be an important difference if your life was on the line.

Maybe there were a lot of words for it. Counterfeit. Bitch. Annie was a lot of things and, if all of them, then not really any of them, not completely. Who was that Annie who sniffed him for a carrot, touched his lips with hers, kissed the air when he scratched her withers? That was in there, too. Like any complex being, she could be very different depending on the context. How essentially anything were any of us? Okay, it was an old question, but Bird, for one, believed that people, and animals, too, became something essential. You were born into it some and you lived into it some, and though most people, most animals, didn't change much, we could change. How much of his time, how much of his life would he bet on that in Annie? In some frightening moment, all of it?

"She's an asshole," said Bird, "but she's my girl."

"I like that," said Paddy.

"You just going to spend all your time up here in this little ring doing tricks?" said Bob.

"I don't know," said Bird. "It's training, isn't it?"

"Her face changes as she watches you," said Paddy.

Bird looked at Annie. Would you walk quietly through the woods if it made Bob make squeaky noises?

No, Bird.

"Have you ever been on her bareback?" said Paddy.

"Please, not on my property," said Bob.

Paddy had Bird get on the fence while holding Annie's lead line. It was the same, simple routine he used for the other things. He raised the line. If Annie backed up or moved away, he kept holding on, but as soon as she stepped toward him, he let up a little, and as soon as she brought her butt toward him, he released the pressure on the line completely. Once she understood what he wanted, it took about two minutes; all he had to do was get on the fence and Annie walked up next to him. He hopped on.

"Boy, she learns fast," said Paddy.

Annie walked out and stood in the middle of the little ring with Bird on her bare back.

"Is my life on the line yet?" said Bird.

"Maybe," said Paddy.

"Maybe?" said Bob. "Now what?"

"Now we just stand here for a few weeks," Bird said.

Repercussions

*More often than not a cosmic cataclysm is unleashed
by some futile gesture that nobody has noticed.*

- - Mahabharata

Aside from all the other problems in dealing with Rumi, Bird didn't want to mess with the chemistry in the pasture. In the past, whenever he gave anybody besides Annie attention it only created friction. Whoever he'd bothered to throw a carrot would be at the fence the next day, pushing for more, screaming when he took Annie out of the corral and, inevitably, Annie had new wounds from nips and kicks. Then Annie misbehaved during their ride. As much as he wanted to be kind to all of them, he couldn't. It just got everybody pissed off.

So for that little bit of attention Rumi garnered from Gail, Rumi paid the price. Dummie chased him. Precious bit him. Tasha lectured him. Though now he spent more time standing by himself, more time with Annie, and for the first time began watching rumbles.

Herds, however small, are full of subtle politics. Dummie had always preferred Precious to Tasha. Precious looked more like him; she was younger and more pliant. He stood closer to her in the cold, offered her small attentions, nipping gently at her neck, sometimes even trying to mount her. Well, who even wanted that, but it was attention, and now, everybody seemed to be getting a little from somewhere, everybody but Tasha. Sometimes now she wandered over to Rumi and Annie. Bird noticed the shift.

"Another great alliance?" he said to Annie, who knew by his tone, by the way his body pointed toward Rumi and Tasha, that he was talking about them.

She nuzzled Bird's ear. Carrot. First things first. Carrot.

Rumi was exhilarated that Gail had petted him and taken him out. He really didn't have any thoughts about it, no plans, he just wanted her to come back. Then, in the following days, when Bird came for Annie without Gail, Rumi grew crestfallen.

"It's called waiting," Annie said to him.

"You've only made his life worse," said Tasha.

"Hope," mumbled Rumi.

"Hope sucks," said Precious, circling them.

"They'd give a day's oats for it," Annie said to Rumi.

Dummie roared up the side of the pasture fence, thundering, chest out; he threw his head. He was a huge thoroughbred, still young, still fast. He was the most magnificent horse and the most ignored. He felt it deeply.

"You prefer rage?" said Annie.

"Dummie's a gelding," said Tasha. "He'd feel it anyways."

"What should I feel?" said Rumi.

"What you'd feel anyways," said Tasha. "You can't have the female Hum. I've seen this a hundred times."

Of course we must remember that none of this was conversation as we know it, but like Dummie's raging, a jumble of emotions and dispositions, a semiotics indicated by posture and mutter, the tilt of an ear, the nod of a head, the ripple of lips, the raising of a tail to defecate or urinate in one direction or another, and not done once, but repeated and repeated so as to be clear and impossible to misinterpret.

"She might come again, once or twice. But you're somebody else's. Somebody who doesn't care. Hums don't care," Tasha said.

"Bird," said Annie.

"Bird," said Rumi.

"She's not Bird," said Tasha. "She'll stop coming. Nothing changes. Sometimes it looks, for a little while, like something is going to change, but give it a little time. Nothing changes."

"I changed," said Annie.

"You didn't change," said Tasha.

"I'm changing," said Rumi.

"You're not changing," Tasha said. "You're just being foolish for a while."

Now Dummie came charging into the center of the circle, hitting Rumi with his chest and scattering the others. Annie spun and pinned her ears. Dummie struck out. She bared her teeth and hissed, spun again and put a back hoof in his neck. Dummie reared, came down and lunged at her, but found Rumi there.

"You idiot," said Dummie. His chest expanded. He looked like a mountain. But he didn't lunge at Rumi. He tried to circle around him to get at Annie, but Rumi backed up between them.

"I can do this," hissed Annie.

"We," said Rumi.

Dummie struck him with a front hoof. Rumi tumbled. Annie stepped between them before Dummie could come down on Rumi, who bounced to his feet. Dummie backed up, planted his back feet, readying for another strike. Annie was about to spin for a rear kick when Rumi squared off in front of Dummie.

"I know your real name," Rumi said.

And Dummie stopped.

"I know it," Rumi said. "Wiley," he said softly. "Your Hum, a female Hum, called you Wiley."

Dummie backed away, snarling. It was one thing to be called Dummie, and another, much worse, to be an abandoned Dummie who was once Wiley, once named and loved. He exploded. He ran the length of the pasture, pushing against the fence. He turned the corner and ran and ran, screaming. He tore at Precious, and then Tasha who collapsed in the far corner of the corral. Dummie ran and screamed and frothed until there was nothing left. Then, finally, he hung his head and walked beneath the awning. He stood, facing the road.

Precious went to him.

"Get away," he said.

And she stood outside, swaying, not knowing what to do.

"It's a good thing it's not raining. We'd never get in there now," said Rumi.

"How did you know?" said Annie.

"He dreamed it," said Rumi. "I felt his dream."

"He's really not very wily. More dumb than wile," said Annie.

"It's just a name," Rumi said. "His name that no one uses, except in his dreams."

"Did you ever think you'd feel sorry for Dummie?" Annie said. She thought of Obleena then and worried, worried that Bird's Other would not have the persistence to take on Rumi. She thought of her own foal and wondered if he had a Hum or was abandoned now like everyone here but her. And how long before Bird one day just stopped coming.

"I just need a little attention," Rumi whispered.

"Yes," said Annie, "just a little." She wandered toward Tasha who lay folded on her legs, her head stretched onto the dirt. Annie touched Tasha's ear with her nose.

Tasha barely lifted her head. "I want to die," she said.

"No," said Annie. "No."

"Leave me," said Tasha.

Annie backed away.

"Why is the world so bad?" said Rumi.

"It's not bad. It just is," said Annie.

"Why?" said Rumi.

"Don't ask why," said Annie.

"The Great Caregiver must be very busy in other places," Rumi said.

Then, later, Bird came in his rumble, alone.

Big Ring

*Is it any surprise, then, if knowledge can only
become manifest through enigma?*

- - Satapatha Brahmana

Bird sat on Annie in the middle of the little ring. After a while he slipped off and took her to the pasture where he released her and hurried away. She always got really irritable when Bird put her in the turnout, so she wouldn't let him touch her; she even tried to bite him if he did. At night, Manny, Bob's stable helper, opened the gate and she ran into her open stall. In the morning Manny threw alfalfa into the stall; later Bird came and got her out and they walked to the little ring where they stood, then ran through their routine, only now, at the end, Bird brought Annie to the fence, hopped on her, and they walked to the center of the ring and stood there.

When Bird first imagined having a horse, he hadn't imagined it being like this. He thought the horse would be his buddy. They'd ride together into the hills and he'd turn her loose to graze while he sat in the sunshine reading or thinking near a burbling stream; his horse would wander to him while he was lost in thought and nuzzle his ear. That was the other horse, the one that didn't exist. Now he'd been with Annie a couple years and she still chased him out of her pasture at the end of the day. He wanted to give her a big, loving hug around the neck and instead she tried to kill him.

Now, sitting on her bare back in the middle of the small ring, he wondered if he'd ever get to give Annie a hug. Maybe she just wasn't that kind of horse. She had other qualities. She was smart and agile. And she didn't hate him, not really. For Annie's part, it was true that she didn't

105

want Bird hugging her. For starters, horses don't hug. And her neck was connected to her chest, where her most hurtful memories lasted the deepest. Then, at the end of the ride, she didn't want to go into that big pasture by herself, she wanted to stay with Bird, hang out, eat grass, and that's why she got so mad at him when he put her in there. Bird was so stupid that he thought she got mad at him because she didn't like him. Why would you get mad at somebody you didn't like?

Standing bareback in the middle of the ring, Bird learned that he could now ask Annie to do the same things he'd asked her to do by using his hands only now asking with his feet. A heel on her left shoulder and she spun right, a heel on her right and she spun left; touch her left rear and she moved her rear end right, touch right and she moved it left. She could turn completely around like that or just take one step, so if he moved his feet back and forth, she danced. If he put his feet forward, she backed up, touch her side and she walked sideways. Touch her behind the leg and she kicked out, left then right, back and forth, the Spanish dance. For a carrot, she'd touch his knee with her nose, right or left. Raise the lead line and she bowed her head. It was all really easy. Easy for him. Easy for her. It took time. They got to be together.

In that little ring everything was fine. Bird even learned to trot and lope bareback without falling off. To feel Annie move out without anything between his legs and her back, to feel her muscles stretching smoothly and powerfully beneath him in rhythm, in rhythm, in rhythm; there were moments, some moments, when they felt as one, completely one, together one in a moment of heaven.

Who knows how long it took for all this? Sometimes Bob drove down his driveway and stopped his truck and watched. Sure, Bob thought Bird was nuts, but what was the point of saying anything? Even Bob had been worn down. And then one day Paddy came again.

"Think she could do all that in the big ring?" said Paddy.

"I'd have to get her through the woods," said Bird.

"How long do you think it will take?"

"A year?" said Bird. "Two?"

So one day when they were all done in the little ring, Bird brushed Annie and gave her some carrots, then, as usual, let her graze a bit, and then, instead of leading her to the pasture, led her to the dark opening of the woods. They stood there a long time. Then Bird took one step in. He asked Annie to follow. He waited a long time. When she finally moved one hoof, he gave her a carrot and then put her in the pasture. In a matter of weeks he was standing with her ten yards inside the woods. Bob came riding up with Gray Dog from their workout in the big ring and stopped in front of them.

"Don't tell me," said Bob. "I don't even want to know."

Every day Bird asked Annie for one more step and she gave him one more step and that was it. If Bird was patient, Annie was stubborn. Time passed. Bob sold Gray Dog and bought a horse named Ranger. Bird and Annie stood a little deeper in the woods. Bob sold Ranger and bought a horse named Arapaho. Bird and Annie stood in the little clearing halfway to the big ring. Bob sold Arapaho and bought a horse named Rapid. Sold Rapid and bought a horse named Firelight. Sold Firelight and bought a big red horse named Cody. Cody was a big, sweet boy and one day while Bob was cursing him for his lazy lope, Annie and Bird showed up at the big ring.

"You walked here like that?" said Bob.

"In a manner of speaking," said Bird.

"Are you going to take two years to walk back?"

"I hadn't really thought it through," said Bird.

"You have to do it on her back," said Bob.

"Why?" said Bird.

"You're going to go on trail walks with your horse?"

"Maybe it will be an unusual relationship," Bird said. He took Annie into the big ring and walked her to the center. The woods loomed all around, the traffic from the road rushed by, Hum noise from the restaurant across the stream. Bird stood with Annie, then ran her through her ground routine. He brought her to the fence and hopped on her back. Annie swirled and danced, pranced, trotted, loped out.

Bob watched. Bird stopped in front of him and Cody. "She doesn't like me," Bob said.

It was true. Annie didn't like Bob. He moved too quickly and he was too demanding. He expected his horses to read his mind while his body was saying a dozen contradictory things. But she'd known him a long time now and he left her alone.

"I don't get it, but Paddy should see this," Bob said.

Bird hopped off Annie and they walked through the woods back to the stables.

"You showed off for Bob," Bird said to Annie as she grazed outside her turnout. He couldn't quite figure it out. Desire, fear, even jealousy seemed like simple enough emotions for an animal, but when it came to performance, Annie often acted as if the whole business was beneath her; he could almost feel her eyes rolling as she ran through her routines; and then there were moments, like down in the big ring in front of Bob, when she seemed to take pride in it all. Did it matter? It might, if he could unlock it.

Think like a horse, Bird. Dump the silly, abrasive sounds. Move patiently, touch, listen, smell, watch, live always in a split second from flight, even now, under the gentle sky, on the green grass.

Boy, when a horse ate grass it sure looked good. "You sure like grass," said Bird. He plucked a piece of grass and chewed it. It didn't taste that good. Kind of bitter.

Annie raised her head, her mouth full, green fresh grass sticking out the sides of her cheeks.

"You going to show off for Paddy tomorrow?" said Bird.

Bird, tomorrow is another day.

And so it was. Bird walked Annie down to the big ring where Paddy waited. Paddy held a video camera (back then, not so very long ago really, video cameras used tapes).

"Oh, please don't," said Bird.

"You'll learn a lot by watching it," said Paddy.

"I'll just mess up."

"Pray for mistakes," said Paddy. "That's how you learn." Paddy might have been a big old red neck horse trainer, but she was really good at it.

So Bird led Annie into the center of the ring. Annie backed up, performed side passes, danced, spun, Spanish stepped. Annie ran around cones and jumped over obstacles. Then Bird got on her back and they did it like that, Paddy waving that camera and cheering, "Oh man!" and "Holy cow!" Bird barely managed to stay on when they jumped, but Annie just held him steady, easing up and straightening out when she felt his weight shift dangerously. Bird knew; she was doing it for him.

There was a ditch at one end of the ring, near the road, and in it a live oak tree, surrounded by railroad ties three deep.

"Take her into that ditch," said Paddy.

"We've never done that," Bird said.

"Just ask her. She'll do it," Paddy said. "That horse will do anything for you."

Bird took Annie to the edge of the ditch. The wind blew in the leaves of the tree. Cars and trucks roared by. Annie lowered her head and sniffed at the railroad ties. Her shoulders quivered.

"She's scared," said Bird.

"That horse isn't scared!" yelled Paddy. "Don't believe it for a second."

"I'm scared," said Bird.

"Of course you are," said Paddy. "Her head is down. She's going to do it. Ask her again when she raises her head."

Annie sniffed the ties some more, then raised her head. Bird touched her sides with his feet and then, slowly, Annie put down a leg and lowered her front end into the ditch, then the back. They stood under the tree, the railroad ties as high as Annie's chest.

"Bring her out," said Paddy.

And Annie lifted them out of the ditch.

"Holy mackerel!" said Paddy. "Okay, one more thing."

At the same end of the arena, in the other corner, sat a big, yellow backhoe that Bob rented to move some new sand into the big ring; it had a huge shovel and black tires six feet tall. Bird had kept Annie away from it as much as he could the whole time they were in there.

"Get on top of one of those tires, call her over, jump on her back and gallop down the center of the ring," said Paddy.

"It's a monster," said Bird. "A dragon." He petted Annie's neck. "Are you afraid of dragons, Annie?"

Annie'd had her eye on it the whole time. It was a big, unusual thing. Looked something like a rumble, but there was no Hum in it and it was sleeping.

Bird slipped off Annie and led her over to the machine. She sniffed it. It didn't wake up. Holding on to the lead line, Bird crawled up into the cockpit, then out of it, onto the tire, balancing there. He raised the line and Annie walked over to the tire. He raised it again and Annie brought her butt toward him and stood underneath him. Bird felt like he was diving off a cliff. What if she moved? What about his genitals? But by now it looked like everybody was reading each other's minds.

"Put your other hand over them," Paddy said.

Bird took the lead line in his left hand and cupped his genitals in his right. He stepped off the tire and plopped onto Annie's back, touched her haunch with his foot and off they tore down the center of the ring.

"Yahoo!" yelled Paddy. "Yahoo!"

Annie skidded to a halt at the end of the ring, then she and Bird trotted back to Paddy.

"Amazing!" said Paddy. "Do you have any idea what you've accomplished?"

"She did it," said Bird.

"You saved that horse's life," said Paddy.

Annie was hot now, sweating from the workout, though not tired. There, she felt. There. Enough.

"I wish you could see her face while you're on her," said Paddy. "I've never seen anything like it." She held up the camera to shoot Annie's face, but then Annie pinned her ears at her. "Ha!" said Paddy.

"She's kind of amazing," Bird said.

"You were both pretty amazing," said Paddy. She took the tape out of the video camera and handed it to Bird. "When you watch this, you'll see that your weight is still too far forward. That's why you're bouncing. Get your heels down more and don't hold on to her with your thighs."

"More to learn," said Bird. He laughed.

"It's good you laugh," said Paddy. "I don't know anybody else who laughs when they ride."

"If you were me you'd have to laugh," Bird said.

110

"Now ride her home," said Paddy.

"I don't think so," said Bird.

"Put your weight in her and walk home!" said Paddy.

"She's not done with me today," said Bird. "She's a complex, sentient creature."

"It's a good thing I don't know what that means," said Paddy. "She'll do anything for you. Now walk back."

"You don't know her like I do," Bird said. He side passed Annie to the gate, unlocked it, then he and Annie walked the gate open, turned, and Annie side passed the gate closed.

Look at that," said Paddy. "Come on!"

"Okay," Bird said.

"Call me when you learn something new. Teach her to trot in place and run backwards."

Bird laughed. "She can already run backwards." He started Annie up the hill. Annie walked calmly underneath him. Good thing there was so little wind. The woods didn't seem to breathe so much; there was less predation in the air. It almost took her this long to realize that Bird wasn't walking in front of her, but rode her. Bird on her back. Where was Annie in all this?

They reached the little clearing and Bird stopped. He'd done a lot of things in his life that had exhilarated him. He was a pretty good athlete as a kid. Scored touchdowns, dunked basketballs. Won big games, even championships. Earned degrees. But right now, at this moment, he never felt better about anything in his life. Paddy was right. It was amazing. Look how far they'd come. A little patience, well, a lot of patience, a lot of time. How many years? But what a day. He and Annie. This was the Great Exhilaration. What a day!

He petted Annie's neck again. "Annie," said Bird. "Sweet Annie. Think we can make it?" Their sweat blended from her back to his seat. Bird's legs moved with her breath. It was as if they were one.

Annie took a deep breath beneath Bird. They were not one. She was Annie. He was Bird. He touched her side with his foot and urged her forward, onto the forest path that led back to the stables. A butterfly

111

dropped in front of them, flitting across Annie's face. She spooked. She threw Bird off and ran back to the ranch.

Rumi, Too

Live in every moment as if you are saying farewell.

\- - Gautama Buddha

Bird came in his rumble, alone. The other horses, who didn't watch rumbles like Annie did, didn't look up, though Rumi watched Annie and then tried to follow the rumble. It was hard to watch a meaningless thing. Then, as Annie predicted, Bird appeared over the hill and walked to the pasture. Then another rumble came up the road. It didn't have a top. Annie looked at it quickly, raising her head and perking her ears, the way you looked toward danger, and Rumi followed her motion, jerking his head toward the rumble too, and there, in the topless rumble, Rumi saw Gail. It was her! Rumi hopped up and down. They come in rumbles! They come in rumbles!

By the time she came over the hill Bird had Annie out of the pasture. She raised her head from the carrot bowl and briefly pinned her ears at Gail. Carrot. It didn't matter that she had a bowl of them in front of her. Important gestures needed to be made. Gail went to the tack box and brought Annie a carrot, which she accepted grudgingly but without malice.

"Annie is still Annie," Gail said.

Yes, Annie was still Annie and that's how Annie liked it. She liked hearing her name. But now Rumi was practically dancing at the fence. Everyone was watching now. Dummie and Precious stepped forward together from the feed bin. Tasha walked to the center of the pasture.

"Hello, cutie," Gail said to Rumi. She petted his nose. "He sent me a dream," she said to Bird. "A dream that I came to see him."

"Rumi?" said Bird.

"Rumi," said Gail.

Rumi, yes! Rumi, Rumi, yes! Rumi, Rumi! Rumi danced. He nuzzled the halter that hung buckled to the top rung of the fence.

"Think he wants to get out?" said Bird. "He's pretty worked up. You might need help."

"I think I can handle him," said Gail. She unbuckled the halter and went in. Rumi pushed his head into the halter, almost knocking her down. She laughed. They walked out.

Annie pinned her ears at them. Fine, Rumi, you're out. Now stay away from Bird.

"Tie him up a little farther away," Bird said.

Gail didn't like being told what to do, but Annie was growing irritable and Rumi was jumpy, and there were some two thousand pounds of anxious horses out there. She tied Rumi to the top of the pasture fence; she gave him far too much rope and used the wrong kind of knot; as jumpy as he was, his head should have been secured and most horse people used a slip knot that you could release quickly by just pulling the end, but Bird knew he'd ruin this by telling, teaching, directing; for years Gail had avoided horses, as much as anything because of the people; horse people were bossy know-it-alls; Bird didn't like the know-it-all part either; it was one of the reasons he kept Annie out here, away from all the other horses and owners, but the bossy part, well, sometimes you had to boss a horse; somebody had to be in charge and as much as he loved Annie, she made some very bad decisions when she thought she was in charge.

Don't be a know-it-all, Bird. Annie was looking at him. She'd learned how to untie that slip knot in about two days; she could even take the padlock off the tack box if it wasn't locked; she just watched Bird do it; she didn't have hands but she could knock it with her nose till it fell off. Any horse could unbuckle the halters that hung on the fence and if they wanted you to take them out they did it right in front of your face.

Gail got Bird's curry brush and cleaned Rumi, brushed his tail and mane with the thick pronged mane and tail brush. Rumi was so happy his ears drooped like a donkey's.

"Guess he likes it," said Gail.

"I guess," said Bird. He saw she hadn't taken her ring off. "I worry a little about that ring," he said. She ignored him.

Now Tasha was edging up toward the fence, standing between Annie and Rumi. Gail walked over to her and offered her a carrot. Tasha stepped toward Gail and sniffed the carrot suspiciously, then took it. Gail cleaned the crust from Tasha's eyes with her index finger.

"Look how she's softened," said Gail.

It was true. Tasha's brown eyes relaxed and her lips pushed slightly forward.

For Annie's part, this was all getting a little too cozy. She hit Bird between the shoulder blades with her nose.

"You and I are going for a ride," Bird said.

Annie wasn't that crazy about going for rides except that everybody else was so jealous that she got to do it.

Gail petted Tasha's forehead, then went back to Rumi. "Do you think I could clean his feet?"

"All their feet are a mess," said Bird. "But who's going to pay a shoer?"

"A farrier," said Gail.

"Yes," Bird said. The ranch had one, but individual owners contracted him. Bird had his own, a woman he used from back in the Bob days.

He put some carrots in Annie's bowl, got the hoof pick and went to Rumi. He touched Rumi's left shoulder and ran his hand down his leg. Rumi gave him his foot. Bird cleaned the dry mud from Rumi's hoof and frog, the soft back center of the hoof. "You can do this," he said to Gail.

"Yes," she said.

And while she did, Bird saddled Annie.

"Let me walk him a little," said Gail.

Annie had taken the bit and Bird stood in front of her holding her reins. His shoulders sagged. Where could this go?

"Come on . . ." and Gail looked in Annie's eyes. "Bird," said Gail. She walked up to Bird, lifted her right hand and ran her fingers across the feathers on the left side of his hat. "She calls you Bird."

Annie's ears twitched.

"Or whatever a bird means to her," Gail said.

"How would you know that?" Bird said.

"Rumi. Last night, in that dream."

Lots of people talked about horses being telepathic, but as soft-headed as Bird was about the whole animal cognition thing, he was a long way from buying horse telepathy. Horses were extremely tactile and subtle. For all the talk about Clever Hans not being able to really do math, for him to answer mathematical problems by reading unintentional signals from his trainer, well, that's amazing enough. Bird figured that Annie could read his body that well. And doing that, reading those subtle cues, often knew what he felt or what he wanted to do even before he did. Back home, his animals sometimes scattered before he even knew he was mad. All of that could be explained away behaviorally if you wanted to be that narrow about it, and Bird didn't. But telepathy?

Gail on the other hand, she saw ghosts though she didn't believe in them and though she didn't believe in telepathy either, her cats and dogs sent her dreams. In one dream she was a many-armed Sarasvati, handing out pet snacks. One old dog, who was angry that she brought in a new one, sent her a dream that she took the new dog for a walk and came back without him. Stuff like that. Besides being an anarchist, she was a surrealist; for her, explanations were like the mist that shrunk the incredible shrinking man.

Annie looked at Rumi. She felt it. Rumi was thinking about Gail all the time, sending himself, bringing her, dreaming of her.

Bird looked at Annie. "Bird?" he said.

Yes, Bird. Bird, felt Annie.

And somehow Bird felt it, too.

Gail untied Rumi; it took a long time because of that clumsy knot she'd tied, and she led him across the road into the open. Bird saddled Annie and followed. Then Rumi began hopping from his front legs to his back legs. Rumi, yes! Rumi Rumi, yes! Rumi yes Rumi! and Gail started to lose control; she tried to circle him around her but he kicked out. Annie quickly moved forward, Bird and all, stopping in front of Rumi. Calm down. You'll blow it. And Rumi stopped.

"What happened there?" Gail said.

"I guess she sent him a calm dream," said Bird.

Tasha was at the gate now, nudging it with her nose.

"She wants to come out, too," said Gail.

"How many horses that we don't own do you want to take care of?" Bird said. "When their owners find out, they'll want to charge you for doing it."

Gail led Rumi back to the pasture gate and gave both him and Tasha a carrot. "What do they say where you're from?" she said. "Day at a time." She unlatched the gate.

But some trouble arose. Tasha pushed against the unlatched gate and knocked it into Gail. Rumi panicked and pushed the other way, Gail in between. Bird loped Annie over, dismounted, and shooed Tasha, but then Rumi poured through the opening and ran in, tugging Gail along. "Let go!" said Bird, and Gail dropped the lead allowing Rumi to pound off into the pasture with the lead line flying behind. He shut the gate.

"You all right?" he said.

"Yes. They didn't try to hurt me."

Later he might tell her, make sure the gate is clear of other horses. Rumi had to be taught to stay behind her and never run through the gate. She had a rope burn on the palm of her hand, thank the Gods she hadn't wrapped the lead line around it; you could be dragged, even lose fingers as well as her ring. But now was not the time. If she came back again, maybe then. Maybe she'd already learned it. He'd known her a long time. He always knew what she was feeling, but he could never predict what she'd do.

Gail held Annie's reins while Bird went into the pasture and took the halter off Rumi whose eyes burned toward Gail. Tasha ran up and down the other side of corral. He'd never seen Tasha run before. Dummie and Precious stood taut just outside the awning. Things had changed in there.

When Bird got outside the gate again, Gail said to him, "The depth of that feeling."

"In you?"

"In them. In all of us. Everything."

"A little attention goes a long way," Bird said.

She touched Bird's cheek. "Bird," she whispered.

Annie muttered.

"Sorry," Gail said to her. "But I accept some things and you're going to have to accept some things."

Bird wondered what those things might be. Annie saw it a little clearer. She knew there was going to be trouble with this Gail - Rumi business when she instigated it. Change.

Gail went off in her topless rumble, Rumi watching. She slowed, waved to Rumi, and then was gone.

Bird mounted Annie again. "So, Bird is it?" he said.

Annie's ears shifted slightly toward him, then went back.

"I guess you're going to be in for an interesting afternoon," he said.

Bird's noise. He couldn't know she felt there was never anything interesting or uninteresting about an afternoon. But on the other side of the hill above the pasture, she stopped, raised her head and perked her ears. Bird cocked an ear, too. It was Dummie, screaming and screaming.

Bird's Brain

Are you afraid of this happiness?

- - Majjhima Nikaya

It only took Bird ten years to figure out that Annie gave him trouble to keep him near. It only took Annie a few days to figure out it would work. When she acted up, it prolonged the ride. Bird wouldn't end the ride until she behaved and she misbehaved for as long as she wanted to be with Bird. She could run and buck all day.

Though Bird felt something deep in his seat about Annie. Just like her ability to hold a part of herself separate from her performance in the ring, when she spooked in the woods there was something going on that was not quite sincere. Eventually, as she frothed and raised her tail and snorted, he thought she might actually have bought her own act, but he could feel, beneath him, even deeper than her hot, shivering electricity, something that wasn't really scared, something that was about him and not the woods. Unfortunately for Bird, back then, his feelings were more perceptive than his brain.

But slowly he learned. If Annie spun downward unexpectedly near the top of a steep hill, throwing Bird sideways and forward—it was almost impossible to stay on if a horse did that—she always stopped, braced her feet, and threw Bird back on. The first time Bird hung on her neck, puzzled, but after that he began to laugh. He knew she'd saved him. It took him a decade to figure out that she planned the whole thing. Got you, Bird. Saved you, Bird. Get it?

It took him a long time to realize that Annie made plans. At a crossroads, Annie might try to head down a path that led away from the

119

pasture, only to choose an even shorter path straight home at the next juncture. There didn't seem any other way to explain it: she knew about the second choice when she made the first one. She was thinking ahead, and somehow using a cognitive map.

But way back, on Bird's most exhilarating day, when Annie dumped him on the ride home, he hadn't quite figured out that Annie would do one thing wrong every time. No perfect rides. No perfect workouts. And if it didn't come early, then it was going to come late. Bird fell on the video cassette when he hit the ground that day, broke it, and never saw that amazing bareback ride in the big ring. No one ever did. Bird didn't even bother to tell Bob. Paddy did. Bob didn't believe any of it, or much of it, but for the part about Annie dumping Bird on the way home.

"That horse will never change," said Bob.

"She's already changed completely," said Bird. "Well, a lot."

The day of the Great Exhilaration, after Annie dumped him, he walked out of the woods to find Annie munching some grass near the horse bath. She lifted her head and stared at him like she'd never seen him before in her life. But she let him walk up to her. He picked up the lead line and led Annie into the pasture, pulled off the halter and scooted out, though Annie didn't chase him that day, she just stood. All of that time. All of that work.

"Annie, Annie, Annie," said Bird.

Herd of one, Bird, felt Annie.

"Herd of two?" said Bird.

Herd of one.

Even Bird felt that.

120

My Hum

*It is the emotion that steals the heart . . . the liquid
path toward the bazaar of love. Going there is as dangerous
as diving into waters from which one may never emerge.*

- - Rig Veda

If Bird missed a day, Annie waited for him at the gate. This was the case every Tuesday. On Monday this ranch closed to its members, only the ranchums and helper-hums came and dropped alfalfa over the fence, morning and evening. Monday was day three of the second four days. Tuesday, day one, Bird came. He came two, three, four times, then one, two times, then the third day the ranch closed and no Bird. Day four she waited at the gate. And Bird came. It was day one again. Time was not one thing. There was moon time and sun time, the time of the four weather changes, the time under the shifting stars each night and each year, time of rain, time of wind, feed time, roll time, time to lie in the warm mud, time to be alone, and time for Bird to come, Bird Time.

If he was going to be gone for more than a day, he told her. He'd say, "I can't come" or something else that wasn't "Good-bye, Annie, I love you. I'll see you tomorrow." If he didn't say that, she knew she'd have to wait, maybe as long as several cycles.

Now Rumi waited, too, though he didn't really know how to wait. He waited for the rumble with no top, inside, a woman, she didn't wear birds, but grew a mane that was both black and gold. For Annie, Rumi was always some kind of pain to have around and now he was this new kind of pain.

"I love her," said Rumi.

121

"Please go let the world feel you or something," said Annie.

"She doesn't smell like Bird," said Rumi. "Like flowers."

"Horses wait," said Annie.

"Honeysuckle and sage," said Rumi.

Well, that was the smell. "You can't be waiting and hurting all the time," said Annie.

"I'm sending myself to her," said Rumi.

"She doesn't always come with Bird," said Annie. "You know that. Maybe once every two cycles."

"Maybe more!" said Rumi.

"Count a cycle, then start waiting," said Annie.

"I can't count!" said Rumi. "I don't count! I love!"

Tasha walked over. She spent more time with Annie and Rumi now because Dummie and Precious had been brooding and moody. Though something was up with Dummie; during the last ranch-closed day the helper-Hums took him away for a little while and when he got back his eyes got wider and his ears perked. Right now Annie felt she could do without both Rumi and Tasha.

"Nothing changes," said Tasha. "He's still babbling, only now he's babbling about different things."

"Some things have changed a little," Annie said to her.

"I'm going to have a Hum," said Rumi.

"A pat on the head, a carrot, it changes nothing," said Tasha.

"You came to the gate too!" said Rumi.

"And got a carrot," said Tasha.

"She brushed me!" said Rumi.

"Hums come and go. Take it one carrot at a time," Tasha said.

"Bird," said Annie.

"Bird will not last forever," said Tasha.

"A lot has changed, but not Bird," Annie said.

Now Dummie came thundering up with Precious behind. "My Hum is coming for me!" he said. "Ha! Soon! Ha! Soon! My Hum!" He panted. "Taking me with her! Away!"

"What will you do?" Annie asked Precious.

"Maybe I'll breed again," she said.

"Everybody is pooping twice as much," said Tasha.

"A change?" said Rumi.

"This place stinks of hope," Tasha said.

Dummie and Precious ran around them. "My Hum! My Hum!" said Dummie.

"At least he's not biting anybody," said Annie.

"Another change," whispered Rumi.

The two red horses pounded off, nipping at each other's backs.

"They won't breed her again," said Tasha. "She's too old."

Rumi had his nose in the air, quivering.

"You're feeling something," said Annie.

"Dummie is going far away, alone," Rumi said. "It's sad."

"You don't have to stand there like an idiot with your nose in the air to know that," said Tasha. "First they stop coming around. They don't start coming around again after that. If they show up, it's to get rid of you."

"You're still here," said Annie.

"Lucky to be left alone."

"Poor Precious," said Rumi.

Annie didn't know what to feel for Precious, not really. Precious had been mean, then, after Dummie, she left Annie alone. Her daughters were gone, still broodmares. But there was Rumi, feeling his heart out for Precious who would beat him up in a blink.

Tasha walked away, turned back for a moment. "This will pass. Worse things will happen," she said.

"That's change," muttered Rumi.

"For the worse," said Tasha. "What little change happens, it's always for the worse."

The Good Horse

To give your horse a large, spacious meadow
is the way to control her.

- - Shunryu Suzuki, Zen Mind, Beginner's Mind

When Annie ran with her head up and her tail in the air, there was fire in her eyes, but other times, running dead out, head down and flying, her eyes went calm, as if meditating or in a dream, and in time Bird felt it too, the brush along the trail racing by in a blur, her hooves pounding, blasting out, heart and mind, the absolute peace inside a torrent, there, where horse met God, and then, for the moment, inseparable in trust, he too became calm, running full speed together, balls out satori. Heaven.

The day after the Great Exhilaration he began again, this time on her back, to walk into the woods, one step a day. After their workout, whether in the small ring or the big one, the big arena to which he still walked her, there and back, on the lead line, Bird got on Annie's back and took her to edge of the woods. Bob found them there, about twenty yards in, a month after the Great Exhilaration.

"That won't work," Bob said.

And for once Bob was right. Eventually Annie blew up, or pretended to blow up, and Bird took her to the clearing or back to the big ring and ran and ran, he even let her run to the arena if she wanted, but never home, not downhill in those woods and not home; those were Bird's rules and he enforced them now with quiet resolution, without anger or panic. He hopped on Annie, stroked her neck and said, "Okay Annie, here we go, if you want to fight, I'm ready," and usually the readier he was the less she fought with him, though sometimes she just had to go crazy and Bird just

124

had to ride it out, and it had gone beyond whether he was going to keep her or get rid of her or whether or not she would ever let him hug her. Every day Bird came back and they rode, until one day some strange people came and walked all around and put up signs, then more; and more often more and more strange people came and one day Bird arrived with yet someone else who helped him put Annie in a trailer and they left. Bob had sold the ranch and moved to Santa Fe.

She never missed Bob for a moment. It was a long ride to the new place, which was much different; there were a half-dozen rings and hundreds of horses in stalls; there were no woods, just a lot of open space and some big hills. Paddy was there.

Bird lived much farther away now; she came to understand this; she felt the distance in the drive and the weariness in his seat, as well; he didn't come every day anymore but every other day. She grew to accept it. The other horses in her pasture, the far pasture closest to the ranch entrance but farthest from the central facility, those horses came and went and she had little to do with any of them. The rings here had more things to do in them, obstacles to jump, poles to race between, barrels to ride around, and all that was fun enough. Sometimes Paddy came by and yelled at Bird while he was riding; sometimes Bird took Annie out on the trails and there he found out that Annie didn't just blow up in the woods, but anywhere she chose, especially if approached by a madly flapping butterfly, and wherever they went Bird found some open area to take her and run and run and run until they were both coated with foam and sweat.

Paddy was training horses for the movies then and on those days Annie and Bird joined them and ran through sprinklers, jumped trenches, ran around bulldozers, braved huge flapping tarps and crazy loud sounds like blowing whistles, explosions and gunfire.

"You see," Paddy said to Bird after one of those sessions, "that horse isn't afraid of anything."

"Shouting men," said Bird.

"We're all afraid of shouting men," said Paddy, "if we have any sense."

"Butterflies."

Paddy looked right at Annie. "You aren't afraid of butterflies!"

Annie twitched her ears. Maybe. Maybe not.

It went like this for a year, broken up only by some big event that Paddy threw. Hums came from all over and the air filled with the smell of burned flesh, not horse, but cows, pigs, chickens. She saw cattle trailers for the first time; they brought the moos in and the Hums and their horses chased them. She smelled the cows and then smelled their burning flesh.

Then the riding contests began. Flying lead changes, pole riding, side passing, backing around obstacles, barrel racing, all the stuff that Annie already did, but Annie and Bird didn't enter any contests because Bird told Paddy that Annie would win every one.

"It wouldn't be competition," said Bird.

"You think so," said Paddy.

"I know so," said Bird. "I'm watching it now." What would be the point of taking ribbons and trophies away from people who really wanted them? What he and Annie had was not about measuring what they could do together against somebody else.

Bird saddled up Annie and they watched from outside the ring. It was all rather festive if, to Annie's mind, if not Bird's, a little ridiculous. But then, at the end of all the contests, one of those famous horse listener cowboys walked into the huge ring; he had one of those wireless microphones, and he put a hundred dollar bill in the middle of the huge arena. Whoever could get their horse to step on that hundred dollar bill could put it in their pocket and take it home.

You have to know a little bit about horses to know how hard that is. Horses have acute senses. On top of that, their ears can rotate separately, like independent radar dishes. The way their eyes sit at the side of their heads, they can see in both directions, about 355 degrees while staring straight ahead, but they can't see behind their butts and they can't see directly in front of their faces. This is why jumping fences is such an act of faith for a horse, because when she makes the leap she's lost sight of the fence and must make it blind. So the horses couldn't see that dollar bill, not only was it in front of their faces, but looking down, their noses were in the way. The trick has to be taught, and then performed, tactilely, teaching the horse to step by indicating with your toe.

One after another the contestants brought their horses to the center of the ring and danced around that hundred dollar bill. Nobody could do it, that's why the cowboy put that hundred dollar bill out there. He never had to give it away. After the last contestant failed the cowboy walked into the ring and put his arms in the air. "Well," he said, "I guess you all have something to learn." That's when Bird rode Annie into the ring, prancing.

Of course, by this point Annie knew exactly what they were supposed to do. Bird let her spy the bill by tilting her head, then stopped in front of it. He tapped her behind the knee and Annie stepped on the hundred dollar bill, then she picked it up in her teeth, brought it to Bird's knee and put it in Bird's left hand where there was a piece of carrot waiting. People were so stunned they didn't even cheer.

"Shit," said the cowboy. He hadn't turned off the mike.

Bird gave him the hundred dollar bill.

"You won it," the cowboy said.

"I didn't enter the contest," said Bird.

After that Paddy told Bird he should show Annie or enter some competitions.

"Would I have to dress up?" said Bird.

"Yes. But you could win some trophies and money. Some people have a knack, some don't. You do. You could start training maybe."

"Other horses?" said Bird. "Annie would be jealous."

"She's a horse," said Paddy.

Well, Bird didn't do any of this horse stuff for trophies or money. In fact, in that moment, he couldn't say why he did it, even less so why Annie did. When he sat on her, he was futureless. He loved her, even if she couldn't love him, yet, or ever.

"I just like sitting on a horse," said Bird.

"You like sitting on that horse," said Paddy.

I just like eating carrots, felt Annie.

As the year went on the only difference was that Annie began to watch the rumbles as they rolled into the ranch and she learned Bird's rumble and now, when he arrived, she was waiting for him, ambivalently, at the gate. He always had a carrot, even though everybody told him not to start with carrots, don't reward before the workout. He had a carrot and she was at the gate when other people were lucky to drag their horses out of their stalls. He didn't have to chase her to put the halter on her, in fact, she lowered her head into it; they could do this with Bird on his knees. Then he led her down the road along the pastures into the saddling area, though when he put her back, she still tried to bite him, after all, she was Annie, it's what she did.

But the whole thing had a feeling of impermanence about it, and one day it took a bad turn when Bird missed his day, then another day, and then another. She was not so much of a counter then, but for counting the beats between lead changes, but now she counted the days and four went by three times. Some girls came to her pasture and tried to catch her, but she ran away from them. She watched the road. Another cycle of four went by and for the first time in her life she worried. She ate much less. Paddy noticed. Sent the girls again, but Annie ran away. She thought about Bird. She wanted Bird to come.

And then one day as she stood alone at the back of the pasture she heard a familiar groan, looked up, and saw Bird's rumble. She watched it go into the ranch. Then across the pastures, she saw Bird walking with her halter. She stood. She trembled. She hated him. Fuck you, Bird. Show up out of nowhere. She wanted nothing to do with him. He could chase her till tomorrow.

She watched him come up the road, then approach the gate. He looked in. Looked across the huge pasture. "Annie," he said.

And Annie took off like a bolt, but not away from him but toward him. Bird stood in front of the gate, ground glued, stupefied, as a half-ton of crazy Annie built up speed and thundered at him. Annie hadn't decided anything except that she was headed for Bird, and Bird was beyond decisions. If she hit him doing forty he was a goner. The world disappeared. What could Bird do? Run away? He stood as Annie grew larger in front of him, running at him.

Annie thundered down. The air was hooves. And then she pulled up, skidding to within an inch of Bird's face, her nostrils throwing steam.

Bird! Bird! Bird! Who could tell whether it was love or hate? Even Annie didn't know.

"Annie," said Bird. "Sweet Annie. I missed you. I'm sorry. I had to go away."

He stepped toward her. She stepped back. He offered her a carrot that she sniffed suspiciously. Then she took it. Whatever you feel, carrots are carrots. Her breathing calmed.

"You missed me," whispered Bird. He had another carrot. "I will never leave you," said Bird. "I will always come back." And then, it was hard to tell, because it was an impossible thing, but water, he'd swear, tears, dripped from the inner corners of her eyes. "Oh Annie," said Bird. And he stepped forward and put his arms around her neck. And she let him. She heard an odd sound from him, something she never heard before, but when he stepped away he had water in his eyes, too.

"I love you, Annie," whispered Bird.

Well, maybe once every decade she'd let him put his arms around her neck. After being together almost every day for ten years, he meant a lot to her, in fact, without ever realizing it, he meant everything.

After a couple of day cycles, Bird put her in a trailer again and moved her to a new ranch, this one, now, where he came six times a week; first there was Bernard and Howard, Precious and her daughters, and then this little herd of Dummie and Precious, Rumi and Tasha. And now with Rumi and Gail, Bird's Other, trying to work out this new thing.

Commitment

He has shaken out his robe
there is nothing in it anymore.

- - Rumi, "Omar and the Old Poet"

Before Bird and Annie left Paddy's, Paddy asked him a favor. There was a woman there named Rosie with a gray roan mare named Ida, Rosie's first horse. Paddy found the horse for Rosie and it was always Paddy's policy to get you a horse that might be too much for you at first, but if you stuck with it you'd have a horse you wouldn't outgrow, a horse you'd grow into and keep. But Ida started giving Rosie trouble in the ring, crow hopping and taking off; then things got worse and now Rosie couldn't even get Ida out of her stall. Every time Rosie came to the stall, Ida pinned her ears and tried to bite her.

"What do you want me to do?" said Bird.

"Get that horse out of that stall," said Paddy.

"Can't Juan do it?"

"She bit Juan."

Juan was Paddy's wrangler.

"You could do it," said Bird.

"But I'll just do it," said Paddy. "Rosie can't do what I do. You'll figure out something that she can do."

Bird liked Rosie. She was thin, gray-blonde, a little cranky, probably pretty cute up to ten years ago. Bird walked over to Ida's stable with her. He liked Ida, too. Ida was athletic and stubborn and liked to run. She was a pretty horse, if a little stocky for his tastes. Ida pinned her ears and bared her teeth at Bird.

"First problem is she's in the stall," said Bird. He didn't like isolating horses in stalls, but Rosie wanted to show Ida, so she couldn't have any nicks or bites on her, she had to be clean as a whistle.

"I have to get her out of the stall," said Rosie. "Every day."

"That's the problem," said Bird.

"What's the solution?" said Rosie.

"Don't put her in the stall," said Bird.

That solution was unacceptable.

"She's not happy to see you," said Bird.

"Why should she be happy to see me?"

"Exactly," said Bird.

"I'm just going to sell her," said Rosie.

"Before or after you get her out of the stall?" Bird said.

"I'm just going to get some easy horse."

"You're not going to show an easy horse," Bird said. Horses, like every other person and animal, came as a package deal. With intelligence, talent, and athleticism came fire and complexity, and trouble. On top of that, mares were usually more trouble than geldings; Bird believed that females were more complex than males across the board; sex was more complicated and had more consequences, they went through more physical changes, they had to bear young, feed them, protect them, teach them, give them up. He told all this to Rosie. That aside, Ida was still in the stall.

"This is a great horse," said Bird. "I've watched you."

"You watch me?" said Rosie.

If this went on much longer it was going to turn into a seduction.

"Let's get some carrots," Bird said.

"Everybody says not to do that," said Rosie.

"I don't care what everybody says," said Bird.

Bird came back with some carrots and stood in front of Ida, just outside the reach of her teeth. Ida hissed and snarled and pinned her ears. Bird stood.

"This is great," said Rosie.

"She can't do it forever," Bird said.

Another thing everybody said was that horses had very short attention spans, less than a second. If that was true, they could sure string together a lot of short attention spans. Around now Ida'd been spitting at him for a couple of minutes. One trainer told Bird that horses had learned that most humans got fed up after thirty seconds, so if you stuck with something for over thirty seconds the horse would always give in. Tell that to Annie who could fight with Bird for hours.

Bird stood calmly in front of Ida. Finally, she put her ears up a little. Bird pulled out the carrot. She pinned her ears and Bird put the carrot away. She pulled her head back into the stall and put her ears up. Bird pulled out the carrot again. Her ears went back down and he pocketed the carrot. You know how this went. Eventually she sniffed the carrot and finally she kept her ears up and got it. In a half hour Bird was in her stall, gave Ida a carrot, put her halter on her and led her out.

"Great, now my horse loves you," said Rosie.

"She loves carrots," said Bird. "You can do it."

And she did. In fact, a month later Rosie and Ida won their first show ribbon. But in those last weeks, every time Bird walked past Ida's stall on his way to get Annie, Ida nickered to him and he always gave her a carrot. Turns out she did like Bird.

Mares liked Bird and Bird liked mares. Stallions did not like Bird. He got along with geldings okay. In time Bird came to believe that sexuality communicated across species; certain movements, smells, postures, attitudes, other unnameable if not unknowable things, were peculiarly male or female, some of it biological, some of it cultural, and that animal species possessed culture, some of it inherited, some of it passed on and learned, some of it adapted or even invented: mating, migration, nest building, child rearing, hunting, avoiding predators, fighting, dominance, submission, socializing and social hierarchies, marking territory and maintaining it, finding food and telling each other where it was, recognizing danger, communicating danger to their group or herd, and lots more.

Animals, like people, might be gay or straight, or something on the spectrum in between. Just watch. Most people, in general, didn't watch anything very closely. Scientists and philosophers watched too closely and too restrictively to see anything. Sometimes animal trainers were like that too, letting what they thought they knew get between them and what was in front of their faces.

For his part, Bird's great grandparents were shepherds. Inside him lay generations of herding hooved animals, sitting in open fields for days, watching.

Bird once had a dog, actually it was Gail's dog, a brown hound named HD after a lesbian Modernist poet; she was the dog who sent Gail her dreams. HD the dog didn't like anybody. She didn't hate them. She didn't bark at them or bite them. She just didn't bother with them. If you tried to talk to her she went to a corner, turned her back and rolled her eyes. Bird loved that dog. He loved his cats, too. He loved the feeling of a house full of cats lounging, loved the way cats filled a room. He loved to watch his beautiful Mucha Plata dance around him like the Queen of Sheba.

You might want to say that Bird was good with animals, but he wasn't, particularly. To return to the sexual thing, male birds and male ungulates hated him. The reason was simple. He moved like they did, like a dominant male, and more like a heron or an elk than a cat or a wolf, more challenge than threat. And he didn't back down. On the other hand, it attracted the females, especially since he usually carried food. It got him into trouble. It was fine to have cows following you around until the bull showed up.

If it took Bird a decade to get to Annie, well, it took him two decades to get to Gail. Though like Annie, Gail found Bird the best of a bad bunch. Sometimes it was nice to know he'd be there for you; other times he was the last person you wanted to see. And if Bird was perfectly willing to let you do whatever you wanted, he was equally unwilling to change. If you hung around Bird long enough you found that he accommodated you so completely that eventually you were doing the same things he did. Getting Bird to make the bed was the last step before not caring whether or not the bed got made anymore. You didn't make that bed, now sleep in it.

You just had to leave him. In fact, you couldn't live with him unless you were in the process of leaving him and you couldn't leave him either because when you did you inevitably found yourself in a worse situation, with somebody more demanding, more dependent, less faithful. Gail hated loving Bird. It riled her sense of unconvention and anarchy. Bird loved that about her. She was beautiful and difficult, in fact a woman who if in her youth was striking, now, as she aged, and the complexities of life grew into her face, she became gorgeously deep, drawing you into her features like a whirlpool; like in a Hindu story, men fell in love with her instantly, something she found, of course, a tremendous burden.

This is not so much a story of Bird and Gail, but of Annie and Bird, yet seeing as you have witnessed the simmering love between horse and man, you have naturally wondered about Bird's Other who witnessed this love, this transformation of Annie, a transformation that had, as well, transformed Bird into a man wiser, more manly, more loving, more calm. What was it between man and horse, human and horse? And was there something for her, of her, there? Gail both felt and denied the odious comparison of the two relationships, and has come, now, to the pasture to groom Rumi for a mixture of unknowable reasons, curiosity, jealousy, a desire to touch the mystically equine thing that Bird, her lover, touched, to know something, to forget something, to separate herself and to investigate what held them all together. One thing else, there was a message on their home phone from a movie agent.

Bird looked up from grooming Annie when Gail's convertible came up the road. Rumi ran to the fence. Again, it had been some time for Rumi, too many cycles. Annie froze him. Calm down. Don't blow it.

It had been a long time since it last rained. The atmosphere was hot and dry and a hot breeze floated sultry from the northeast. The hills stretched out thirsty gold-brown under the ugly, dry air. Gail got out of her car and petted Rumi's nose. Brought him out and tied him to the fence.

"We need rain," said Bird.

"I called your cell," Gail said.

But of course Bird's cell was in his truck, turned off. He only turned it on to call Gail or Marlena. Bird wasn't that fond of communication in general. He didn't like movies or TV or music or the radio; he got plenty of all of it without even trying.

"He looks forward to seeing you," Bird said to Gail.

"I dreamed we took a trail ride," she said. "Me and Rumi. He sent it."

"He gets all worked up."

"I get here when I get here. He likes it."

"You'll never take a trail ride if you don't spend a lot of time with him," said Bird. "His owner should sell him."

Annie lifted her head and sneered at Bird. She didn't like his tone.

"That movie agent called," said Gail.

"Amy?" said Bird. "I think her name is Amy."

"You better find out," said Gail. "She sold your book."

That was the book he'd written fifteen years ago, his little story about teaching, about a teacher reaching out to some unreachable kid and, in the end, failing to help him.

So what happened?

Recently there'd been a hit movie about a debate teacher and his debate team; it made a lot of money and won some Oscars and suddenly Hollywood producers sent their staffs of readers scouring the flotsam and jetsam of the written word for another inspirational teacher story. Teacher hero scripts and books were being gobbled up. A reader for a producer who made independent films had found Bird's teacher book on the internet. The producer wanted an option on the book. It would need a happy ending.

"It will never be made," said Bird.

"Money," said Gail.

"On the back end," said Bird. "We'll never see any."

"No free option," said Gail. "It's on the message. There's money up front."

"Money?"

"A little," Gail said. "Help me with his hooves."

Bird moved over to Rumi who stood calmly now. It was no big deal. If Bird saw his life as a fairytale, and often he did, with the gift of things he loved everywhere around him, it yet was not the kind of fairytale where you write a book, it gets sold, a movie is made, money rolls in, a career occurs, expertise is acknowledged, hard work and merit are rewarded. In fact, most of the time he observed the opposite, so let it pass, concentrate on life, love the things around you; you're probably better off. But a little more money is a little more money. It was nice that something nice might happen, even a little of it. And as he cleaned Rumi's feet, the space among those four mammals standing there sighed, it softened and brightened just a little, Annie could feel it.

"What would you want to do with a little money?" Bird asked Gail.

"I don't know," she said. "Buy a horse?"

Joy and a Terrible Wind

Roar, lion of the heart,
and tear me open!

- - Rumi, "The Debtor Sheikh"

Buy a horse? They could sense the change. The managers came down the hill to the pasture and watched the horses. A vet showed up and checked Rumi's feet, his teeth, his heart; gave him shots. When Bird showed up, even Dummie and Precious pushed to the fence now, shouldering Rumi away. Bird had to chase them to get to Annie. Tasha stood mid-pasture, watching it all. Bird placed some carrots on the ground in front of Rumi after he got Dummie and Precious off of him, and when Annie had her head down at the carrot bowl he threw some carrots across the pasture to Tasha.

Bird didn't even use the lead line anymore. Annie knew what to do, though sometimes she did what she wanted, like when she ran along the outside of the pastures just to make a point, or when the grass came in the winter and she walked past the carrot dish and trotted right to the sprouting grass on the hill. She could open Bird's locker if she wanted. She could even unlatch the gate. When Bird came she met him there, unlatched the latch, and walked out, offered him a bow, took a carrot, let him hug her, then walked over to the feed bowl or up the hill to graze. Then Bird latched the gate before coming to her and scratching her withers while she ate. She knew better than to open the gate when he wasn't there. Then everyone would get out. It would ruin everything.

They saddled up and rode into the hills. Dummie screamed because he was left behind, because he wanted Annie back in the pasture, the

137

pasture where he believed he was in charge, out of resentment, fear, rage, unfigurable injustice. Rumi waited at the roadside fence, watching for the topless rumble.

There was very little grass on the hills now; the summer had been dry and the autumn still bone dry. Even in the woods Annie had to watch and smell closely for thistle and dandelion in spots of shade or near the dry stream. Bird thought it funny because she was usually all flight out there, but now finding green eatables was deep business. A truck came down the road. Her ears barely twitched. "Waiting to be spooked by a butterfly?" said Bird.

Annie sent a quiver up through Bird's seat. Herd of one, Bird.

Bird laughed.

But then, suddenly, everything around him seemed to breathe. Last night Rumi sent Gail a dream in which the four of them stood in a meadow and everything around them, everything, even the grass and ground and sky and trees, watched them and smelled them, tasted them, touched them, listened to the beating of their hearts. When Gail told Bird of the dream, his heart almost broke. Nothing is perceived that does not itself perceive. Every moment vast and sympathetic, even in the slaughterhouses, most of all in the slaughterhouses. This sympathy made him ache. You couldn't live like that, feeling that much. But now, on Annie's back, in the dappled light, he felt it again. He touched Annie's neck. This was more than anyone could ask for, this eternal moment, this paradise. He made it a prayer. Oh Bird! felt Annie. In the old days she'd have bucked him off.

When Annie and Bird were done he brushed her, cleaned her eyes, then he opened the gate and Annie walked inside. He gave her apples, took his last hug, said good-bye, then stood outside the fence and gave her the last few carrots when she nuzzled him. He was so easy.

Then there was the peace of the day in the sun. A feeding in the late afternoon. A black, quiet night. Gray dawn. Breakfast. Then Bird again. It had happened ten thousand times. She couldn't know that she would never see him here again, but no one could.

Today after he left things got chaotic. Dummie raged up and down the fence, chasing Rumi when he could, while Precious scoured the ground for carrot crumbs. Tasha tried to find a quiet corner. Annie wandered to the open feed bin on the upper end, closest to the gate. Rumi, then Tasha, found her. They spoke in the way of horses, in their bodies with steady repetition, tail and shoulder, head and breath.

"When?" said Rumi.

"I don't know," said Annie. "Everything is complicated for Hums."

"Soon?"

"Sooner or later, what's the difference?" Tasha said.

But Annie'd seen things go into motion like this before. With Hums even the simplest things required great buzzing, interminable flailing and noise. There was commotion toward Rumi and around Rumi now. It would be better. Better for Bird's Other, better for Rumi. It had taken her long enough to realize it, but there was satisfaction in her life with Bird; let them all have it, let them all share it; she'd done her part, one horse and one Hum at a time.

"Rumi," said Annie. "It's happening."

Rumi shook with pleasure. "It feels good," Rumi said.

"Nothing will change," said Tasha. "You're not going anywhere. You'll still be here all day almost every day."

"I'll be cared for!" said Rumi.

"Every two or three cycles. A carrot. A pat on the head," said Tasha.

"I once thought it didn't matter," said Annie.

"Everything matters!" said Rumi.

"Nothing matters," Tasha said.

"I think about her and she thinks about me," said Rumi.

The hot wind swept in and blew across their faces.

"The wind is bad," Rumi whispered.

"I hate that wind," Annie said.

"Just let it feel you," said Tasha.

"I am!" said Rumi. "That's why I know," he said, not understanding that Tasha might bait him in more ways than a nip on the butt.

A rumble came up the road and Annie lifted her head.

"Bird never comes back the same day," said Tasha.

"You never know," said Annie.

"That won't change," muttered Tasha.

139

"Something is changing right now," said Rumi. "On the back of the wind."

The hot breeze shifted again, dry and hot. The horses turned their backs to it.

Dummie burst from under the awning and rumbled across the pasture. Precious came up to them at a trot. "What's that smell?" she said.

They put their noses to the air. It was unfamiliar, a little like the smell of a passing rumble.

"I know it," said Tasha. "Smoke."

"On the back of the bad wind," said Rumi.

If you are an animal, then the elements are born inside you and you remember them from the lives of your ancestors, the grass, the earth, the sun, the rain, the plains, streams, woods, air, wind, earth, water.

"Fire," Tasha said.

Fire

The blazing flame shall not be quenched, but from south to north every face shall be scorched by it.

- - Ezekiel

Fire is the earth. Fire is the air. Fire is the sky.

- - Maitri Upanishad

As the day wore on the wind grew hotter and the smoke thicker, pouring in over the western hills. Hums came in rumbles with trailers. There was much commotion. Ranchums scurried and ran with hoses. Sprinklers shot off all around. Atop the broodmare hill the ranchums placed big plastic buckets and metal water troughs along the outside of the fence and filled them with water, then brought horses and released them inside. At a pasture above them and across the road, a rumble with a trailer came, loaded the horses, and left the ranch. More rumbles came with empty trailers, then left the ranch with trailers full of horses. Bird didn't own a trailer.

"You've seen this before," Annie said to Tasha.

"Yes," Tasha said. "It ends. They all come back."

Below their feet, in the dry grasses outside the pasture, the small furs and the small leapers began to stir, sniffing the air and moving cautiously up the eastern hill behind the pasture. Above them hawks took wing, scouring the air, some diving to pick off the small furs.

"I want out!" thundered Dummie at Annie. "Let me out!"

"It's far too early to panic," muttered Tasha.

"When will it be time to panic?" said Rumi.

"There's time," said Annie, who understood panic as well as anyone, but her panic, if true and mad, always contained a certain glee as well, it had never been a panic of the heart, something she felt this fire could do to her, to all of them. But letting Dummie out wouldn't solve anything, not even for him. And he was expending energy, sucking smoke.

"Stay calm," she said. "Wait." If Bird could come, he would. She wanted Bird, but she might have to wait.

Rumi moved nervously at the fence. He glanced at Annie and seeing her standing quietly, he stopped and stood.

Then, below the western hill, Annie saw the leapers emerge from the brush and follow the trail around the lower pastures until they were almost to Annie's. Her four friends, and they had two fawns with them. She went to the fence where they paused in front of her, noses in the air.

"Bad," they signaled. "Running."

"Where?"

"Away. Beyond fire. Away."

A cloud of black smoke rose into the sky beyond the western hill. Annie knew deep in her memory that the wild woof packs and the death hiss would be waiting there for the prey that fled the fire.

"The threats," she said.

"Run behind the small furs." They'd hope there would be plenty to feast on running in front of them and while the predators were busy, then they'd run.

A gust of hot wind brought smoke and ash over the pasture. The leapers jolted, moving in six different directions, then steadied themselves and moved up the hill in unison, beyond the training hill and into the brush.

Tasha came to Annie and looked up toward the broodmare pasture as the ranchums crowded more horses into it.

"They shouldn't put them on that hill," whispered Tasha. "Fire travels uphill."

"If it comes," said Annie.

"If it comes," said Tasha.

"It's coming!" said Rumi.

Precious followed Dummie now, pounding about. She squealed. "It's coming! It's coming!"

Annie moved to her. "You never listened to him before. Don't start now."

They looked to the hills, but still there was just smoke and heat.

"We must run!" screamed Dummie. "Run! Open the gate!"

More rumbles with trailers came and went, though it seemed many more were leaving than coming. Annie looked to the top of the hill behind the pasture where the managers' rumbles sat silently next to their barn. Sirens wailed in the distance. Horns. And now, over the distant hill, the first sky rumbles circled.

A rumble with a trailer came for the broodmares at the lower pasture across the road. Precious screamed. She'd been a broodmare. They had room. They should take her. But now she wasn't breeding, wasn't valuable to anybody. Nobody owned the rest of them, or if they did they were far away. Where was Bird?

Now the first line of flame came over the ridge. It looked like a bright stripe, like a long, thin sun, the air vibrating above it. Sirens. Sky rumbles criss-crossed in the air above, dropping water on the flames, but the fire advanced and grew until it looked like a bright, flailing wall of light. A small rumble with a trailer came to the pasture just below and loaded those horses, a sorrel, a bay, and a little paint. A Hum pointed at Annie's pasture.

"What about those?"

"They aren't ours. There's no room."

The wall of flame came down the mountain and disappeared behind the near hill, then began its climb back up; it threw black-red smoke. Ashes filled the air. Sky rumbles buzzed everywhere, dropping water across the hill. Dummie roared at Annie again. "Open the gate!"

"You're safer here," said Tasha.

"No one is safe anywhere!" screamed Precious.

"That might be right," said Annie to Tasha.

"Yes, it might," Tasha said.

Rumi ran to them now. "I'm frightened," he said. "I'm panicking now!"

143

"Yes," said Annie. "Yes." Where was Bird?

The first arm of the giant fire approached the ranch, burning below the broodmare hill, its pasture filled with horses and surrounded by water buckets and ranchums with hoses. It was all happening very fast. The flames topped the near hill, spread. The air filled with red burning ash and hot smoke. They were surrounded by a wall of fire on three sides and it rained fire. Then the flames roared up the broodmare hill. Some ranchums ran, others fell down and didn't get up. The horses screamed. The fire came over them and Annie saw them running against the fences, wailing, running on fire until they fell. She heard the screaming above the racket of the sky rumbles and the roaring flames. Around them, it was as if the ground had come alive with running small-furs, though now the air was so full of smoke and burning ash that there were no longer any birds of prey.

Where was Bird?

The five horses stood.

"Open the gate!" said Dummie.

"It's safest here," said Tasha.

"Safe?" said Rumi.

"Just safer," Tasha said.

"No grass in here," said Annie, realizing. "Nothing to burn."

"But us!" said Precious. "We burn! Horses burn!"

"Open the gate!" Dummie screamed.

"He can choose," Annie said to Tasha. She ran to the gate and mouthed the latch open. Dummie pushed by her. Then Precious. Rumi rushed forward. "No," Annie said, and Rumi stopped short.

They watched as Dummie and Precious burst into the flaming field, dodging between the patches of flames, circling. It seemed as if Dummie was almost drawn to the fire, by bravery, by madness. He dashed toward the fire, Precious at his heels.

"Away from the fire!" screamed Annie. "Run away!"

"Hums!" screamed Dummie. "Hums!"

She knew then that he would run to the barns, to Hums, for protection, through the fire and to his death, Precious following. She led Rumi to Tasha. "Don't follow me," Annie told him. And Tasha stepped between Rumi and the open gate. Annie didn't even understand why or what she was about to do. Deep in her memory, before time, she had been born to lead, and that was all she felt; she must lead them.

Now the fire burned around Dummie and Precious, sparkling ashes falling on their backs, only kept from igniting by their sweat. Annie charged toward them. She hit Dummie with her chest and when he turned on her in anger she fled back toward the corral, Dummie on her tail, screaming in fury, and Precious behind him, maddened and bewildered. But when he saw the open pasture gate he veered off, this time running down the line of the fence. Miraculously, it led down the road to the ranch entrance where the fire had yet to burn. The two red horses veered toward the narrow corridor beneath the pasture where there were no flames and disappeared.

"We should have run," Rumi whispered.

"No," said Annie. "Tasha has seen this before."

"Come to the center," said Tasha. "Lie down. Stay close. Butt to the fire. Head out all the way down where the air is coolest. If you feel fire on you, roll." Of course, she didn't say this so much as do it. She walked to the center of the dry, dirt pasture where there was nothing to burn. She lay down as flat as she could, stretching her head away from the fire, tucking her mane beneath her neck, her tail beneath her body, her nose as close as possible to the earth. Annie followed, tucking next to her, and then Rumi.

"Hope," whispered Rumi. "Hope."

"Wait," said Tasha.

"Bird," said Annie. Where was Bird?

The flames circled them on all sides now, burning away the dry grass. The three horses huddled there in the center of the dry pasture as ash, black smoke, and fire filled the air. There the three horses waited, surrounded by fire as the wall of flames swept down upon them.

Bird on Fire

The universal fire is here within.

- - Brihad Aranyaka Upanishad

Were Bird by himself when the fires started, he would have got in his truck and driven to Annie. But he had a home to protect, a family. The radio said there were fourteen fires burning, fires everywhere and a big one burning west of his house, several canyons away. Television news told him almost nothing; pictures from the air of the hills on fire, mansions burning; the sky reporters didn't seem to know what they were looking at or where they were. Fire engines screamed up and down his road.

Marlena was away at college now and he called her, took a short list of things she might want saved if he had to evacuate, musical instruments, some art. He got his flash drive, a couple books, gathered some clothes and laid them on the bed. The last time he'd been forced out he'd forgotten clothes. He closed the windows and when cats came to the door he locked them in, so far two of the five, his favorite, his silver Maine Coon, Mucha Plata, still out.

He broke a privacy rule, went outside and stood at the base of the eight foot retaining wall, under the window of Gail's office that she reached by a ladder from the deck. Usually, like now, she pulled the ladder up so you couldn't get to her at all. She opened her window and looked down.

"Fire everywhere," he said.

"How close?" she said.

"I'm afraid."

"That's when you're at your best," said Gail.

"Think about what you want to save," he said.

"Everything," she said.

He drove down the road to the General Store where the canyon dwellers often met in the parking lot to pass information. He avoided the panic guys who always said it was all going to go, went up to a guy in a baseball hat who had just bought two big plastic containers of water.

"What do you know?" said Bird.

"They're suggesting evacuation at the bottom, but I figure that's just so they can get fire trucks up and down the coast without people getting in the way," said the man.

"Have you heard where it is?"

"Two, three canyons down. That's a long ways."

"Where two canyons down?" said Bird.

The man didn't know. But Bird knew these canyons. Their mouths might be several miles away, but they met, like a triangle, at the top of the mountain where Bird's house sat at the bottom. He came back and told Gail he was going to try to check on Annie.

He headed up the canyon, away from the ocean, toward the Valley. It was quiet now, the fire engines somewhere else. The air sat on the canyon like in a sauna. Then, near the top, about five miles up, he found a big fire burning out of control between him and the ranch, moving east, away from his house. He felt the wind for the first time, dry and hot, shaking the oaks. He couldn't get to Annie. The road to the ranch was blocked by flames sixty feet high. He tried to call, but the ranch phone was out. He turned back. Someone might trailer her, if not, he knew she was in one of the safest pastures in the canyon, bare inside, the vegetation around it pruned low to the ground. Still, now he felt sick with worry and fear.

Back at his home a police car moved slowly down the road, blasting a loudspeaker, suggesting that people begin evacuating voluntarily. He parked his truck, saw his neighbor, Norm, an iron sculptor, watering the front of his house.

"Are you leaving?" said Bird.

"No," said Norm. "They just don't want people in the way."

"In the way of what?" said Bird.

"Them," said Norm.

These old canyon dwellers would stay till the last, guarding their homes against sixty foot flames with garden hoses until it was too late.

Bird went back inside his house. He got another cat in. Not Mucha Plata. The electricity went out. He checked his electrical box. It was fine, but out, so the blackout was canyon wide. He went back to Gail's office.

"You should get ready to go," he said.

"The fires never get here," Gail said.

"I'm going to see where it is," said Bird.

He got back in his truck and drove to the top of the mountain behind his house. It was a winding, switchback road; it took some time. Some residents were moving things from their homes into their cars and trucks.

"Are you getting out?" he asked one couple.

"Just getting ready," the woman said.

"Have you seen it?" said the man.

"Up that way," said Bird. He pointed toward the Valley. "About five miles, not moving this way. I'm going to the top to look."

In a mile he reached the top where several canyons and their roads came together. There he saw the fire in the adjacent canyon, heading up the slope, black smoke and a wall of flames reaching to the sky. In this wind it could burn an acre in three seconds. It was too close. Panicking some, shivering, he drove back down the hill. He stopped when he saw the couple again. "It's right there," he said to them. They looked at him silently. "It's coming," Bird said. On the way down the mountain he ran into fire trucks on the way up, sirens screaming. He pulled over and let them pass, then drove to the fire station to try to get information, but no one was there.

Back home, Gail was out of her office now, gathering some framed art from the walls.

"Get your necessities!" said Bird.

"We're just getting ready, in case," she said.

Bird went outside, opened the bird cages and released the birds.

"What are you doing?" Gail screamed out the window.

He didn't answer. He came inside, put the lab rescue rat in a small cage. He found another cat at the door, not Mucha Plata. He retrieved the huge plastic carrier, made for big dogs, and gathered up four cats one

148

by one and put them inside. They yowled. But his cat. His horse. Where?

Gail found him there at the door. "Bird," she said.

"I'll put this carrier in the back of the truck with everything else. You take the rat and the dogs."

"We haven't even been told to go."

"We don't want to be caught in a line of cars when that fire hits," said Bird.

"I don't want to leave unless we have to," Gail said.

"Okay," said Bird. "You get things ready, I'll take them down." He got Marlena's spare sitar and carried it down to his truck, her electric piano, some guitars. He took the clothes he'd put on the bed, then the ones Gail had gathered. Some bathroom stuff. Then statues, paintings, cat food and dog food, finally some food and water for themselves.

Back inside, Gail stood near the door, surveying her emptying house. She put her hands on his chest. "People don't die in these fires," she said. "The homes get saved. They get out."

"Before it's too late," said Bird.

"I can't. I'm not leaving everything."

He took her hand and led her upstairs, then to the back of the house where her ladder took them atop the retaining wall and to the roof. There was smoke in the air now and red hot ash fell. They climbed the ladder and stood on the roof of their home, and from there they saw the first flames rising at the top of the mountain.

"They'll stop it up there," she said. "We have hoses."

"It will be in the trees," said Bird. "Everywhere."

"You go," she said. "I'll follow if it gets here."

But that was impossible. She could die there, or if not, then whatever they had ever been would die the moment he left, no matter what or how much was burned or saved.

"Your work. Have you saved your poems?" he said to her.

"Let them burn" she said, "or not."

He took her back down to her office and using her laptop battery got her work transferred to a flash drive. Fire engines poured up the canyon now, sirens screaming, and headed up the hill. On the road below, police loudspeakers now called for everyone to get out.

Bird turned to Gail then. "The house will be saved or not," he said to her. "It doesn't matter. We have to save our lives, our animals' lives."

She said nothing. She helped him carry the cat carrier down and put it in the back of the truck, put the dogs and the rat in the back of her car. Then they locked up the house as more fire trucks poured up the hill behind them with their horrible sirens. Helicopters now lopped above, pink flame retardant streaming from the copters onto the mountainside. Hot ash fell. Bird put his hands over his face. "My cat," he said.

"Maybe we'll be lucky," said Gail. "She'll be lucky."

"Annie," Bird said. How could he have not been prepared? And how could he have prepared? He took Gail's hands. He said, "I'll follow you out."

But when they got to the cars she turned again. "My ring," said Gail.

"You're not wearing it?"

"I took it off."

"Why? Why take it off?"

"I just did. I don't know why. I wasn't thinking straight."

"Where?"

"I don't remember," said Gail.

"You don't know?" said Bird.

"I don't know!"

"The bathroom?"

"I don't know! I have to go back."

"It's too late!" said Bird.

"I've got to go back!" she screamed at him.

He grabbed her. "It will be here or not! We have to go!"

"My ring!"

Across the road a hot ash settled in a cypress tree and the tree exploded in flame.

He pushed her toward her car. "I'll follow you," he said.

And she got in her car. Started her engine. Finally in their cars, they headed down the road toward the ocean, their backs to almost everything they owned, their house, his cat, her ring, his horse. They were lucky to live at the bottom of the mountain. Of those who stayed this long, they were the first ones out. Now the road was silent, but in forty minutes it would all be different. The fire swept the mountain, the homes, the people, the line of cars that filled the road trying to escape. The fires were everywhere and bigger than anyone had expected. There were not enough fire trucks or helicopters or firefighters. There was not enough water. The winds howled, fueling walls of flame, a firestorm. Nothing could stop it. When the world burns like this there is nothing anyone can do. They drove down the canyon toward the ocean, but even the ocean was no escape.

Ash

*How irresistibly sacrifice is transformed
into massacre.*

- - Roberto Calasso, Ka

*Tomorrow will bring its own worries.
Today's trouble is enough for today.*

- - Jesus, Gospel of Matthew

The air filled with the roar of engines and fire crackling through dry bush and weeds. In the distance, a Hum shouting, barking, and the cries of horses. As the flames advanced to the edge of the pasture, Rumi stirred and tried to get up.

"Wait," said Tasha. "Wait. There's nothing we can do."

To calm Rumi's whining, Annie let out a low mutter, like a mother would give a foal. "Calm," it said. "Calm."

The wall of fire advanced to the fence and crackled in the dry grass at its edge. It roared up toward the sky. Yet as ashes fell around them the sky quieted. No more sky rumbles. The screaming of Hums and horses in the distance stopped. Now only the roar of flames, the intolerable heat. Above them, the flames swept the managers' barn, then their rumbles. The rumbles exploded with a roar. Rumi quivered. He said, "Mother, Mother, Mother." Annie licked his neck. "Be still," she said.

Night fell with little relief. The horses waited and finally the flames burned down and fell away. By dawn the fire had moved on. It had not come into the pasture, but burned all around it. The earth lay barren

152

under a coat of black ash, smoke still rising from the embers. In some spots, where the charcoaled trees and shrubs had begun to cool, white ash clung like feathers and floated like snow, a landscape of black and white.

"This is certainly a change," said Rumi, very quietly.

Annie looked around, struggling to her feet. She shook off the ashes that covered her. "Water," she said. She stepped carefully in the ashes around them. She sniffed the warm ground, then stepped. She didn't know anything about ashes. They flew into the air as she walked; they floated, fell.

She checked the troughs, then the water fount. The bins were dry, the metal still hot, the water steamed away; the plastic bowl beneath the fount had melted, but the trigger trickled out a little water when she touched it with her nose. She licked the water, then walked back to the center of the pasture where Rumi and Tasha stood. "A little water," she told them.

The three took turns at the water feeder. It was very quiet.

"What do we do?" said Rumi.

"Wait," Tasha said. "There's water. Wait."

"We need food," said Annie.

"Wait," said Tasha. "Someone will come. They always do."

"No one came for us," said Annie. "Who will come?"

"Who?" said Tasha. "Bird?"

Annie didn't know what to feel or say.

"I can't feel Bird," said Rumi. "I can't feel his Other. I can't feel anything."

"We can wait if we find food," said Annie. "I'm going to look."

"I'm staying here," Tasha said. "Stay in one place. Stay together. Safety in numbers." The creed of any herd.

"I'm frightened," said Rumi.

"Stay here," Annie said. Someone must make choices and take risks for the sake of the herd, no matter how small.

Annie walked out the gate, smelling for threats, but she saw and smelled nothing but smoke. She'd been everywhere on the ranch with Bird and everywhere for miles around, but everything everywhere had burned. She walked up the rumble trail. All the wooden fences were gone, the metal ones melted. She avoided the broodmare hill, where nothing stirred and where she knew they were all dead. She walked to the training hill near which the managers' barn once stood. Only Hum rubble there. The two burned out rumbles, other melted machines.

Down the hill, at the center of what was once the ranch, the huge barns had burned to the ground. There was the stench of burned flesh, burned hay, and corpses of horses and Hums. The hills behind them, once covered with open stalls filled with horses, were barren now, nothing on them but melted fences and the occasional dead horse. The outdoor arena was gone, just sand covered with ash, the covered arena a pile of charred rubble, its aluminum roof flattened on the ground, its naked steel girders like blackened ribs. The huge hay barn and all its hay had burned up. The air was still. There was nothing. Nothing standing. Nothing alive.

Annie knew that Mick and Adele kept food at their far corner of the ranch area and she knew where they kept the carrots, maybe more, maybe oats. She walked around the flattened arena to their outdoor stables. Annie found them. Without a trailer they'd stayed to the last, losing everything to save what they had: two old dogs, five horses, themselves. She sniffed Adele. Then Mick. But they wouldn't awaken. Good-bye. Thank you. Everything burned. Even Hums. No one alive. Could Bird be like this? She had nothing in her memory, not her deepest most primordial memory, that answered this. Only survival. The carrot can. She opened it, lifting the lid by the handle. Some carrots inside.

She reported back to Rumi and Tasha.

"A carrot," whispered Rumi. "A pat on the head."

"One carrot at a time," said Tasha.

They followed Annie to the can. Tasha kicked it over and spilled out the carrots and the three of them ate.

"What else?" said Tasha.

Annie opened the oat can, but it was empty. "Nothing else," said Annie.

"We'll find something else," said Tasha.

"I've been everywhere."

"What'll we do? What'll we do? What'll we do?" said Rumi. He shivered.

"Calm down," Annie said.

"We just wait," said Tasha. "Stay put. The first rule of being found."

"We have to leave," said Annie.

"We have the awning still, and water," said Tasha. She began to walk back toward the pasture.

It's said that horses are stoic beings. It is only true in a very limited sense, and even in that sense, more due to our inability to read them. They are great hearted. And more than any other domestic animal, spend time alone, by our choice, not theirs. Thus, they are contemplative, philosophical in the sense that they are more accepting of fate, and though capable of unpredictable flight, in times of need or crisis there is no creature more steady, more reliable. Now, they had to rely on themselves.

They stood again in the center of their pasture, surveying the devastated landscape.

"We must go now," said Annie.

"I'll wait," said Tasha. It was the only home she'd known for years and years.

"Oh, Annie. Oh, Annie," said Rumi. His head sank to the ground. The fire broke everything for him. He'd been so close to happiness. Now he'd never have a Hum. He would die. He'd have nothing.

"Stop it," said Annie. "We need you. Send. Feel."

"I'm waiting here," said Tasha.

"We need food," Annie said. She walked away from them toward the drooping gate.

"Annie!" squealed Rumi.

Tasha walked to the water fount. "Don't worry," she said. "Someone will come. They'll come or not whether you worry or not." She pressed the lever on the fount. She pressed again. But the trickle of water that once meant the trickle of life no longer flowed at all.

"No water," said Rumi. "Annie!" he screamed again. She was already on the road, heading for the entrance. She stopped. Turned. And he ran to her, shivering next to her.

"Calm down," she said with her body. "Stop."

Then she called out to Tasha. "Tasha," Annie called. She walked back to the edge of the pasture where Tasha stood behind the fence. The two touched noses. "We need you," said Annie. "You know things."

"Nothing will change, whether I come or not," said Tasha.

"So come. Be with us. You know things. Come."

Tasha walked away from Annie and went back to the water fount. Again she nudged the trigger with her nose, but the faucet was dry. She raised her head and sniffed the ashen air. "Let's find a streambed," Tasha said.

Water

It is just water solidified that is earth, that is atmosphere,
that is the sky, that is gods and men, beasts and birds,
grass and trees, animals together with worms, flies, and ants; all these are just
water. Reverence water.

- - Chandogya Upanishad

Annie knew of a stream below the ranch that ran along the other side of the rumble trail. Along that trail once sat horse barns and Hum barns, but no longer. Now they were burned to the ground, the rumbles, trailers, and horses, too, gone. The stream ran with water in the winter and spring, after the rains, then went dry in the summer and autumn, but trees grew along it, big oaks, and created shade for grass that grew under them almost until the rainy season. If she weren't too spooky, Bird let her go in there and munch.

The three horses left the ranch and followed the rumble trail. The land was devastated around them, the other ranches burned out, the barns gone, as well as the usual surrounding rumbles. The trees that once lined the stream and dropped a canopy of limbs covered with spiny live oak leaves, uneatable even in the best times, now hung with blackened bare arms, a spiny, morbid tunnel over the dry streambed. They looked for a spot that showed the barest hint of moisture, smelled for it, and that's when they spotted Precious. She lay unmoving and stiff at the foot of a rumble drive that led to a burned out ranch. Tasha sniffed her, then Annie sniffed.

One of her legs was broken and crushed. Tasha figured she'd been hit by a rumble, then caught by the fire.

"Poor Precious," mumbled Rumi.

"She might be better off," said Tasha.

"Do I have to sniff her, too?" said Rumi.

"No," said Annie. "Let's find water."

They walked in the morbid dry streambed. They walked and walked. Beneath the ash, dust lifted into the air and settled on their hooves. "There," Tasha pointed with her nose. "There." Annie pawed the ground. Ash floated up, dusty and black and fell down again, upturned and white like dry snow. Again and again until it seemed that all was dust and ash, dust and ash in their throats and they were thirstier still.

Annie, and Tasha, too, knew there might be water at any of these burned out ranches; it came out hoses and spigots, though they hadn't the words, nor the knowledge of how to make the water come from those things. Annie pictured the handle atop a spigot.

"I'll try to find a water-giver," she said.

"Don't leave," said Rumi.

"It's the first place the hunters come," said Tasha.

In particular the wild woof, coyotes, knew to scavenge the waste of Hums. In a pack they could be a threat even to horses.

"It's best to stay in one place and stay together," Tasha said.

"Yes, together," said Rumi.

There would be no change without doing something different. Safety, staying together in one place, was as big a risk as taking a risk. Annie said this with her posture. "Let me try once. Stay here together." She turned up a driveway and followed it past a Hum barn, burned down but for a brick tower that she could see once burned wood inside, but now everything all around it was burned down. There was a burned rumble. Inside it, the bones of a Hum, stripped. Wild woof had come already.

She watched the sky for birds, but there were none, not the small prey, nor the big predators, not even vultures. She walked toward where there once stood barns, her ears perked for the growling or hooting of wild woof, her nose flexing the air, but now, nothing but ash here. Though near the burned down stalls, the smell of flesh. She chose not to see the horses burned and then torn apart. But things had survived. Some predators had survived.

At the edge of the melted barn she found a spigot. She raised her head to listen and smell. She inspected the horizons. Then she lowered her head and mouthed the handle. She knew something must move to make change. When Bird moved the handle, then water came. She pulled at the spigot handle with her teeth and lapped the opening with her tongue, but nothing came out. She tried again. No water.

She scoured the ranch for danger, then walked back to her little herd.

"Nothing," said Tasha.

"Nothing," Annie said. "Death. Wild woofs came."

"Already," Tasha whispered.

"Hope," Rumi whispered.

Tasha lowered her head and swept the ground with her nose.

Then Annie remembered an old palm tree that sat above a deep, stagnant water hole; the water hole was under a narrow, wooden bridge that she always gave Bird a bad time about crossing. Sometimes, when Bird brought a woof with him, the woof ran down the cliff to the water hole and splashed around, then came out soaked and smelling like mud and hot plop, which seemed to make the woof very happy. "I know a place," she said. "This way."

She led them back to the road, up and down a hill, then to a narrow trail. So often she'd dreaded this trailhead, because it meant crossing the bridge, the sky falling away all around her. Now it meant something different, the possibility of water. The trail was once a narrow path through wildflowers and chaparral, bending oaks and eucalyptus, but now the land around it lay scorched, the mountains like frozen waves of black, everything flattened but the barren oak trees whose branches stretched out covered in white ash. They walked for a mile before coming to another dry stream between two ledges. And there, below them, the palm tree stood, now a scorched stump.

Annie remembered that the woof found a way down. She walked along the edge of the cliff until she found the spot where the incline was less steep. Sliding down, their butts almost on the ground, they made it to the bottom and walked to the dead palm. Annie pawed the ground until she found a spot where it became soft. Tasha sniffed at it, then began digging with her front hoof. In time, she found mud. Annie pitched in and in a little while they'd made a small water hole. Again they drank.

"Do we wait here?" said Rumi.

"This is nowhere," said Tasha.

"Food," said Annie. "If we found water like this once, we can do it again."

There were three choices. They could go back the way they came. Farther down the trail there was a fork to the right that led back to the ranch; that's what she and Bird usually did, though once they took the trail to its end, up the hill where stood a huge rumble path and uncountable Hum barns with rumbles in front of them as far as she could see. Bird didn't live there. She could feel that. He didn't even like it. But now it was a place where they might find Hums and help.

It was difficult to communicate all of this. It took time, though Tasha eventually understood what the choices meant.

"Lead," Tasha said.

Annie led them out of the gully and back onto the trail that began to ascend. From the top of a knoll the dark mountains spread out before them, black in the sunlight. Then came a whir from the sky. Annie perked her ears.

"Sky rumbles," she said.

"Hope," said Rumi.

"Trouble," said Tasha. "Unknown Hums."

But Annie led them down the knoll and up another hill. As they climbed, more noise arose. Shouting, the honking and screaming of rumbles, sky rumbles dropping water.

Tasha nuzzled Annie. "We shouldn't go there. These can't help us."

"We must look," Annie said.

She walked to the top of the hill where once the sprawl of a thousand Hum barns buzzed with Hum life, but now the fire was inside it. The little rumbles were gone and where barns burned, giant red and yellow rumbles stood outside. Hums held hoses that spread water on the burning Hum barns. Soon Tasha was beside her, then Rumi, and the three horses stood on the edge of the burned forest, watching the chaos. A big yellow rumble came down the road toward the fire and hesitated in front of the horses.

160

From its window a Hum looked at them for a moment, and then it moved into the fray of burning structures.

"Fire," said Rumi.

"And water," said Annie. "So much water."

"Not for us," said Tasha. "These won't help us."

But there was so much water falling on the fires that some of it streamed down the Hum paths and out the entrance of the suburb onto the huge street that led in. Annie went forward and found a stream of it running into a curb and flowing away. She lowered her head and smelled the liquid, but it smelled unnatural, full of chemicals. She went back to Tasha and Rumi.

"We can't drink it," she said and turned back down the trail.

"Where?" said Rumi.

"Back to the water," she said. And so they went back to the waterhole.

The sun began its fall toward the night.

"We should stay here," said Rumi.

"There's no help here," said Annie.

"Eaters need water too," Tasha said. The wild woof and death hiss would smell the water. They, too, would need to drink. And once there they'd know that prey would come to drink, as well. Tasha knew that. Everyone comes to water. The horses couldn't stay.

They needed a plan. Annie'd made plans before. Plans to fool Bird. Plans to eat grass somewhere outside the pasture or take Bird somewhere where she knew there was feed or carrots; one, two, three steps ahead. Now she needed to think of a goal and how to get it. How to get from this place to where? To Bird.

"Bird's barn," she said, though she'd never been there.

"It's gone like the others," said Tasha.

But they'd been up the hill. Everything wasn't gone. There were Hums still out there fighting the fire. They had to keep moving and find Bird.

"Think of Bird," she felt to Rumi.

"I can't think," said Rumi.

"Send to the Other."

"I can't do anything!" said Rumi.

Still, she left the waterhole and led them back up the trail from where they came, to a narrow Hum road that led to the ranch, then took them the other direction toward some of the ranches that Bird had taken her through on the way to some trails that ran above them in the hills. They were almost unrecognizable now, burned down, though that made it harder for predators to hide there. They entered cautiously and found some very charred hay, little else. Tasha surveyed the hills above. "The fire came from one direction," she said. "Behind some very big rocks, on the other side from that direction, maybe something." She pointed with her nose. "There," she said.

Annie knew the trails. She led them back down the rumble trail, heading again toward the ranch. The day was almost gone and she'd led them nowhere and found almost nothing. She felt it from Tasha. They were exhausted and back at the ranch entrance.

"We're back!" said Rumi.

"You always end up back where you started," Tasha said. "Like a trail ride."

"Why did we leave?" said Rumi.

Tasha didn't have to answer that.

But Annie did. Everything was trial and error. The path to success was a path of a thousand mistakes, a thousand errors. It was how you learned anything, how anything was accomplished. It was always hardest when you were right back where you started, the only difference a lot of hard work and frustration in between. She could not think that, but she knew it, right then, that this is what she and Bird had learned together, and how they had those moments, those heavens, when they were each other. But how, here, could she answer Tasha's argument that there was no difference between doing something and doing nothing, that they should wait, stay put?

"There is no water or food in there," Annie said. It was why they left in the first place. But what if Tasha was right? What if someone had come? "Wait here. Rest. I'll see," she said.

She trotted up the entrance road. She stopped, more exhausted than she expected, hot air beating in her nose. She gazed up at the vacant and parched blue sky and listened for the sound of Hums, of rumbles. Did she hear something? Was there a glint of reflection on the hill, the sun reflecting from the top of Bird's silver rumble? It didn't matter if Tasha was right, that staying was best. She moved forward at a lope, then galloping out, the reflection shining into her heart. There, beneath the broodmare hill, the sun off metal, and it would be Bird, finally, returning for her!

But when she reached the pastures, they were barren. Beneath the broodmare hill she found an old sheet of foil caught on the limbs of a blackened manzanita bush, shining as the wind lifted it up and down. Once she was afraid of such things. It was almost fun to be afraid of them. Now, now it was just a piece of foil, something she'd mistaken for Bird's rumble. But more than that. Somehow that piece of foil shining in the sun struck her as something very dire.

She returned to her tiny herd. "Nothing," she said.

Along the road in the other direction lay undeveloped area, once all scrub brush and rocks, now only rocks. Following Tasha's logic, she led them to a trail along a cliff and eventually stood across a ravine from a huge rock formation, pocked with caves.

"There," said Annie.

"On the other side of that," Tasha said.

"How do we get there?" said Rumi.

"Caves are not good," said Tasha. "Things hide in them."

"Things we can eat?" said Rumi.

"Things that eat us," said Tasha.

"We have little choice," said Annie. The sun had begun its late afternoon descent. They'd eaten almost nothing since the fire. There was nothing else around them.

"We can't get there!" said Rumi.

Annie looked at Tasha. "One trail at a time," she said. For a moment she thought of Bird. Pictured him. Smelled his hat. If he could, he'd be here. She felt it. But that he was not here meant that she might never see him again. "Follow," she said.

She led them along the cliff edge until another trail dropped into the ravine. She took them down it, though it led away from the rocks. Tasha and Rumi hesitated. She stopped, looked at them and moved forward.

Get to the bottom, one trail at a time, then worry about going up the other side. Feeling this, Tasha followed and Rumi followed her. Soon another trail led down and back and they found a switchback that took them into the ravine.

Down there, in another dry streambed, they dug for water and found it. Annie was getting good at knowing where to look, under trees and where the ground was darker. They drank, sucking thick, dirty water from the mud, but water nonetheless. They rested there for a while. Fighting the urge to lay down there, to stay, Annie began walking and found a path that ascended to the rocks and caves.

They had to leave the trail and walk across solid rock to get behind the formation, balancing precariously. Annie and Tasha had to keep Rumi in between them or they'd find him left behind somewhere, whimpering. They got behind the big rocks and Tasha was right; the fire had burned around them, leaving some scrub grass and weeds at the base, not much, but a little. They grazed in the low autumn light.

"Can we stay here?" said Rumi.

Annie sniffed the air. Burnt flesh and blood. "I don't think so," she said.

Around another boulder she spotted a cave. Inside, two of the leapers, she recognized them, knew them, and the two fawns, partially eaten. Then she heard movement. Her eyes adjusted. Two death hiss cubs.

She turned to the others. "We must leave now," she said.

"Meeee-oooow," came from the rock above her. "It's too late."

The Cat Doctrine

Sitting, she proceeds afar;
Lying, she goes everywhere.

- - Katha Upanishad

The puma might already have leapt on Annie's back had not Annie been facing her or if she'd turned to run, but she raised her head and backed up. The others might have run, maybe should have, but Tasha held true to safety in numbers; it could not work in the future if it didn't work in the present. The cat paced above them on the rocks. Annie'd seen her before, at night, in the field beyond the pasture when there were plenty of small furs and small leapers and no need, as the death hiss had indicated to her then, to risk her life on large, more dangerous prey like horses, or even adult leapers. And though communication in situations like these was difficult, if not futile, it was not impossible; you'd know if you ever saw a mouse in front of a cat, facing her and shielding his eyes, begging for his life.

"You have food," indicated Annie.

"But for how long?" growled the death hiss.

Rumi jumped and tried to run, but Tasha stepped in front of him. "Safety in the herd, safety in numbers," she said to him.

"Too late," the death hiss said. "Too late for one of you."

But she hadn't taken one of them yet, and if she could have done it easily, it would already have been done. Death hiss had a wicked sense of desperation and play, as if killing were a dance, a negotiation in front of the inevitable, as if prolonging the only outcome were itself a pleasure, and as if the moments where life and death hung in the balance were moments both casual and intense, as if they couldn't concentrate at all except in those moments fraught with everything that counted, and those moments needed to be contemplated, savored, shared with the victim in ritual, as if taking a life and giving it up were somehow a mutual affair.

She displayed her huge, sharp teeth, raised a paw and turned it upward, opened it, gazed at her own long, extended claws. She licked her paw casually. Picked something from it with her teeth. Spit it out by running her tongue against her upper lip, then blowing. She turned the paw forward again and licked the back of it, the side of it. She stood, paced the top of the rock, returned and sat down again. She was above them. Their backs were vulnerable.

"We can hurt you," said Annie. She pinned her ears and showed her teeth.

"My young ones," the death hiss said. "I have young."

Annie hissed at her and the predator hissed back. She stood again. Paced in front of Annie, back and forth, then sat. She licked the side of one paw and rubbed it on her ear, first one side, then the other. She purred. "Clean," she said. "Always clean."

"We can hurt you," hissed Annie. She raised a sharp fore hoof.

"You can't hurt me," the death hiss said very slowly. "You cannot. I have young," she said again. "Surely you understand."

Annie showed her teeth again.

The death hiss raised her upper lip and displayed long, sharp incisors like fangs. "Yours are nothing," said the death hiss.

"Your young," said Annie. "If we hurt you."

The death hiss got up and paced again, sat again, raised her paw and extended her claws. "I'll take the smallest or the oldest," said the cat. "Not you."

There was only one way out, over the rocks, and the death hiss had it cut off, a calculating hunter and clever, cutting off escape while offering a way out to her most dangerous nemesis, lowering her odds. It was an old, old meeting of predator and prey, deeper than a million years, fraught with display and intimidation.

"I can wait," said the predator. "I can wait and wait."

Annie backed up until she stood with the others. "We'll have to run," she whispered.

"Together," said Tasha.

But staying abreast was impossible. Over the top of the rock ledge they'd have to go single file.

"Oh yes," said the death hiss. "Run. It's no longer up to you who lives and dies, but up to me."

Now Annie spoke only with her body. She'd pound her front hoof four times, then lunge toward the cat. At that moment the others would run past her, Tasha first, then Rumi, Annie, the best fighter, following. But Rumi couldn't keep the plan straight.

"I can't think," he said.

"Just follow," said Annie

"Stay together," said Tasha.

"I'm too afraid."

"You're not," said Annie.

"Oh, he is," said the death hiss. "I can smell it. It smells good. Fear sweetens the flesh."

The animal almost lounged in front of them now. She appeared distracted. She lay down, got up. Again she licked her paw and rubbed it on her ear. She looked down at them, holding them in her gaze for a moment, then went back to preening.

"Four, lunge, run," said Annie to Rumi.

"Follow me," said Tasha. "Just follow."

The death hiss gave no indication whether she understood them or not. She had them. At least one of them. She was in her own ritual now, in her own time. Everything was on her terms. She looked up. "The fire has been a lucky thing, for now," she said. "Until I must move on with my young. You must die anyway, why not help me?"

This was the time, while she was preoccupied with her reverie. Annie raised her hoof and the death hiss curled her lips, snarled, again displayed her long, pointed, killing teeth. Annie brought her hoof down. One. Again. Two. The cat watched bemusedly. Three. Annie paused, raised her hoof again. Brought it down. Four! She lunged at the death hiss, ears pinned, teeth bared. The cat jumped back, startled, and Tasha was off, already past her. Rumi hesitated. Annie turned and bit his butt. He lunged forward, but too late. The death hiss was on his back, her teeth in his neck, and took Rumi down.

A Flaming Sea

As fire he is everything.

\- - Prasna Upanishad

At the ocean highway, cars were piled up in a long line, heading away from the flaming hillsides, but barely moving. They covered every lane and in between, five or six deep, leaving a single lane for fire trucks and fire crews to head the other way, toward the fire. Besides the sirens and helicopters, there was honking and shouting. Everyone was trying to go somewhere, but where and why? If the fire took the canyon, then it could sweep into the developments on the other side and everyone would be evacuating right into it. If it burned unstopped down these hills, it would be on them soon. Shouldn't they be headed the other way, trying to get behind it?

Bird got out of the truck and ran to Gail's car.

"This is crazy!" he said. "It's the wrong way!"

"You want to try going the other way? Good luck."

"Try to get in the lane closest to the beach," he said.

"It's the slowest," she shouted.

"It's a way out," said Bird.

He checked on the cats and got back in the truck. He didn't think Mucha Plata would live. He tried not to imagine her death. Annie. Had he known it would be this bad, he might have got to her somehow, done something, even stood there with her in the center of the pasture. No, he couldn't have done that. He had to do this. Die with Gail. Die as a statistic in a disaster.

People weren't cooperative. Gail following him now, he practically had to ram his way through the lanes, but slowly they made their way to the lane closest to the beach. Above him the top of his canyon was engulfed, and behind, in his mirror, he saw the first wave of fire burn down the hills and over the firefighters, taking the road and leaping to the beach homes on the other side. The line of cars crawled. There was panic all around. People waiting inside their cans of death, helpless, now oddly quiet, not even any honking; families, pets. It's what happens. Disasters happened and then there was nothing you could do.

He hung out his window and yelled back to Gail. "When you see an opening, pull over!"

"Pull over?"

"Don't stop in front of a house. Get in a line to the beach."

But they were stuck in front of a house now. If the fire caught them here, maybe they could run for it, but they'd have to abandon the cats. They inched forward as a wall of flame leapt to the bottom of the hill behind them, nearing the line of cars. It advanced. But as it did, Gail found an opening beyond the beach house and left the road. Her car immediately got stuck in the sand. Bird was calm now. He got out of his truck, grabbed Gail and the rat cage and got them into the truck cab, then he went back for the dogs who he lifted into the truck bed. He threw the truck into 4WD and drove onto the beach as the fire swept down. Around them, people abandoned their cars and ran with their children and pets to the beach as the fire leapt the road, igniting Gail's convertible, other autos, and exploding into beachside homes. They fled to the water. And that's where they stayed, the ocean at their backs, watching everything burn.

Rumi's Prayer

Far back, far back in our dark soul
the horse prances.

- - D. H. Lawrence

Rumi screamed and fell, the death hiss clinging to his neck. If she slipped her incisor under a bone and broke it, or opened a vein, he'd be done. Turning back, Tasha spun and kicked, but her hooves flew too high over the cat's head. But Annie knew how to strike out with her front legs. She ran at the death hiss, kicking out with her sharp front hoof, hitting the cat in the ribs. But the death hiss didn't even lift her head. Screeching, Rumi tried to roll as the puma tore at his neck. Annie struck again, but it was as if striking rock or mud, the cat's muscles both falling away from the hoof and rejecting it too. Her strength, her concentration, was so powerful, so horrible.

Tasha kicked again.

"Run!" screamed Annie.

"No," said Tasha. "The herd."

And then Annie struck out, hitting the cat on the head. This time death hiss looked up and when Annie kicked her again the predator rolled from Rumi's back.

"You," she said. She faced Annie. "You," and she raised up on her hind feet, front paws up and claws out, she hopped toward Annie. Leaped.

Annie struck her in the chest, one hoof, then the other, and again. While the cat rolled and got to her feet again, Annie bent and bit Rumi until he got up. But now, her head lowered and vulnerable, the death hiss flew at her. Before the animal could sink her teeth, Annie threw her head

171

and flung the death hiss off. She spun and drove the frozen Rumi forward after Tasha over the rocks.

"Run!" said Annie

"Where?" cried Rumi.

"Just run!" Tasha said.

Once on dirt, at a dead run, the game was up, nothing could catch a horse. But they had to put some distance between themselves and the cat. Tasha, tired, slowed, and Annie pushed her forward. Rumi slowed, Annie bit him. They ran, they ran, they ran, and finally stopped, their bodies covered with sweat and foam. Safe from the death hiss and worse off than ever.

Later, in the dark and far away, they lay in a dry streambed, the ground still warm from the fire. The wind, quieter now, was yet dry and hot, pushing from the wicked dry direction. Around that, the fire still raged and smoke hung in the air; there was little to smell but that of burned things, though in the distance, howls. Coyotes.

"Yippers," said Tasha. "Wild woof."

"We're too big," said Annie.

"Not if they band," said Tasha. She licked Rumi's neck wounds like a mother licked her foal while Rumi whimpered and muttered.

"I can do that, too," said Annie.

"One can while the other watches," Tasha said. "Sleep, too." She struggled to her feet. She'd watch first. She wasn't young. The day had taken much out of her. Another day, maybe another, and that might be it. Tasha knew this herself. And Annie knew. Maybe they should have stayed and waited. But Tasha said nothing of it.

Annie left Rumi and walked up to her.

"Everything is gone," Tasha said.

"The firehums," said Annie.

"No one in the barns."

"There can't be fire everywhere."

"Why not?" said Tasha. "It's been everywhere we've gone."

"We'll find Bird."

"We won't find Bird."

"We'll walk until the fire ends."

"We can't walk that far, Tasha said.

"And live there."

"We cannot live there."

"We must stay together," said Annie. "And live."

Back and forth, back and forth, two horses breathing their uncertainty into the fire night.

"Live," breathed Tasha. She lowered her head and rubbed her cheek on her leg, then raised her head again. She looked at Annie. "Why live?"

Annie ran her lips along Tasha's neck, up and down, once, twice, then stopped. "Because," she said.

"Then lead," said Tasha.

Annie went back to Rumi and licked his wounds as he groaned.

"Stop it," said Annie.

"I need," said Rumi.

"We all need. I can't be your mother." Though she felt then as if she could. She licked his neck.

"Tasha," said Rumi.

"Tasha cannot be your mother," Annie said. "She's weak already. She needs us, her herd."

"I'm miserable," said Rumi. "Pain."

"If you act miserable, you feel miserable," Annie said. "Start feeling something else."

"Something else?"

"Brave," said Annie.

"I'm not brave."

"If you act brave, you'll feel brave. You're not a foal. You're an adult. Start contributing to this herd."

"Other than fear and mistakes?" said Rumi.

"We all fear. We all make mistakes. Trial and error. Learn."

"Learn," whispered Rumi.

"Feel for Bird," said Annie. "Send to his Other."

Back and forth, back and forth, in the language of horses, their bodies, their noses, their smell, their tongues, their breath.

Rumi quieted and put his nose in the air. He lay like that for quite a while, nostrils quivering, feeling the warmth. Finally, he whispered. "The horse is faster than the mind. Underneath everything is a horse and a horse is everything. The sun, the wind, the earth. All animals. All plants. All things."

"Even Hums?"

"Even Hums. Even fire."

"And water?" said Annie.

Rumi hesitated. "And rain."

"Everything us. A horse. Inside," said Annie.

"Yes," Rumi said.

Tasha came over to have Annie relieve her. "What's he doing now?" she said.

"Praying, I think," said Annie.

"Your Great Caregiver is doing a lousy job," Tasha said.

"He must be very busy someplace else," whispered Rumi.

"Maybe he's a gelding," Tasha said.

"Maybe she is making a new, baby world," said Annie, "somewhere else, and expects this one to grow up and get by on its own."

"Too much to expect from us," said Tasha.

"Can you feel Bird?" Annie said to Rumi.

"He's behind the fire," said Rumi.

"His barn?"

"The fire is in the way of everything," Rumi said.

Tasha lay down and Annie got up. "Don't lick him anymore," said Annie. "Don't baby him."

"I'm an adult now," said Rumi.

"You escaped the death hiss," said Annie.

"Brave," Rumi said.

"A brave horse," said Annie.

"An adult now," said Rumi.

"Dream to the Other," Annie said.

Annie stood and took watch. Until now there'd been little time to think, and now, with time for it, she found that Tasha was right, she was better off without it. Licking Rumi reminded her of her foal, the colt she would never see again. So it happened. One day you never see them again. It might have happened with Bird, somewhere behind the fire,

174

unable to get to her. Maybe dead, like Mick and Adele. Never coming back. Since the fire they'd seen no Hums at all but the firehums. Maybe they were all gone. Maybe not. Maybe the death hiss was right. Why survive at all? But the death hiss did not give up. She continued to hunt for her young. Because.

Here is a horse, standing in the middle of ash. Nothing in sight. Nothing for miles but her own hope. First you learn to wait. Then you learn to hope. Then hurt. Then? Then?

She was the lead mare. A gelding couldn't lead, especially Rumi. Getting Rumi to follow was hard enough. Tasha was wise, important, but old and getting weaker. Annie was smart and strong and had to lead. They could work together. They must work together.

She stood watch longer than she should have, but it was important to let Rumi dream and Tasha sleep. She didn't wake them until the shining eyes of the wild woofs had her surrounded.

Once Gods

The world of the Gods is obtained by knowledge.

- - Brihad Aranyaka Upanishad

They circled the horses quickly. Annie counted two groups of four. Eight. They moved back and forth, each one constantly changing directions, around and around, feigning in, circling quickly, trying to dizzy the horses, trying to tighten the circle. They whined and panted, almost singing. "Food here. Water. Let us eat. Let us drink." They were small, but in a pack; if one of the horses was too weak, too dizzy, they could charge. They panted, let us eat, let us drink.

"Water in the streambed," said Annie. Was there a leader? She couldn't read them, couldn't tell.

"Water," they whined. "Food."

"We're the food!" said Rumi.

Tasha and Rumi were on their feet now and Annie backed into them so each horse faced out. Now there were no blind spots and they didn't have to turn their heads to watch the wild woofs. Annie hissed and kicked out. The circle widened.

"Water here," said Tasha.

"Water here. Water here," whined the wild woofs.

Even the horses could feel their desperation, the whining, not the joyful howl after a kill, but desperate whining and whining.

"Dig," said Tasha to Annie. "Give them water. Dig."

Annie pawed at the streambed. A big coyote lunged at her bowed head. She hissed and kicked him. A leader? She stepped back.

"Water here," she said.

"Water, yes," they whined.

It didn't make sense, but they were mad for want of everything. Yet as the mud slowly emerged from the dry bed, the wild woofs stopped to watch. Annie pawed the ground.

"Get ready," Annie said.

When the muddy water appeared, the pack pounced blindly forward and the horses ran.

An hour after horses are born, they can stand. In another hour they can run at their mother's side. They are born for it. These three ran across the charred hills until they could run no more. Tasha slowed to a trot. Rumi and Annie slowed. Finally, they walked.

"How many times can we do that?" said Tasha. "Not many more."

"Let's find a rumble path," said Annie.

"Hums?" said Rumi.

"I don't see any other way," said Annie.

"Hums could be help or danger," said Rumi. "Help or danger."

"Hum at a time," said Annie.

"Hum by Hum," Tasha said.

Rumi's ears wriggled every which way. "You say funny things," he said to Tasha.

"It's all funny or none of it's funny," Tasha said.

"I was brave," said Rumi.

"You were brave," Annie said. And she led them.

By dawn they came upon a rumble path. The three of them walked slowly now, letting the sun warm them. The night burned off and soon it was hot again, though finally the air was still, if deadly still; the wicked, dry hot wind had finally lain down. They followed the path down the slope until they came to yet a bigger one, one big enough for rumbles to go in either direction. Around them, as they walked, white ash formed over the burned out hills, over the naked scrub oaks, the stumps of pine and eucalyptus, the cindered cypress trees, the blackened scrub and manzanita, black with a coating of white ash like snow, and that as far as they could see.

"I'll need a streambed soon," said Tasha.

"I know this road," said Annie. "We'll come to one in time."

They walked. Then, in the distance, they saw a line of rumbles, quiet and unmoving.

"Look!" said Rumi.

"Nothing is moving," said Annie.

"Caution," said Tasha. "Much caution."

They came upon it from behind, a long, long silent line of rumbles, some of them pulling trailers, all of them burned. Some of the rumbles still had burned Hums inside. Some of the trailers were open and empty, others still had trapped dead horses in them; more horses and Hums lay dead on the side of the road. Not even the scavengers, not even the vultures had come for them yet; the sky was empty of birds. Not even predators had been here. Nor Hums. Hums always came to help each other and there were none here. These were all bad signs. She felt it from Tasha. "Bad signs. Much caution," Tasha said.

They walked single file along the line of burned out rumbles and trailers. The line stretched for a furlong. Finally, it ended and the horses stopped. A line of ants came onto the road and wandered to the first rumble.

"Ants," said Tasha.

"Life," Annie said.

Rumi lowered his nose to the road and sniffed above the ants. "Once, they too were Gods," he said.

"What does that mean?" said Tasha.

"I don't know," said Rumi. "I just feel it."

"A prayer?" said Annie.

"It's all prayer or none of it is," Rumi said. He put his nose on Tasha's.

But what Annie felt is that if this could happen to Hums, then it could happen to anyone, to everything; it could happen to Bird.

"I'm going inside one of these empty trailers," she said.

Tasha raised her head and looked around the naked hills. Horses never liked trailers. They were unnatural, tight, noisy and claustrophobic, blinding your sight, your smell, your tactility; they trapped you, almost motionless, an animal born to run, born to see for miles, and once inside you never knew where you were going to end up. Deep in the hearts and memories of horses, months in the dark bottoms of swaying ships, cramped stalls, and this, this death, the price of the contract to work with Hums.

"Caution," said Tasha.

"There might be food, even water," said Annie.

She walked the line again until she found an empty trailer, a long one like for the polo ponies. She didn't see the ponies. The rumble was empty, too. She stepped into the dark chamber, waited, smelled the thick air. Her eyes adjusted, then she walked in, slowly. One by one she passed the empty tie-ups. At the front of the trailer was the storage area; piled tack, saddles and bridles, and food bins. She opened one with her teeth. Alfalfa. And to the right, some Hum water in small plastic bottles. She turned and walked out.

"Some food. Hum water," she said.

Tasha came to the back of the trailer. Rumi followed. Tasha gazed in for a long while. "One at a time," she said.

"You first," said Annie. "The food is at the very end."

"I know these," Tasha said.

Slowly, Tasha went in.

"You next," Annie said to Rumi. "Do you feel anything?"

"Death," said Rumi.

"Anyone can feel that."

"Everything is still here, but dead," Rumi said.

Rumi was holding up better and beginning to feel more things now, but it was hard to know what he was feeling; it didn't come out clearly in horse.

"Bird?" said Annie.

"Rain," said Rumi.

But she could feel that, too. The air had begun to slide in lightly from the west, a hint of moisture on its back.

Tasha emerged. She carried a Hum water in her teeth. She crushed it, then sucked at the water. "Like that," she said to Rumi.

Rumi hesitated at the mouth of the trailer. It just wasn't any place a horse would go voluntarily. Annie nipped his butt. Instead of lurching forward he straightened up and looked back at her. Then he raised his head and walked in.

"Brave," said Annie.

"Geldings, they're all the same," Tasha said. Already she looked more refreshed; her eyes more clear, her head held higher.

"This is bad," Annie said to her finally.

"Yes," said Tasha. "The Hums come for their own, alive or dead."

So the Hums couldn't get here, or there were no Hums anywhere. A world without Hums? Without Bird? If they could get to the end of the fire. Annie looked to the sky where one of the tiny, stiff birds that left white trails crossed. They were unnatural enough to be Hum stuff. But they never came close to the ground. A sign, though, that there was something else still going on. Bird. She remembered him again.

Rumi stuck his head out the back of the trailer and Annie went in. There was yet some alfalfa. The Hum water was hard to get at, too warm, and not enough of it, but something. When done, she walked out and the three of them stood in the midday sunlight.

"There might be more of these other cans," said Tasha. "Food and water. We could wait here."

"It's so exposed," said Annie.

"Wait in a trailer at night," said Tasha.

Rumi shivered. "Urr-ruu," he said.

"Yes," said Annie. "Death hiss or wild woof could trap us inside." And she was driven. Driven to find Bird. She rotated her ears. She heard something in the distance.

"Do you hear that?" she said.

But Tasha was old and couldn't hear as well as the others.

Rumi perked his ears. "Something," he said.

"Rumbles," said Annie. "The other way. Up the road."

They stood listening. Then came the lop-lop of a sky rumble over a distant hill. It came into view, moved into the valley beyond, rose again.

"A Hum in the rumble," whispered Rumi.

"Yes," Annie said. She looked at Tasha who was always reluctant to do anything but stay put. "We find them or they find us."

Tasha's eyes followed the floating rumble. Her nostrils worked the air. "They're not looking for us," she said.

"Maybe," said Rumi. "Maybe for horses, Hums, anything."

They could keep traveling. Move away from the Hums. If the Hums were everywhere, as before, they'd run into them soon enough. If not, they could follow the sun's path. Maybe there was somewhere that hadn't burned, maybe other horses would gather there. Maybe there were yet wild horses, or horses could become wild again, every horse knew that. But Tasha wouldn't survive it. How long could they move from Hum wreckage to Hum wreckage scavenging for scraps? How lucky would they be? Here were Hums. That meant more Hums. Still Hums about. Their fate, the fate of horses, had been tied to Hums for a long time. If she knew of a place to escape to, a place to go, a place they could reach, but she didn't.

"We find them or they find us," Annie said again.

Tasha listened and listened. Anxiously, Rumi pawed the ground and watched the sky.

"Not our Hums," said Rumi.

"Something," said Annie. "A start."

Tasha lowered her head. She sniffed Annie's shoulder, then gazed about at the blackened earth surrounding them. "Lead," she said.

Annie took them up the rumble path. Another, smaller path jutted off in the direction of the sound. They followed the sound up a hill. The sky rumble appeared again, closer this time, but spun off in the other direction. Annie followed the sounds, louder now, rumbles and the shouting of male Hums, men. She hated shouting men. When she rode with Bird, if she heard men shouting she went to the moon with fear. Men who shouted were dangerous for horses. Tasha knew this, too. But as they came over a ridge they spotted the encampment. Rumbles. Trailers. Male Hums. Woofs. Two huge corrals with horses crowded inside. They hesitated there, watching, the three of them jointly fearful and curious, wondering whether to stay or go. Then one of the Hums looked up and spotted them.

Wiley, Hero

We were rescued like a bird
from the fowler's snare
Broken was the snare
And we were freed.

- - Psalm 124

Was he the horse who was sacrificed, or the sacrificer
who killed the horse?

- - Satapatha Brahmana

They did not have to be caught. Annie led the others down the ridge and into the encampment.

"Look at this," one of the Hums said. He wore a black hat with a bill like a duck. "Now we don't even have to catch them."

"Two of these are pretty," said another one.

"It's all just horse flesh," said the first.

Annie led Tasha and Rumi to the less crowded corral.

"These are well trained. It's a shame," said the second Hum.

"Horse flesh is horse flesh" said the black hat.

"These are worth more."

"To who? They got owners. We got to get rid of them before that all starts up."

Inside the corral was very crowded. Dozens of horses pressed against each other. There was a little stale hay on the ground, a tub of water that was hard to get near. A big brown-red horse pushed his way through to it, drank, then raised his head. Annie saw him over the backs of the crowded horses.

"It's Dummie," she said to Tasha and Rumi.

"Safe," said Rumi.

It was difficult for Annie to believe that Rumi could hold any affection for Dummie when all Dummie had ever done was beat him up. Annie couldn't care less if he was there or not, but Tasha wanted information. They worked their way over to the water tub amidst the murmur and rumor from the crowded horses mumbling to each other back and forth; too packed, too crowded, but some hope; Hums here, doing things, some water, some food. Annie pushed through and let Tasha, then Rumi, drink, then she drank. The water was fouled with dirt, saliva, and bad hay. Then Dummie saw them and made his way through the herd.

"Well," said Dummie. "See?"

"See what?" said Annie.

"Me," said Dummie.

"We're here, too," said Annie.

"It seldom matters what anybody does," said Tasha.

"But sometimes it matters," said Rumi.

"It didn't matter, we're all here," said Tasha.

"All lucky," said Rumi.

"Precious," Tasha said. She'd been right. Dummie told them Precious had been hit by a rumble. The fire came down. He had to run.

"What happens here?" said Annie.

"New Hums," said Dummie.

More Hums, these on two-wheel rumbles, firing guns, herded five horses into the camp. Rumi jumped at the gunshots. Rumbles with big wheels and no tops circled the newcomers who ran in panic outside the corrals. The Hums lassoed them, then pushed them into the pen. A furlong away, a sky rumble groaned and chattered at the air above them, descending, slapping wind and dirt toward the corrals where the horses screamed and pushed each other to the back fence. A Hum jumped out and another jumped in, then the thing roared back into the air. The noise and havoc spooked the frightened horses who whinnied and banged on each other. It was difficult for Annie to glean much information from all the fear and panic, and even hope.

Annie stood between the panicky horses and Rumi. "Stay calm," she said.

"How?" said Rumi. How?"

"Brave," said Annie. She ran herself against him, once, turned and rubbed against him again until he stood.

"I don't like this," mumbled Rumi.

"No," said Annie.

Slowly things calmed down again.

Dummie pointed to the trailers. "In them," he said. "At night."

Tasha looked suspiciously at the trailers. "Tonight?" she said.

"That corral first, then this one," said Dummie.

"All of them?" said Tasha.

"Most," said Dummie.

Tasha turned to Annie and Rumi. "Let's stay away from the gate."

"I'm going to be first!" said Dummie.

Tasha turned away and Annie led her and Rumi to the farthest corner from the gate. She fetched some hay and brought it to them.

"I don't like this," she said.

"The trailers aren't horse trailers," said Tasha. "Moos." Cattle.

Annie surveyed the corral again. Across the way, a big gray mare recruited two fours of horses, eight, pushing them, moving among them, placing her head over their necks. Another four watched her curiously, choosing whether or not to join up. Safety in numbers. Best led by the best leader. The gray was a lead mare. She might be more than just shoving and biting. She might know something.

"See her?" said Annie.

"Yes," said Tasha. "You're already enough to deal with. I don't need her, too."

Rumi placed himself beside Annie. "I don't want to submit to someone else," he said.

"Just information," said Annie. "Dummie can't be right."

"He's Dummie," muttered Tasha."

"Wiley," said Rumi.

"Dummie." That went back and forth for quite a while.

"Wait here," Annie said to them. She made her way through the crowded corral filled with the rumbling of hope and fear, across the dirt pasture to where the big gray surrounded her growing herd. The gray turned and faced Annie when she spotted her, and recognizing the power and intelligence in Annie's movement, raised her head and expanded her chest. "Join or challenge, choose now!"

Annie lowered her head.

"Join," said the gray.

Annie moved forward and let the gray nibble her neck. "Is this place good?" she said.

The gray backed away. Questioning could be as troublesome as defiance.

"What is this place?" said Annie.

"Not good," said the big mare. She was powerful, but not subtle.

"Cattle cans," said Annie, meaning the cattle trailers.

"Escape," said the gray. "Join me."

Annie walked to the metal fence and pressed her neck against it. Maybe some of them could jump it, but not most; she wondered if she could, yet to fail would surely mean injury or death. A herd, together, might force it down, but how would anyone get them to do that?

"How?" said Annie.

"When there's a chance."

But there might never be a chance. The gray was all leadership and defiance, but not much else. Yet she would lead. That might be enough.

It took a while for Rumi to get it. He'd felt the badness around him, but he didn't know why. These Hums weren't trying to help the other Hums. They were gathering horses, but not to take care of them. Not in these corrals. Not in those trailers. They were trying to sell them before their Hums found them. Sell them like cattle. For food.

You might find this beyond the reasoning power of a horse, but in fact a smart horse, most likely a mare who had to think about feeding and protecting and teaching a foal, who had it in her to lead a herd from pasture to water to pasture and to avoid danger, has learned to make connections. If some domestic horses moved from feed to water to feed without making any connections, a mother and lead mare had to know that some things were food and others not, and must act toward those things as if they were food, things that she feeds her baby, milk, alfalfa, grass, carrots, dandelions, apples, and must act to procure them for her child, or in the wild, remember the way to water, to pasture, to high ground. She must have a general idea of food beyond any particular food, of place beyond any particular place, must have internal maps and understand direction. It was not a matter of logic. Annie had smelled cows and smelled cow flesh on the breath of Hums. They ate cows. And they behaved differently toward them. Treating horses like cows, keeping them in tight pens and carting them away in cattle trailers, could only mean one thing.

"Moos are eaten," Annie said to Rumi.

Rumi's nose quivered.

"We die anyways," said Tasha.

"I've led badly," said Annie to Tasha. "You were right."

"Now lead us out," Rumi said to Annie.

Annie touched Rumi's head with her lips.

He whined slightly, feeling her despair. "Please," whispered Rumi. "Lead." Rumi, who could barely follow.

Annie gazed at the scarred hillsides around them, at the swaying backs of the trapped horses. Lead. Lead how? Where? In the past she'd laid her little tricky plans to tease Bird, but nothing like this; now she had to think ahead. Far ahead. Not too far. They had to get out. Get away. Then the next thing.

"I'll check the gate," said Annie.

"Don't make any friends," Tasha said.

Annie understood. She worked her way slowly along the fence, looking for weak spots. It was new and metal, not chewable, not wood. The gate was padlocked. She nuzzled the lock, bit it. It wouldn't fall open.

The black-hatted man watched her. Laughed. "Smart one," he said. "Smart, dumb, they all taste the same I guess."

Hum sounds. Not caring Hum sounds. She walked away. Here was the only chance, at the gate, when it opened. And Tasha was right. No friends. They couldn't save the herd. They had to break from the herd to save themselves and their only chance was their last chance, at loading.

She returned and told Tasha and Rumi.

"Are you afraid of bangs?" said Tasha. Guns.

"No," said Annie.

"I am!" said Rumi.

"Don't be!" said Annie.

"There won't be an opening," said Tasha. "They make a fence to the trailer."

"Not as strong," said Annie. "We can knock it down."

But they'd need Dummie.

That night the Hums loaded the opposite corral onto the cattle trailer. Tasha was right again. The Hums built a narrow fence right from the gate and up the trailer ramp. They fired guns and drove the panicking horses into the dark tunnel where there were no tie-ups or stall spaces. The horses were packed tightly, body to body, unable to move. The three companions watched the trailer drive out, the dismal eyes of the horses shining through the trailer slats.

They went to Dummie.

"Get away," he said. "Leave me alone."

"These Hums aren't saving us," said Annie. "Did you watch?"

"There are a lot of us," he said.

"Did you watch?"

It took a very, very long time, into the dawn, past morning, and into the afternoon, after the rumble returned with the empty cattle trailer. The sky rumble descended, rose, came and left again. The Hums on noisy rumbles ran new horses into the other corral. Around them, as the captured animals panicked and hoped, almost as one, Annie spoke to Dummie in the simple, repetitive way of horses. Dummie was even more difficult than Rumi, and first it all had to be explained, over and over, and then he had to be convinced. The herding, the bangs, the moo trailers. Dummie didn't trust Annie and had it not been for Tasha he might not have wavered at all. He gazed down at Rumi.

"Do you believe this?" he said.

"Yes," said Rumi.

"Not new Hums," said Dummie. He surveyed the packed corral of horses. "They all believe in the new Hums."

187

"They will be slaughtered and eaten," Tasha said.

"Tell everyone?"

"We can't even convince you," said Annie. "They'll have their chance."

And Annie gave him her plan. Dummie would, in fact, be first at the gate, but he'd knock out the narrow fence with his chest. The horses would break out and the gray mare would no doubt take over immediately. Annie and Tasha and Rumi would break from the herd, Dummie following them. The Hums would chase the herd, not the strays.

Again, this took a very long time. Break down the fence. Don't follow the herd. Follow me. Again and again. It was simple and arose out of their natural tendencies to break out, to flee, but for the last part, not following the herd. For one, it was a second step, something that came after something else, something distant in time and place; it had to be imagined and held in thought, and worse, it ran against the basic instinct to stay with the group, find safety in the herd.

"Are you herd bound?" Annie asked them. In fact, she knew the geldings would be.

"I'm afraid I am," said Rumi.

She'd have to be on his shoulder, driving him.

Dummie was mulling it all now. "What if I won't do it?"

"I'll do it myself," Annie said, though she knew she might not be capable. She waited. Already the sun began to lower in the sky. Soon it would be night and too late. But her history of standing up to Dummie ran horrifically between them like a torrential stream. How would Bird have convinced her to cross it? Ask gently and wait. "We need you," she said.

Dummie's pale eyes shifted. "Need me," he said. He shook his head, then raised his chin. He looked at Rumi. "What is my name?" he said.

"Wiley," said Rumi.

"What is my name?" he said to Tasha.

"Wiley," said Tasha. It was nothing to her either way.

Now he eyed Annie. His head rolled one way, then the other before he lifted it again. He said to her, "What is my name?"

But she had fought with him for over a year, giving him nothing. If she gave in to him easily now, he might simply take his name and walk away with it, abandoning them.

"Are you herd bound?" she said to him.

"What is my name?" he said.

"Can you remember what to do?"

"My name!"

"Can you do it?"

"What is my name?" he screamed.

"Wiley," she said quietly. "Your name is Wiley."

They were silent for a while. Finally, Wiley said, "When it's dark, at the gate," and walked away from them.

Annie went to the gray then who had a herd of twelve now, geldings and mares.

"I don't need you," the mare said.

"Be ready. You will have your chance," said Annie. Of course, that took some time.

Annie led Tasha and Rumi into the milling herd of horses. The sky rumble left for the last time. It meant there was another place to go. It meant more Hums. Somewhere. If more Hums, then maybe Bird. They waited there patiently, in the way of horses, watching the sun sink, watching the shadows of the hills stretch onto the corral. The air turned gray and the Hums began to set up the narrow fence and back the trailer up to the gate.

Rumi twitched. "Will Wiley do it?" Rumi said to Annie.

"Yes."

"Can he remember what to do?"

"Yes," said Annie. "He's smart enough."

"He's smart?"

"It's why I called him Dummie," Annie said.

And then Wiley came prancing to the gate. The Hum in the black duck hat watched him bemusedly and then walked away, waiting for the night to fall. For the first time in months, clouds gathered in the sky and obliterated the emerging stars, covering the nearly round moon, creating an odd, lavender-gray glow.

Annie felt Tasha heaving next to her, sending out her resignation. They could be shot. Or they could fail. Or they might escape. To what? More death hiss. More wild woofs. Starvation. More bad Hums.

Tasha sniffed the air. "Rain," she said.

"One crisis at a time," Annie said to her.

Tasha looked at Annie. Her ears went back gently, then came forward again. "Good-bye, Annie" said Tasha.

"No," said Annie.

But now the Hums had begun to surround the corral. Annie counted four. Two, one of them the black-hatted Hum, extended the trailer ramp and secured the temporary fence from the corral to the ramp. Two others stood outside the corral and began waving their arms. The horses milled.

"Be still," said Annie. "Stay together."

It happened fast. The men outside fired their guns. The horses panicked and raced back and forth against each other. The gate flew open. And Wiley stepped up. He ran out the gate and between the narrow fences, and then up the ramp and into the trailer.

"Oh, no," said Rumi.

"Dummie," said Tasha.

The other horses pushed at each other, forced by the Hums toward the gate. Annie would have to get up near the front of the herd now very quickly because at the back of the herd she'd be too late, even if she succeeded to knock out the fence, and they'd easily be rounded up, but the whole corral of crowded horses now rampaged between her and her opportunity. She hadn't planned enough. She hadn't planned for Wiley to betray them or fail. She'd misread him and led poorly again.

"Follow," she said, though she now led by instinct and desperation alone, because she'd led them wrong every time, but someone had to lead. Maybe they could push their way to the middle of the crowding bodies. Maybe they'd get lucky.

"Hopeless," Tasha said, but followed.

The Hums waved and fired their bangs. Horses screamed. Annie pushed into the plunging horses who now merged through the gate, into the narrow chute, and began to be driven up the ramp.

Then Wiley emerged from the back of the trailer. From the top of the ramp he flew at the fence, striking it with his front legs. It went down in a heap, the Hums shouting and running.

Annie'd been right. The horses poured out the opening, scattering, and in a blink the big gray mare began circling them as the Hums ran to their rumbles.

"Let's go!" Annie said, and led Tasha and Rumi into the back of the herd and then in. "Stay close!" she said, but already Rumi began to run confusedly, pushed by the bodies around him. She couldn't even spot Wiley now, but the gray mare headed out with her herd in the direction of the rumble path; a mistake, they'd be too easily followed by the Hums.

Annie broke away with Tasha as the rumbles came forward to circle the teeming animals, but Rumi, confused, stayed with the other horses. "Run!" she said to Tasha and headed back into the herd, finding Rumi, biting his rear, turning him, then riding his shoulder, nipping at him until he broke out with her, finding Tasha waiting at the base of the hill. The other horses pounded away, the Hums following on their noisy rumbles, but for one, the black-hatted Hum, who spun his two-wheel rumble toward Annie, Rumi, and Tasha.

"Scatter!" screamed Annie, but they could not. Away from the others it was confusing enough. Rumi and Tasha froze as the Hum circled them, yelling and spinning his lasso. They should back up, butt to butt, like they did with the wild woofs, but everything was too noisy, too wild. The Hum screamed, "Heyaah! Heyaah!" He'd get one of them at least, if not drive all three of them back into the corral.

Annie stepped toward him. She pinned her ears and hissed. The Hum dropped his lasso and raised his gun. And then Wiley, having spun away from the back of the herd, came pounding down on him. The black-hatted Hum spun at Wiley who reared up. The gun banged, one, two, three, four and Wiley came down over the Hum, crushing him between himself and the two-wheel rumble.

"Run!" said Tasha.

But Annie hesitated. Rumble engines whined in the distance as the other Hums chased the herd. Annie walked forward and sniffed Wiley's cheek.

"Get up, Wiley," she said.

"I can't."

"Get up."

"I can't."

Back and forth. Back and forth. Blood oozed from Wiley's neck and his ear.

"You saved us."

"Yes."

"I'll find your Hum. Wait here."

"Yes," said Wiley.

"I'll find her," Annie said. "She's coming."

"My Hum," Wiley said.

"She's coming. When you awake."

"Yes, my Hum," said Wiley. "Coming for me."

"Wiley," whispered Annie. "Your name is Wiley."

"My Hum," said Wiley. "My name." His breath rattled in his throat and he died.

The air grew as thick with moisture as it was with darkness, as if everything, sky and earth, were ash. Annie nuzzled Wiley's cheek. "Thank you, Wiley. I'm sorry."

"We should go now," Tasha said. "They'll be back."

Annie turned up the hill, overland. "Away from the Hums for now," she said.

"Above the mud when the rain comes," said Tasha.

And soon a drizzle filled the air. They trudged up the mountain in the dark, picking their way between blackened sage and ash covered rock, finally settling down on the leeward side of the hill, behind a boulder that blocked the wind. The rain came down.

"Butt to the wind, wait it out," Tasha said, as she always did when it rained.

"Who will be next?" said Rumi. "Who will be next?"

"As Wiley would say, me!" Tasha said.

"You have work to do now," Annie said to him. "Dreams to send."

Now finally, far too late, the rain poured from the sky, lifting the siege of the fire against the land. It drenched the three horses on the mountaintop, their bodies pressed against each other for heat. Rumi tried to maneuver to the middle, but Annie licked him like a foal, then coaxed him to the other side of Tasha who was tired and shivering. They lay down together, huddling against the cold and rain.

"Rain will make grass," said Rumi.

"If we live so long," said Tasha. "Anyway, tomorrow there'll be water."

"We need food," said Rumi.

"I'll take care of that," said Annie to Rumi. "You find Bird."

Rumi shivered next to Tasha in the hopeless rain. Annie laid her head over Tasha's neck and muttered into Rumi's ear. "Send for the Other," she felt to him.

"A dream," Rumi said softly.

"Yes," said Annie. "A dream."

Lost and Found

For everyone who asks, receives. Everyone who seeks, finds.

- - Jesus, Gospel of Luke

Every time in my learning that I felt a breakthrough, I opened the doors and found my horse saying, "It's about time, I've been waiting for you."

- - Dominique Barbier

That night, far away, as everywhere the rain lay down on the fire, Gail was awakened by lightning and thunder, and a dream. She and Bird stood in their house burned down, their things destroyed, nothing of their lives left but ashes, and with them stood three horses.

"Living in our house, though burned, with three horses," she said.

"Now all we need is a house and horses," said Bird.

"I didn't dream it myself. It was sent."

"A horse sent it."

"Rumi," she said. "I wouldn't dream that."

"What would you dream?" said Bird.

"It was like a barn. I wouldn't dream of living in a burned barn," Gail said.

They'd spent a night and a day and another night and day watching the fire rage in the hills above them, before the rain came in, slowly piling up over the ocean, the air growing thicker, saltier, the sky expanding toward the earth, gray, then purple, and then the first drizzle, the first drops of rain. People cheered.

Slowly a kind of community of campers had built up on the beach, watching the fire burn in the hills above them and beyond, toward the city. No electricity. Cell phones failed to connect. The wireless internet was dead. Radio news passed along more rumors than information. What few reporters made it into this rugged territory didn't know where they were or what they were looking at; even if they might have, few landmarks still stood.

People shared water and food, talked about their lives, their kids, their pets, their chances, prayed, speculated as to what happened and how.

"It's the end of the world," a little woman said to Bird on the first night after he shared some of his water with her.

"It's not," said Bird.

"How do you know?"

"We're still here," Bird said.

"Be kind," Gail said to him later. "Maybe it is the end of the world."

"I was kind of kind," Bird said. "The whole country isn't burning down."

Worriedly, she worked her hands, her right thumb pressing the spot on her ring finger where she usually wore her ring.

"It was just a thing," he said to her.

"I know that," she said. "But nothing else will ever be the same thing."

He didn't know how to console her for this loss. It was real, undeniable. He didn't even know how to console himself. They were camped out, trapped on a beach with some dogs and cats, some clothes and a few paintings; everything else they'd been up till then somewhere behind the fire. Sometimes one small thing held everything else together. Besides each other, their child, for her it was the ring. For him, what? Annie. He worried again. Did someone get her out? To where? Would she have stayed in the pasture or run into the fire? How long before anyone would get to her to help? How would he find her?

That was before the rain; the sky was jewel blue then and the hills full of fire or blackened with ash and the ocean shined ironically behind them. Bird and Gail slept in the truck cab, the animals in the truck bed. Their dogs, and everybody else's, ran along the beach. They took the cats out one by one and held them. Even the rat. Sometimes they swam, staring at the fires from the flat, cold water. Then the wind shifted. The water grew gray and waves began to hit the shore. People who'd camped close to the water had to move away from the tide.

On the second day Bird began to organize people into parties that might check the homes and cars for survivors or dead, but some uniformed types moved in, checked the burned out homes and cars for bodies, found none, they said, though red paramedic trucks drove up and down the road; they had no information, handed out snacks and bottled water and suggested everyone stay put, stay away from the homes, even their own burned cars.

Now fire trucks reappeared from the northwest, some headed toward the city and others began heading into the hills again. Helicopters and even water dropping planes flew to the ocean and picked up water, then headed back over the mountains.

"So much for the end of the world," Bird said.

Gail said, "We have to let Marlena know we're safe."

"We're safe?" said Bird.

"Yes," said Gail.

"We have to leave here and get somewhere," said Bird. But even if they could get reception, Gail's cell charger was in her burned out car. They wouldn't be able to move up or down the coast highway, now filling again with trucks and officialdom. They had to cross the hills. "The Valley," said Bird. Ten miles away on the other side of the canyon. And if the canyon were on fire or not, now a barricade of red trucks sat at its mouth. Sometimes you just had to wait. Wait and hope. They reassured each other that their daughter was fine. They'd get out of here and reach her. And, like everyone, they told each other that at least they'd survived, maybe they'd get lucky and find their home unburned.

Finally, that night, it rained, it stormed; thunder and lightning; the ocean pushed everyone up from the beach, closer to the road, beneath the burned homes, and Gail woke up in the night with her dream. The rain stopped. They threw the dogs out of the cab and made love.

In the morning the sky slowly lightened. The hills above sizzled with steam. Then the police showed up. From a big city like the one to the east, they were disaster hardened. They bossed people around and knew nothing.

"The lunkheads are here," said Bird. "Let's go find Annie."

"A phone," said Gail.

"The house and the ranch are between here and the Valley," said Bird.

"Not much to pack. I suppose we can do what we're doing here anywhere," Gail said.

They checked the animals, fed them, gave the dogs a short run, then they drove down the beach and shortly were stopped by a police jeep. "Can I help you?" said the policeman.

"Can you?" said Bird.

The officer hesitated. "We're not here to help. We're here to keep order."

"We're just changing camp spots," Bird said.

"Don't leave the beach."

"Right," said Bird. He drove off. "I think this beach goes from Mexico to Alaska."

"Around the whole country," said Gail. "It's hard to know where the beach begins and ends."

It was good to love an anarchist. And losing everything really loosens you up.

"Let's go home," Bird said.

The horses awoke with the dawn on the hill. The rain had passed. They waited for the sun to rise up and warm them. White steam rose from the ground around them, from the ash, from the black wet earth, filling the air with white mist, like standing in a cloud. Slowly they walked down the muddy hillside, found water in the stream, and drank. They found some weeds beneath a boulder.

Annie nudged Rumi.

"Yes, I can feel now," said Rumi. "Bird's barn." He looked downstream, pointing with his nose.

"Let's go," Annie said.

"Does it matter, really?" said Tasha.

"To me," said Annie.

"Hope," Rumi said.

Hope, the thing that came with waiting and made pain. Why not do it here? Why somewhere else? Why move? Annie felt Tasha's despair. Tasha was exhausted, maybe too exhausted. But finding Bird would be better than staying here. She said it in a glance. And Tasha responded. What were the odds?

"If we find Bird's barn," Annie said. "Let's go."

"We'll go where the water goes," said Rumi.

"Follow the stream," Annie said.

"Lead," said Tasha.

And they began to walk. Annie pushed Tasha forward now, staying at her flank, and Rumi followed with his muttering. "What lies beneath the earth? Nothing. What stands behind the sky? The rain. Why does the sky meet the land? To make fire sleep. For who? For us. For horses."

"He doesn't make any sense," Tasha said to Annie.

"He doesn't have to," said Annie.

"If I begin to die, make him stop talking," said Tasha.

"You won't die," said Annie.

"To die in peace," said Tasha. "I'm not that lucky."

"You should ask him to stop talking now, before you die," said Annie.

"Stop talking, Rumi," said Tasha.

"I'm just one little animal asking why," said Rumi.

"We all are," said Annie.

"And no one answers," said Tasha.

"It helps me find and send," said Rumi.

"But where are you sending and what will we find?" asked Tasha.

"Bird," Annie said. "We need to keep moving."

This is how they spoke to each other with their bodies and breath, their tails and teeth, their eyes, their lips as they walked. Then for the first time some lopping sky rumbles passed overhead, heading the opposite direction.

"Rumi," said Annie. "The sky rumbles."

"No, this way," Rumi said.

Bird drove down the beach until he didn't see any police cars, then got on the ocean highway and took the first fire road into the hills. Paved roads would likely be filled with rescue vehicles and barricades. As they ascended he spotted the palisade suburb that sat above the canyon on a plateau overlooking the ocean. It was flattened, black, gray chimneys standing amid the ruins like sentinels. A trailer park closer to the ocean was burned out. From the edge of cliffs they stared down into the canyon; the twisted roads lay naked up and down the hills like string, like snakes. Along those roads the fire had been indiscriminate, taking five, ten homes in a bunch, leaving one.

On the beach it had been different, in the exhilaration of survival, the absence of everything made their hope, if desperate, then more abstract. Now, with the devastation in front of them, the dismal nothing of the blackened hills filled Bird.

"Maybe we got lucky," he whispered.

"We've lost enough," said Gail.

There was more to be said, more about how much loss you can take, more about how much everyone had lost, how the mansions and ranches had burned, the big houses and the small ones, and the squatters' shacks behind the town center, her car, his cat; certain losses, and uncertain ones, his horse, their house.

"It's so quiet," she said.

"The radio," said Bird.

Back in the truck, he turned it on. The world hadn't ended. The fire didn't reach the city. The ocean winds pushed it north and the fire line was drawn above the suburbs in the Valley, the fire increasingly contained by all that it had already burned.

They drove along the top of the cliffs into the State Park, down the hills into County land, and finally back into the canyon. Around them, ash lay on the scorched hillsides and covered the limbs of burned oak trees like snow, the carcasses of deer scattered occasionally beneath the naked limbs of the oaks. They drove onto the road to their house.

On the road to their house the town center had burned. The homes alongside the road were gone: the General Store, the restaurant across the stream from Bob's big ring, the vintage clothing store; the fence to the ring lay around the sand like a blackened necklace. But the cement bridge over the stream still stood and they drove over it toward their home.

In the stream, just down from the burned out restaurant, Rumi perked his ears. "Listen," said Rumi. "Do you hear a rumble?"

The horses stopped, listened. A rumble? "What do you feel?" said Annie. But the noise was gone. It happened too fast.

Bird drove across the bridge and around a bend, then spotted the ruins of Norm's house. Bird stopped the truck. "We should look for him."

"They made everyone leave," said Gail.

Across the way, the canyon fell down steeply again to the stream. There'd been houses on a ledge there, in the woods. Creekers, the homeowners were called, but the woods and their homes had burned away, and now he could see down to the stream that ran brown over the rocks with new rain water. On the road, there were still marks where hoses had crossed back and forth, where a stand had been made, and lost.

"There's rubble," said Bird.

"Our house," said Gail. "They got these people out."

Bird stood. They'd seen no horses anywhere. He didn't know if the new owner at Bob's kept horses.

"Bird," said Gail, "our house. If Norm is under that rubble, he's dead."

Their place was farther around the bend at the base of the mountain, tucked inside it like within a cove. Maybe the fire swept past. Gail took Bird's hand, squeezed it.

"Our house," said Gail.

They got back in the truck and drove, that drive you drive to the hospital when your child has been in an accident, to the vet with your dying animal, that drive into everything and nothingness. When he drove around the bend they found their home burned down, too. Another big maybe had been used up.

They got out and stood for a little while in the heap of burned up things. Heat still rose from the burned barn wood that was once the outside walls, heat, and moisture, too. From the firefight? The rain? The clapboard had disintegrated, the drywall and plaster turned to dust. In the laundry and kitchen, heaps of machines, partially melted. The open field next door was scorched. Bird didn't see Mucha Plata. He didn't want to find her cindered bones. He held Gail's hand. She wept.

"Everything," she said.

Bird kicked at the ashes, but there was little underneath but more ash.

"Where was your jewelry?" he said. He pointed up the hill. "The bedroom?"

"I have my jewelry," Gail said. "It's the ring. I lost it."

"These cinders are still hot, too hot to dig," he said.

"Will there be looters?"

"Likely. They won't find much." He looked around again, but he wouldn't find his cat here. He thought of Annie.

"We should get these animals to some kind of shelter," Gail said. "Find a phone. Call our daughter."

"We'll come back after that," Bird said. "Look for the ring. The ranch is on the way out."

"My dream," she whispered. "I dreamed they were here. Three horses."

But she couldn't have expected to find the horses here, where there was nothing at all. Maybe it was just her way of saying it was hopeless; that they didn't need to go to Annie's pasture; it was just as impossible that they'd find her there. But she didn't say it. She let him have his own impossible dreams.

"Let's go," she said. They got back in the truck and Bird headed into the hills again, headed for the ranch. You could see everything from those hills, everything but horses.

The three horses followed the stream, walking beneath the shadowy arms of burned oak trees until they reached the bridge. They heard a rumble pass above. Was it familiar or was it strange? From where they stood Annie knew that Bob's big ring stood above them. She led the others up from the streambed where the ring lay, its sand almost pristine,

201

its burned fencing lying around its edge. No Hum sounds from across the stream now, no rumbles rushing on the big road. From there they walked the old woods path that once frightened her so, the trail from the ring to the stables. "I know this," she said to the others. At the top of the path the stables were now gone.

Then out the driveway until they stood above the little ring where Bob once parked to watch Annie and Bird standing together.

"You know this?" said Rumi.

"Yes," she said. Once it was her home. Her first home with Bird. "Do you feel?"

"Yes," Rumi said.

They walked down the driveway to the big rumble path, now silent. She didn't know where to go then. She'd never been to the bottom of the drive. "This way," Rumi said. The three walked around the base of the hill past several burned out houses until Rumi felt it, Bird's barn. The horses stood where Bird and Gail had stood only moments ago.

"Not here," said Rumi. "Here. Here. But not here."

"I can smell him," Annie said. She ran her nose along the ashen ground. They looked around. Nothing but desolation. Though in the distance the lop-lop of a sky rumble.

"But I sent," said Rumi. "I dreamed her this."

But it was simply another disappointment. What was there to expect? "We have to think what to do next," Annie said.

"There's nothing to be done," said Tasha and she lay down in the ash.

On the main road Bird and Gail ran into the train of burned out trucks and trailers. Bird drove along beside it, then finally stopped. They walked along together. Some people hadn't even made it out of their cars and were burnt beyond recognition. By now, as well, the stench of death was in the air. There probably would have been scavengers were there anywhere for them to live, but everything was burned; no birds in the air, not even vultures. Among the horses, he didn't recognize any bodies, though it was difficult to tell. He looked inside a few trailers. In some, the horses had burned alive. Others were empty. Then he found the chewed water bottles.

"Look," he said. "Someone was alive."

"But when?" said Gail.

Maybe Annie. Annie was smart enough.

Finally Gail took his hand. "There's nothing we can do here. I can't do this anymore," she said.

"Yes," said Bird. They heard a chopper and then spotted it following the line of the canyon. "We should get off this road," he said.

He drove up the fire road, around the rim of the canyon and then down the private road to the ranch. They found Precious at the foot of the drive of a burned mansion.

"Well, there's one of them," said Gail.

"Yes, not good," said Bird.

Inside the ranch, Annie's pasture was empty, the gate swinging. He drove farther in. The managers' house was gone and their cars burned out skeletons. They didn't see either manager, neither the husband nor the wife, but found the dead horses and ranch hands at the top of the broodmare hill.

"What should we do?" said Gail.

There was little to do. They couldn't even make a phone call. Maybe in the Valley. Helicopters were in the sky now. Eventually they'd spot this, send people. He drove past where the stables had burnt to the ground, the devastated outdoor stalls above, the collapsed indoor arena, and finally to Mick and Adele's. There they found them with their horses and dogs. He'd known them. Annie had known them. He stuttered. Found a can lid and began to cover them with dirt, burnt sawdust bedding, and ash.

"This is stupid," he said.

"No. No," said Gail and bent to help him. That's when she found the can that the horses had raided for carrots, dried orange crumbs at its lip, atop the ash. She said, "Look here."

Bird saw it. "Somebody got carrots," he said. "After the fire." He looked around again, but there were only ashen hills, no life. They finished covering Mick and Adele and drove back to Annie's pasture. They let the dogs run for a bit. Bird shut the gate and stared into the empty corral. He

203

took off his straw hat and looked at the feathers. He touched them. Through all this, though he'd worried about Annie constantly during the fire, it was the first time he realized he might never see her again. "Annie," he said.

Gail touched the back of his neck. "We need to find shelter for these animals," she said.

"Yes," he said.

"And we need to live somewhere."

He'd forgotten. They needed showers. They had to think of the future. They needed to call Marlena, and other friends and relatives to tell them they were alive.

They gathered the dogs and got into the truck. Bird drove to the crossroads that led out of the canyon and into the Valley and there, he stopped. He hesitated. He wanted to turn back. To check the ranch again. To go back to his home. But it was absurd. He made the right turn toward the Valley.

"We have to keep moving," said Annie.

"I'm not going anywhere," said Tasha.

"We have to find Hums."

"If they're around, they'll find us soon enough."

"Let's stay here," said Rumi.

"The wrong people always arrive first," said Annie. She felt it strongly after the bad Hums from the day before.

"I can't go on," said Tasha. "I'm going to die. Here is as good a place as any."

"I'll lead," said Annie.

"No," Tasha said. She breathed heavily. "Not me. Not anymore."

"Don't leave," Rumi said to Annie. "I feel the Other here. I feel Bird."

Annie nuzzled him. "He's not here. Not anymore."

"He'll come back," said Rumi.

"Not to this," Annie said.

"I sent."

"You hoped," Annie said. Rumi had come far, but maybe too far. Waiting became hope, but hope did not become what you hoped for. Dreams were only dreams. She nuzzled him again. He smelled young. She thought of her foal. Of loss. Of Bird. "If we find good Hums they might help," she said.

"They help themselves," said Tasha.

"We should wait," said Rumi.

Annie stepped away from him. "We need to move," she said. "Coming?"

"No," said Tasha.

Rumi quivered. He was so tired. He lay down next to Tasha and put his head over her back.

Annie lowered her head. She'd start toward the sound of the sky rumbles. Find Hums. Hum at a time. Hum by Hum. She wouldn't wait for something to happen to her. They'd become a good herd. Worked together. Now she would miss them. She'd lead, if only a herd of one. She turned from her two companions and walked away, down the road, around a bend, and toward her new life.

"I want to check the house again," Gail said to Bird. "Before the looters, the authorities."

Bird drove on. "It doesn't make sense," he said to her.

"I want to find my ring."

He slowed the car and pulled over. "You've changed your mind? You want to look for it now?"

"My dream," Gail said. "We found the water. The carrots. Somebody did that."

"They weren't there," Bird said.

"I was sent that dream," Gail said.

"Why would they be there?" said Bird.

"Because I feel them."

"We need to call our daughter."

"Another hour. She's all right," Gail said to him. She touched his hand.

"You don't have to use the horses," he said. "I'll go back to look for the ring."

"Bird," she said, "Let's go back. I want to go back."

Bird peered out the windshield at the gray road, almost bright now between the black hills. "You called me Bird," he said to Gail.

"Yes," she said. "You, Bird."

But he wasn't Bird anymore, not without Annie.

"Bird," said Gail. "I feel it."

"All right," he said. "Let's look for the ring." He turned the car around.

When Bird came around the bottom of the hill, Gail spotted the two horses. "My God," she said. "Bird, look!"

Bird parked the truck beneath the wreckage and Gail leapt from the cab and ran up to Tasha and Rumi, lying in the ashes of her home. Bird followed. Rumi stood. He'd felt them. He'd sent!

"My dream," said Gail. "They're here."

It was impossible, yet inside the impossible fact, something was wrong. "Only two," said Bird. He looked around, but saw nothing. If Tasha and Rumi made it, then Annie had to have made it, too. Where could she be? He touched Rumi's forehead.

Now Gail stroked Rumi's neck. "Where, Rumi?" she said. "Where?"

Bird knelt and scratched Tasha's withers. "You'll be all right now, Tasha," he said. He stood up. There was nothing anywhere. "Where is she?"

It was then that Rumi stiffened and began to scream. He screamed and screamed.

"What's wrong with him?" said Gail.

"Trauma," said Bird. He petted Rumi's neck, but Rumi refused to settle. He screamed again and again.

"Easy, Rumi," said Bird. "Easy."

"Maybe if we wait a little," said Gail.

Bird tried to compose himself. These two. How could he be this close? He scanned the blackened hillside, the naked road going up. Across the way, nothing in the ashen debris leading down to the stream. He couldn't say it. He couldn't put words to his loss, his disappointment. "We should look for your ring," he said instead.

He tried to leave Rumi with Gail and walk up the hill, but Rumi trotted after him. Bird turned. Rumi spun away from him, his head pointing down the road.

"Annie?" Bird said.

In the distance, Annie heard Rumi. She stopped. Rumi. Maybe something happened to Tasha and he was alone. She looked ahead, looked back. He screamed again. Really, what more could she do for him? He'd chosen. What could she do? She turned away.

But back at his burned house, Bird suddenly got it. "She wouldn't stay in one place. Wouldn't wait," he said. He didn't even get in his truck, but took off running down the road. Around the bottom of one hill, then another. He ran. Around a bend. Nothing. He began to yell. "Annie! Annie!" She heard him and stopped. And then he came around the bottom of another hill, running.

He spotted her. "Annie!" Bird yelled.

And his horse turned around. She saw him running toward her under his feathered hat. It was Bird.

She ran up the road, her hooves clapping on the asphalt like guns. Bird. Bird! Through the fire. Through everything. She ran. Bird stopped and stood. She raced to him, slid to a stop in front of him, heaving, rumbling.

"Annie," said Bird. "Sweet Annie." Though she wasn't sweet, had never been sweet, had always been much more than that, she let him put his arms around her neck and bury his face there. She let him.

Then he vaulted onto her bare back and headed up the road to his lover and his burned home. Rumi spotted them and began to jump his excited jump, front legs to back, back to front. Rumi yes! Rumi yes! Rumi yes! Yes! Rumi yes yes yes! Gail ran to them and Annie looked at the Other below her. Well, she'd brought Bird and now Bird was on Annie's back, where he belonged.

"Annie," Gail wept, and touched Annie's nose. "Annie," she said, and Annie's ears twitched.

Rumi jumped and jumped.

"Think he's happy?" said Gail.

Rumi yes! Rumi yes yes! Even Tasha got to her feet. She came to Bird and put her nose on his knee. Something. Something had changed for the good.

"I think your horse has water falling from her eyes," said Gail. "She's crying."

"Me, too," Bird said. He leaned over and hugged Annie's neck. "Annie. Sweet Annie," said Bird. "My sweet little horse. I love her," he said to Gail.

"I know," Gail said. "And she loves you."

Bird slid off and went to Gail, hugged her. Annie pinned her ears. "But still not me so much," Gail said. They laughed. "My dream, Bird," said Gail. "Rumi sent me the dream." Then she turned from them and walked up the slope a little ways, where she thought the bedroom used to be. Rumi followed. "You didn't dream about this," Gail said to him.

Rumi yes! Rumi yes! felt Rumi.

"Don't feel Rumi-Rumi-Rumi! Feel for my ring," Gail said to him. "Remember it? Would you like to think about it, Mr. Mystic?"

That didn't mean too much to Rumi.

Gail dug into the ashes with her boot. She spread ash around. Bird went to her. "There's just so much ash and little else," she said to him.

"It wouldn't melt," said Bird. "Not the diamonds."

Rumi stood above her when she went to her knees and dug at the cindered ground with her hands. Bird joined her and now the two of them dug in the ashes of their burned home, the cinders flying and the two of them covered in the warm, black ash. Gail sat back on her legs. "I don't know about this," she said. "Hopeless."

But Annie'd been watching them. They were looking for something in the dust. She was good at that. Annie was good at finding shiny things in the dirt. She walked up the hill and nudged Rumi out of the way. Again, she was going to show him something. She began to paw the ground.

"Your horse is helping," said Gail.

In fact, she was. She pawed the ground, feeling for a different thing, something hard, not ash; she pawed softly at the ground and felt something like a tiny stone. She pushed the ash aside with her hoof and then spotted something. She uncovered the shiny object and she stepped on it. She lifted her hoof. It was the ring.

"My God," said Gail. "There it is! Bird, there it is!" She picked it up and wiped it off, held it to her chest and put it on. "Oh Bird," she said. "Oh Annie. My ring."

Jewel in the Lotus

Om mani padme hum!

- - Tibetan Buddhist chant

*...there's nothing better for the inside of a man
than the outside of a horse.*

- - Will Rogers

With their insurance money and the movie money from Bird's book, they made a down payment on the land that was once Bob's ranch. Bird tracked down Rumi's and Tasha's owners, who assumed the horses had died in the fire or were rounded up by rustlers and sold for meat. A group of them had been spotted by a chopper and caught near the summit chasing a herd led by a gray mare, a famous race horse.

"Do you know anything about that?" Bird said to Annie, petting her forehead.

More than you'd ever want to know, Bird.

"You weren't involved or you'd have been leading," Bird said.

But she'd led them all in her way.

Bird purchased Rumi and Tasha. On Bob's old property, the house and stables had to be rebuilt. In the meantime, they rented a home near Paddy's facility and kept the three horses there where they shared a pasture.

In that year it took to rebuild Bob's old place, Gail learned to ride Rumi. She helped Bird take care of him, if not every day. She always remembered to bring Annie apples and carrots, and she always thanked Annie for finding her ring. For Annie, that worked.

Sometimes Rumi and Gail joined Annie and Bird on the open trails where Annie barely misbehaved, as long as she wasn't mugged by a butterfly. Bird and Gail took care of old Tasha, too; cleaned her coat and hooves, brushed her mane and tail, and in time her eyes brightened.

Sometimes, when Marlena came home from school, the three of them saddled up. With Rumi and Tasha both around her on the trail, especially after all they'd been through together, Annie had to show off how steady she was, how fearless.

Sometimes Bird took Annie out on her own. Sometimes they ran in the hills, ran like the wind, their hearts beating as one, in that heaven. Sometimes they walked and Bird petted her neck. He loved her and she had come to love him, to feel complete when he was on her back and they moved as one. Sometimes they just stood. Man and horse. Bird raised his eyes to the sky. He said, "Thank you." And that's all he had in him.

And sometimes, like the old days, Bird took Annie into the ring to change leads and run poles and Annie figured out whatever game they were playing and tried to outguess him, and Paddy yelled and Bird laughed.

Paddy brought new, untrained riders to watch them sometimes, too, and said to them, "See that horse perform? If you got on her, how long do you think before she'd be riding you? Fifteen seconds!"

"It only took a decade," Bird said.

"You ought to write about her," she said to Bird.

And Bird just laughed some more.

One day when the three Hums showed up, Tasha ran to greet them and nuzzled them all for carrots. Afterward, Rumi ran to her. "You've certainly changed!"

"I haven't," Tasha said. "It just appears that way because you never notice things."

"The Great Caregiver!" said Rumi.

"Bird," Tasha said.

"You're not dead!" said Rumi.

"That hasn't changed," said Tasha.

211

For Annie's part, she was grateful for all Tasha had done during the horror of the fire and after, her experience and intelligence, grateful for all the times Tasha had insisted that they stay put and been right, yet followed and never said a word.

"You were right," Annie said. "About waiting."

"You led," said Tasha. "If not, we'd have died without water. Leading is a kind of waiting. We just had to wait somewhere else." They watched Rumi who danced in the center of the corral. "Safety in numbers, in the herd," Tasha said. "We found Bird."

Rumi danced. Rumi yes! Rumi yes! Rumi! Rumi! Rumi! Yes! Then he stopped and put his nose in the air, letting the world feel him.

"I think he's happy," said Annie.

"He thinks he's happy," said Tasha. "What's new? Nothing." But her ears twitched.

"He has a Hum," said Annie.

Tasha turned a back hoof upward and laid it on the ground, resting, at peace, content. "Carrot at a time," she said softly.

And then one day Bird and Gail came with a rented trailer on the back of Bird's rumble and took them to their new ranch, Bob's old one. A rainy year followed the dry one and the land around the ranch filled with grass and wildflowers, the oaks burst with new leaves and the forest grew around a tunnel down to the big ring below. Bird turned the two big pastures into one and irrigated it with the underground stream that flowed on the property, so when the rains stopped, grass still grew and the horses could graze into the summer.

But soon into that stay back at Bob's old ranch, now Bird's new one, Bird saddled Annie up and turned for the woods.

"Remember this, Annie?" said Bird.

She sure did.

First he walked her around the pastures, then into the small ring where they loped a little, then he took her down across the stables and onto the path that led to the woods and the big ring. Tasha and Rumi watched; at the mouth of the forest, Annie stopped cold.

Not the woods, Bird.

Bird urged her forward.

Nope.

And Bird laughed.

Some things change and some don't.

Ten Thousand Heavens

I don't want to die.

- - Shunryu Suzuki

We live to save each other's lives. This is what Bird did for Annie and he came to believe that she did it for him, too. That's the way of love. Once Bird believed that he could have fallen in love with a thousand different people and done it a thousand times, and then slowly he came to see that he could only have fallen in love with Gail and he had done so in ten thousand different lives, over and over. Remember the last time we were here? I carried you across the river. I saved your life so we could be in love again.

Do you remember our child, the one like this one, brave and smart? She looks like you again. When you went away, how I missed you. How I missed you every time. How I never live long enough to be with you enough. How quickly things change.

And so it was with Annie, too. On Annie's back, every day, the disaster behind them, Bird stroked the neck of miracle. Green hills and a lurid blue sky, he sat on the back of his horse. Thank you for this day. Thank you for this moment on this horse. How can anything ever end?

Annie grew older. She wanted to stand more, run less, make less trouble. Sometimes, in the hills, Bird rode her, dreaming, and Annie, walking slowly, dreamt too. Then Bird found himself standing somewhere on horseback, in some field of yellow with mustard plant and wild daisies, on some hill, the canyon stretching to mountains beyond, peaks of snow. How long had they been standing there?

Sometimes he got off her back and stood with her in that quiet. Sometimes he fell to his knees and clasped his hands. Annie nuzzled his ear, picked his vest pocket for a carrot, then left him alone. One day, coming down to ride Rumi, Gail found him like that, Bird on his knees and Annie near him grazing.

"Bird," she said, "you're an atheist."

"Atheists pray more than anyone," Bird said.

When Gail came down to the corrals, she brushed and cleaned Tasha, took Rumi on short rides. She was less interested in riding than simply being near Rumi, walking with him in the sun. Rumi, yes! Rumi, yes! Sometimes she and Rumi, Annie and Bird, walked through the woods to the big corral and walked around and around silently, the wind in the oak trees, the push of the horses feet against the sand, the saddles creaking so slightly, rhythmically; then the gurgle of the stream, or on the far end, the occasional rush of traffic on the road. They came home, brought Tasha out and let the horses graze.

"How long can this last?" whispered Tasha to Annie.

"Are you afraid?" Annie said. "Of change?"

Tasha looked up. She stood motionless.

Because Annie had begun to feel ill. She didn't know how to tell Bird. A cramp in her stomach. Bird took her to the small ring, but she didn't want to run at all. And the next day she lay down in the sun and when he came she didn't get up. So he went to her. "Annie," whispered Bird. She raised her head. Took a carrot. Got up and shook herself.

Bird called a vet, a woman named Beth, who emptied Annie bowels and stomach.

"A little colic," said Beth. "Let her eat some fresh grass. She'll be fine."

It was spring and Bird stood with Annie for a long time on a grassy hillside, letting her eat. How old was she? Twenty-two? Not that old. Tasha had to be pushing thirty. He petted Annie's neck. She felt better. Almost new. She raised her head and took a carrot. He saw himself in her soft eyes. She lowered her head into his arms.

Then one morning Gail woke him just before dawn. "Bird, I'm afraid," she said. "Something about the horses."

He dressed. Put on his boots, his feathered hat. When he got outside he heard the screaming. Annie lay in her stall, writhing. She rolled and thrashed, her eyes clouded with pain. He got her on her feet and took her outside. She tried to collapse again. He prodded her forward. He got a riding crop from the tack room and hit her to keep her moving. He didn't keep numbers on his cell phone, so he phoned Gail.

"She's colicking," he said. "I don't know why. Call the vet."

Walking Annie, he got Rumi and Tasha into the pasture, got them some hay. And Bird walked Annie, forcing her forward. She tried to lie down; her legs buckled; he struck her on the behind with the crop, walked her forward.

"What's happening?" Rumi said to Tasha.

"Change, I'm afraid," Tasha said.

Bird phoned Gail. "If you hadn't woken up, she'd be dead," Bird said to Gail.

"Do you need me?" Gail said.

"Not yet," said Bird.

He pushed Annie forward. Pushed her. She couldn't even recognize him through her pain, but if she were to lie down, she'd die, and that's what she wanted to do. To lie down. Just lie down. This for an hour until Beth arrived.

Beth evacuated Annie's bowels, then, using a hose through her nostril, evacuated her stomach and bladder. She did it again and again, but everything came out and Annie didn't get better.

"Everything is out," Beth said. "That's all I can do. It's got to be intestinal. You need a specialist." She filled Annie with pain meds, then called for an emergency trailer.

And while waiting, Bird drove Annie forward. For another hour and more, again and again, her legs buckled, she almost went down.

Beth gave her more shots. "That's too much pain," she whispered.

Yes, it was too much pain. She tried to find Bird, but she couldn't see through the blur. When she stood still for a moment, bolstered by the medication, Bird held her neck. "It's okay," Bird said through his tears, "It's okay to die." But he didn't mean it.

When the truck and trailer arrived the driver scratched his head. "We'll never get her inside," he said.

But Beth knew. "She'll go in for him," she said.

And she did.

"Can I stay with her?" said Bird.

"Too dangerous," said the driver.

"She'll make it," said Beth. "The motion will calm her."

Bird followed in his truck on the long drive to the hospital. He could see Annie's ears twitching through the back of the trailer. Annie, curious, ears twitching; it gave him hope.

At the hospital he unloaded her, led her to a stall with a sling that kept her on her feet. The specialist, David Rogan, was a famous horse surgeon; Bird had heard of him. If there was anyone in the country who could find out what was wrong and cure it, it was Rogan. He moved methodically, efficiently, trying the same things Beth did. Bird stood at Annie's head, petting her forehead, stroking her neck. "Annie," said Bird. "Annie."

Rogan stepped back.

"What next?" Bird said.

"Too much pain," said Rogan. "There's something in there. We'll have to x-ray."

"Something?" said Bird. "A stone?"

"If it's cancer, there's no hope," said Rogan. "It could be a twisted intestine. We might be able to operate on that." He scrutinized Bird. "You're about $2,000 in now, after the x-rays. Surgery and recovery will be tens of thousands." He paused again.

"How old is she?"

"Twenty-two," said Bird.

"Well, I'm the best at it," said Rogan. "She might make it."

"Let's find out," said Bird.

Annie wouldn't budge from the stall until Bird led her out. After he got her into the x-ray room he called Gail. "X-rays," he said.

"I better come now."

"Yes," said Bird.

Outside the barns, Bird waited. The day was frighteningly calm, clear and blue. A gray haired woman in high riding boots stood with another vet as a groom ran a tall two-year-old with a golden chestnut coat and a long blond tail and mane. The animal danced and snorted as the groom ran with him up and down the sandy road outside the barns. Bird remembered Annie on that first cold April day, her nostrils flaring and the mist rising from her hot back, how she flew, fire in her eyes, head up, tail in the air.

The woman and the vet watched the prancing colt closely. An evaluation. An investment. The vet nodded. The woman nodded approvingly. She stood across the road from Bird when the vet went inside the offices and the groom led the young stallion to a trailer.

"Your mare?" she said, her gaze shifting to the x-ray room.

"Yes," he said.

"She's older than seventeen?"

"Twenty-two," Bird said.

"I've seldom seen that much pain," the woman said. "How many more do you have?"

"She's my first horse," Bird said. And now, he couldn't help it. He wept.

The woman waited. She turned. She almost walked away. Then she hesitated, turning back to him. "Don't put her through it. She can't make it," she said. And then she did walk away.

Bird waited. Finally the door slid open. He went to Annie, but her eyes were clouded with pain.

"She's pretty drugged up," Rogan said. A vet's assistant tried to lead her to the barn, but Annie stood fast until Bird took the lead line. "She'll follow him," Rogan said, and Bird took her to the first stall in the barn. When she tried to go down, Rogan told Bird, "Let her go. It doesn't matter."

Annie put her head on the ground. Then she tried to roll. "Already," Rogan said. "That's too much pain. I'll give her something more." He came in and gave Annie another painkiller in her neck. Annie calmed and put her head down again.

Outside the stall now, Rogan said to him, "I don't know what it is. Honestly. I mean maybe I could do something. You never know. But you have to decide in the next half-hour."

218

"Can she recover?" Bird said. "If you succeed?"

"Maybe," Rogan said. "Maybe not."

"All right," Bird said. "I have to walk."

"I'll be here," Rogan said.

Bird walked out to the road where he stood and waited for Gail. In a while, her convertible came over the hill and he met her in the parking lot. "Thank you for coming," he said to her. He told her what he knew.

"Not Annie," Gail said. "Not Annie."

He took Gail's hand and stood with her. He didn't know if he could walk to the stall. "I have to do something," he whispered. "For her," he said. Holding Gail's hand he walked with her to the barn. There, at the stall door, Annie saw him. She tried to get up to come to him, but collapsed and rolled. He turned his back.

Bird walked out of the barn. He walked. Then he put his palms over his mouth and screamed. With all he had in him, he screamed. Gail found him. From behind, she put her hands on his shoulders. He turned to her. "All right now," he said.

When he went to the stall again Annie tried to get up and come to him, but she collapsed, rolling on her back, kicking, and then she lay down, her head falling to the floor. Bird opened the door and went to Annie for the last time. He knelt at her head and stroked her neck. Then he sat. She raised her head and placed it in his lap. He held his horse like that. He didn't want her to hear him crying. He felt her breath.

"Good-bye, Annie," he said to her. "I love you. Good-bye. I'll see you tomorrow."

And tomorrow he would return. He would mount her back and together they would run, through the mist, running, the brush along the trail racing by in a blur, the world falling away, her hooves pounding, blasting out, heart and mind, two hearts becoming one, where together horse and man met God in a moment of inseparable trust, running, running, again and again in the last of their ten thousand heavens.

About the Author

Chuck Rosenthal was born in Erie, Pennsylvania; he moved to northern California in 1978 and has lived in Los Angeles since 1986. In 1994, at the age of 43, he began riding horses, and he purchased his first horse, Jackie O, an Arabian Thoroughbred bay mare in 1995. She died on January 17, 2009, at the age of 22. His new horse, La Femme Nikita, is a buckskin Morgan, age 7. He tries to ride six days a week.